# THE SOURCE OF LONGING

## A Novel

Richard Hawley

ISBN: 1501045385
ISBN 13: 9781501045387
Library of Congress Control Number: 2014915932
CreateSpace Independent Publishing Platform
North Charleston, South Carolina

# 1

## LONGING

It occurred to Sloan Fox as he was leaving the house that he actually *was* in retreat.

Running late – yet there had been no running – he had showered in a hurry and did not take time to wash his hair, which, he knew, was overdue. The only laundered shirt was the blue pinstripe with the too-tight neck. In the bedroom's half-light he swiped yesterday's white shirt from the back of his desk chair, looked and didn't look at its starched creases, smudged patches on the collar band. Hell with it, hell with it, hell with it, he told himself as he clumped downstairs.

In the buttery kitchen light, Jen stood at the counter watching the coffee-maker drip into the clear, calibrated pitcher. Sloan looked into the eyes of his son Bart who was weakly slicing sections of banana into his cereal bowl. The boy seemed, Sloan thought, stupefied with sleepiness, and he almost laughed.

"All set to conquer the world?" Sloan said to his son.

Bart looked up at his disheveled father, water from his shower moistening his shirt-front, beading along his hair-line.

"Yeah right, that's me." he said,

"You should really try drying yourself after your shower," Jen said. "It's part of the whole experience. You'd be surprised at how nice it feels."

"Really?" Sloan answered flatly. He felt a reflexive burn of resentment at her sarcasm rising in his gut. "That's a terrific idea. We should buy some towels."

Sloan moved to his wife, awkwardly and closer to her than he wanted to be, in order to pour some of the brewing coffee into his mug. When he removed the pitcher, a succession of droplets hissed and spattered onto the heating element, spraying a faint brown mist over the counter top. Jen stared hard at the hissing burner, then up at her husband.

Sloan looked at his watch. Some beads of water, he noticed, had formed under the crystal. The retreat started in fifteen minutes, and it was a twenty-five or thirty minute drive downtown to the Hyatt. He looked sadly into the impossible coffee steaming in his mug.

"I've gotta run," he said, "I'm way late."

"Since when is eight-fifteen way late?" Jen asked.

Again the mounting burn below his heart.

"It's an administrative retreat today," Sloan said, emphasizing "retreat" as if he found the event, or perhaps the word for it, contemptible.

"What are you all retreating from?" Jen was relentless in her disapproval of the *Cleveland Sun Messenger,* the paper for which Sloan worked. She seemed to take an enjoyment, which he did not entirely understand, in dismissing it. Her question confused him.

"We're not retreating from. We're retreating to." Sloan's fingers found the glossy flier in his jacket pocket. "We're retreating to...'The Organization and Its Shadow.'"

"It doesn't make any sense," Jen said.

"Go figure," Sloan said and swallowed back what he knew would be his only gulp of coffee.

"Now I'm good and late," he said. "First day of the rest of your life, big guy," he said to his son.

"It makes no sense," Jen repeated as he let himself out the back door. "You retreat from, not to..."

Sloan had scalded his tongue and the roof of his mouth with hot coffee. He knew he would feel it, as a kind of reprimand, all day.

Good, Sloan thought, as he made his way into the Parlor One conference room of the Hyatt. Nothing formal had begun. His colleagues, editors and staff writers mostly, were standing or seated, chatting in little clusters around a horseshoe configuration of linen draped tables. He could see insulated coffee jugs, plastic cups of orange juice. Sloan imagined the bitter tang on his scalded tongue.

He was acknowledged, assumed into the gathering with greetings, jokey and incoherent. Someone said: editorial page heard from. The words gave Sloan pause. Was he? He thought about his new post, new title: Editorial Page Editor. For a moment, although he knew clearly what he must do and with whom as the *Sun Messenger* editorial page editor, the idea of the job confused him. Editorial *editor* seemed to him, at least semantically, redundant. Editorials were already "edited" versions of issues and events set forth in the rest of the paper. He was – what? – the editor of the edited. His work was now abstracted from the real and the urgent. He was no longer to deal with news but in creating a mood about the news. Sloan was beginning to feel confined and diminished by this idea when Nora Hick, the book pages editor, said, "Earth to Sloan. Earth to *Sloan.*"

"What am I being," Sloan said, "stupid?" He felt stupid saying this.

There was purposeful movement, an abrading of metal chair legs on the tile floor. Steve Kraal, executive editor of the paper, was standing at a lectern at the open end of the horseshoe. "Friends... friends...if we could begin...if we could find a seat..."

Sloan was struck by the open, unfinished proposition: *if,* if we could begin.

At Sloan's place, at everyone's place, was a glossy folder, its pockets stuffed with printed material: photocopied articles, some schematic diagrams and charts. Sloan fanned through the enclosures, noting on one of them the heading "Self/World."

Sloan sat back. He felt heavy, tired, his awareness deep and muffled behind his eyes. At once he realized he had slipped back into his school posture, padding quietly, anonymously to the rearmost seats of the classrooms and lecture halls at Amherst. With luck he would not be engaged, singled out. With luck, his lack of preparedness and, usually, of interest would go unnoticed. With luck, the clenched feeling in his stomach would dissolve, and he would let himself drift into safe reverie.

The fluorescent light on the white linen made reverie difficult, and Sloan's attention was suddenly drawn to the guest speaker – "facilitator" – seated to Steve Kraal's right, waiting with an attentiveness bordering on mischief. She was striking.

Now she was at the lectern herself, broadly smiling, taking her time. She had a look Sloan had always liked: slight, angular, nicely formed. Her blond hair was pulled back, imperfectly, in a kind of twist so that wisps strayed appealingly about her ears. Her eyes were dark and shadowed with color, lips vividly reddened. The nose was a little hooked, and her upper lip – she was talking now – drew tightly away from good, slightly protruding teeth. This drawing away of her upper lip was arrestingly interesting to Sloan.

She was Naomi Wise, a psychologist, an authority, a handout said, on "organization dynamics." Now she was laughing, and because of the irresistible drawing back of the upper lip from her teeth, and the accompanying helpless down-turning of the corners of her eyes, Sloan laughed, as they all laughed, in welcoming response.

Naomi Wise had begun well – no inconsiderable achievement, Sloan felt, given the quirks and cantankerousness of many of his *Sun Messenger* colleagues. Sloan drew himself a bit more upright to listen. Whatever might be said about organizational dynamics at the *Sun Messenger*, he was now willing, even eager, to watch her, to hear her talk. He could not have articulated it yet, but this was a presence he was pleased to let into his inner world, and with the rising awareness of his pleasure, she had already entered.

Naomi Wise told the editors and executives of the *Sun Messenger* that every organization has a shadow. The shadow consists of everything that was true of the organization that its members, especially its leaders, do not consciously acknowledge. The shadow was not an inert bundle of qualities and attributes, but a purposeful being, a kind of force with intent. When the rational, conscious activity of the organization diverges too greatly from the shadow, when the shadow is negated, trouble erupts. The trouble might take the form of unassignable bad morale, irrational lapses in performance and conduct. The shadow is mischievous, inclined to subversion. Shadow play might include sophisticated dissembling, the anonymous disclosure of embarrassing and illicit behavior on the part of the leaders, the implanting of computer viruses. When the shadow is actively at work, Naomi Wise said, mishaps and crises tend to cluster. Everyone tends to feel on edge, confidence and productivity low.

In a way that both energized him and made him uncomfortable, Sloan could feel the condition Naomi Wise described even as she spoke. He recalled, with a startled unease, the still unattributed prank that embarrassed the paper's editors on Christmas Eve. Over a rather dull editorial in the late edition which mildly approved a court ruling that the Salvation Army could solicit donations inside city hall despite the administration's objections, a bold headline appeared stating: SANTA KICKS MAYOR'S ASS. The intended headline, which Sloan and others had seen in the final lay-out, had been SALVATION ARMY PREVAILS. The prankster had not been discovered. Technology services were unable to determine the computer terminal from which the headline change was directed. There seemed to be no lapse in supervisory protocols. For a time there was a worrying belief that someone outside the paper's computer network had cracked the security code, although most of the staff felt only an insider could have managed the substitution. It had fallen to Sloan, on Christmas Day, to compose the correction notice. Only Jen had heard him laugh crazily over his lap-top at the impossibility of making the confession of error anything other than an extension of the prank's intent.

> An editorial headline in the Dec. 24 late edition, SANTA KICKS MAYOR'S ASS, should have read: SALVATION ARMY PREVAILS. The editors regret the vulgarity of the suspected prank and are vigorously investigating the lapse. The *Sun Messenger* further regrets any embarrassment caused to the mayor, the Salvation Army or to any other party mentioned in the editorial.

Sloan e-mailed the correction to Steve Kraal. He couldn't resist asking: should we also regret any embarrassment caused to Santa?

Naomi Wise stopped mid-sentence at the lectern and looked out with kind puzzlement at Sloan. He realized with a hot flash of embarrassment at the back of his head that he was inappropriately grinning. There could be no explaining. He willed his face to go blank, bent over his pad as if to make a note. Naomi Wise resumed speaking. Sloan wrote, for some reason in microscopically tiny script: am I the shadow, the shadow, the shadow --

Naomi Wise began answering questions. The shadow, she explained to the *Sun Messenger* staff, was a finding of the Swiss depth psychologist Carl Jung. Sloan scanned his memory, Amherst again, a seminar: Psychoanalysis and the Twentieth Century Mind. Freud, Jung, Ferenczi, Reich. But what exactly was Jung? Sloan had not thought or read deeply at the time. There was an impression of Freud as grimly, powerfully logical; deep instincts channeled, as if hydraulically, into compromised outwardly acceptable behavior. Unconscious frustration, conscious anxiety. But Jung? The psyche was brighter and livelier; the unconscious more crowded, somehow containing whole mythologies, whole destinies. Sloan didn't really know.

Naomi Wise said that Jung was mainly concerned with the personal shadow, but that institutions and organizations revealed shadow activity as well; much more needed to be learned. There was a hand-out, on the personal shadow, quite good, she said, included in their folders. And now, perhaps, would be a good time for a break.

Sloan remained in his chair, riffling through the documents in his folder looking for the article praised by Naomi Wise. The piece in question, "Honoring the Shadow: Integration and Individuation in Mid-Life," was written by Chandru Lott, a Jungian analyst in Santa Monica. Sloan poured some coffee from one of the thermal urns, took a sour sip, then began reading deeply into the essay; the opening section of which was titled, "The Shadow in Dreams, Mistakes, Obsessions." Sloan thought: *this is very clear, this is smart* – and at the same time had to will himself to continue reading. Something insistent within wanted him to put the article aside, turn physically away from it, get up and leave the table.

> Because the shadow presses dark and culturally forbidden content onto conscious awareness, it is easy to think of the shadow as a "dark side," as dangerous wishes and illicit destructive urges.
>
> While the shadow does indeed contain such material, it also includes the heroic, perfected, "larger-than-life" qualities and aspirations the waking persona is unable to imagine or admit. We worship heroes because we cannot bear, or are repressively afraid, to be heroes.

Naomi Wise had resumed her place at the lectern. Sloan was immediately drawn to her words – but at the same time troubled. He found his response to the agreeable progression of her thoughts exactly like his response to the shadow article. Something was accurately and unsettlingly striking an inner target. Then, just for an instant, Sloan saw it. If I am free and clear to think and feel this way, to take in and to be my whole crazy, unsavory self, then where are the boundaries? Where does it stop? And then, even more unsettlingly: how will I know what to do, how to *be* with anybody? Sloan suddenly felt uncomfortably weak, adrift. Then, just as suddenly, he sat up straight in his chair and told himself that he would no longer drink, or he would drink less, before dinner.

Naomi Wise held her listeners fast. Even while he was reading during the interval, Sloan had heard his colleagues' approval through the din of chat: "this is deep stuff," "incredible," "she's good." Naomi Wise was illustrating the shadow at work in the organization.

"Take bigotry," she said. "Or that we don't have any bigotry in our lives. That's right isn't it? We are all open, good, modern, liberally educated people here. Look, I can see it in your faces. The Civil Rights movement was not lost on you. I read your paper. I know your editorial positions.

"There is still bigotry, but it is *out there*, in infuriating pockets, brutalizing the police, wrecking the poor city schools. But it's not to be found, in fact it is vehemently denied, it is *out*lawed at the *Sun Messenger*." Naomi Wise paused; she smiled penetratingly into the eyes of one listener after another.

Again, softly, "Am I right?

"Oh, but what has been happening, what have you been feeling since I brought up the subject, since I said, 'bigotry'?" She paused again, and Sloan could feel the rising unease. "I am looking out at two black faces and – what? – fifteen or sixteen white ones around these tables. Is it now a little unpleasant, or more than a little, that I have raised the subject of bigotry, of race?" Without turning to look at her, Sloan pictured Rasheel Giddings at her seat, imagined her discomfort.

Sloan considered the phrase 'is it now a little unpleasant'. There was something, he thought, old-world, vaguely European about Naomi Wise's manner of address.

"And now maybe," she continued, "some of you are thinking, 'I wish she would stop.' Yes?" Sloan was glad for her laugh, the upper lip so appealingly drawn back from her teeth.

"Let me tell you. Whatever feelings have just surfaced are just the tip, tip, tip of your shadow business about race. Unless you are somehow utterly unlike any other people in the United States, you are unconsciously loaded with racial concerns. There is fear, fear about difference. Fear, and also resentment, about acceptance, or the lack of it. I don't know how much, if any, racial anger or aggression there is in your offices. But I do know this – and how strange and dangerous to talk about it. There is *desire*. There is a subterranean current, a pulse of desire across racial lines, at your paper, in the place you all come to work every day." Sloan sensed the arrival of laughter in her eyes, but it did not come.

"Only the tip, the feathery edge of the shadow. The whole of the shadow includes everything about race that is felt and feared and desired that *The Sun Messenger* can't acknowledge or publicly admit.

"The most important thing to realize is that the danger does not lie in whatever race-related feelings and impulses might be unconsciously at work in your paper. No, the danger comes when the denial of those feelings becomes an institutional posture, a righteous certainly, company policy.

"Because whenever something soulfully alive is denied altogether, that truth goes underground and starts making itself known in the strangest ways. The worst, the most vicious race relations in this country occur not in the pockets and regions of society believed to be the most racist. The worst outrages occur in those places that have declared themselves forever enlightened and thus beyond primitive racial feeling. So it's not in Mississippi farm towns, but at elite liberal colleges and universities where the racial shadow erupts. That's where crosses are now burned at night. That's where the hate mail and hate e-mail are anonymously dispatched. And you know a peculiar thing? It is now likely to be minority students themselves who are secretly provoking the self-righteous and the enlightened." Naomi Wise paused. "Isn't that interesting? It's an amazing thing, the shadow.

"You can count on the shadow being on the prowl whenever something important and true in the organization goes unidentified or is denied. I don't know the personnel or the personnel issues at *The Sun Messenger*, but I certainly wouldn't be surprised if the people in top management weren't itching to let someone go, maybe even to let a lot of people go. Rarely are such desires, such wishes openly expressed, nor are they always consciously acknowledged by those who hold them. For just as none of us generous souls wants to harbor any racial fears and desires and resentments, no one in this room wishes to be anything other than a good, fair, supportive colleague. Right?

"I hope you all would feel this way about your colleagues. But if you do, and if that is all you allow yourself to feel and to admit, then you may be unleashing a frenzy of doubt and fear about job security. Again, as with racial feelings, stated concerns about poor job performance from overly demanding executives are not the organizational problem. No, the problem is the smiling inability to acknowledge the fact that, yes, there are some terrible contributors among us and everyone would be happier if they would leave or get fired. When the wrong hands are on deck, or in charge, for that matter, the shadow goes into high mischief mode. Before long all authority, even duly constituted authority doing perfectly reasonable things, is mocked and questioned. A maddening climate is created in which every conceivable ineptness goes unaddressed or is forgiven. In an organization unwilling to acknowledge its critical disapproval and aggression, everybody finds himself and herself walking on egg shells and not quite knowing why."

Sloan's thoughts raced confusingly as he summoned up images and circumstances to corroborate Naomi Wise's propositions. Not because her words were aversive, but because they were now too much for him, he felt an urge to withdraw, to find an excuse to exit the conference room and go home. No – not home. It was not yet noon. He pictured his empty house in the forlorn light of mid-day. There would be breakfast dishes on the counter and in the sink, crumbs on the sticky plastic tablecloth. Sloan felt a wave of deep and unfamiliar sadness, a kind of sadness that made him feel helpless and exposed, like a little boy. He willed his attention back to Naomi Wise.

"This is a lot to think about," she said with what seemed to Sloan infinite thoughtfulness and concern. "And you know I could add sex to the picture." She widened her eyes in a way that suggested sorrow. "We carry out, or at least try to carry out, our organizational life as though we had all tacitly consented to be eunuchs until it is time to go home." There was some laughter. "And of course there is no sex at *The Sun Messenger.* We don't even joke about it much anymore, because that might be harassing somebody. No, we don't flirt, touch, ogle, or consort on company time. We banish such thoughts, or at least keep them to ourselves. Because that's appropriate, right? It's only proper. But there's a problem in organizationally neutering ourselves. I don't have to say what it is, do I?"

Naomi Wise was looking, Sloan believed, directly at him.

"The problem is that we are not and cannot ever be neutered. Because sex is sex, the shadow finds a way to take charge of our lives. Deny sex and we become helpless, we become fools.

"And on that very peculiar note" – she was already laughing – "we should have our lunch!

"So how was it," Jen asked him as he stepped into the bright, cluttered kitchen, "the retreat?" She spoke the word "retreat" as if it could only have been pretentious, silly.

"Actually," Sloan said, feeling strangely spent, "it was interesting. It was kind of amazing." Immediately Sloan wished he had not said it. Now he would have to elaborate, and he did not want to, especially at that moment in the kitchen to his wife.

The atmosphere was heavy with the aroma of something insistent and faintly sour. Sloan glanced at the stove and saw broccoli and onions sizzling in the wok. Another stir-fry. Sloan's stomach clamped tight. He wanted to ascend up and out of the kitchen, to make his way to his chair in the corner of their bedroom, maybe to flop down on the bed, lie still in the darkness until it was time to eat.

"Bart coming home?" Sloan said, he hoped cheerfully.

"Of course he's coming home. He lives here." Jen turned away from Sloan. She began paring a slippery white brick of tofu into little cubes. "He's at practice."

"Go team, go Bart," Sloan said as he moved past Jen and out to the hall closet. He heard her say, "e-mail from Henry today."

Henry. Sloan felt a tightening below his heart. He pictured the rangy, slouching figure of his older son, the sharp, appealing bones of his cheeks and chin. He imagined that he was looking directly into Henry's imploring, apologetic eyes. Sloan knew at once that Jen's mention of the e-mail was a kind of summons to talk about Henry's precarious position at Miami University of Ohio where, as a freshman, he seemed to be failing to thrive. For a moment Sloan's head was flooded with images of college, of courses and credit hours, lecture halls and examinations in blue books, waxy dormitory corridors, vast cafeterias, shabby cluttered rooms smelling of stale socks, bunk beds, stalls of steaming showers. In the dark hallway Sloan could not imagine Henry, himself, anybody wanting to be in a college.

"I want to hear about it," Sloan sang out in a voice loud enough to carry into the kitchen. "But I'm absolutely whipped. I'm going upstairs to crash for a few minutes before dinner." He said this with an exaggerated cheerfulness he did not feel as he lunged up the stairs. His steps on the carpeted risers were heavy and loud, or perhaps he merely imagined they were, so that he was not able to hear all of Jen's response, or complaint, from the kitchen: "you go crash...retreat... takes it out if you...your son...drop out..."

Sloan closed the bedroom door and lay down on the bed. *Drop out.* Was Henry going to quit, was that the e-mail? From the outset, Henry had not seemed to like Miami much. There was little pointed complaint, but there was an ominous absence of enthusiasm in his periodic phone calls and e-mails. He seemed to Sloan less discontented than sad, flat, unaccountably lost. Or, Sloan told himself, that's just the way I imagine he is. Sloan recalled Naomi Wise talking about the universal tendency to project unacknowledged psychic business onto others. *I am* – Sloan was aware that he was mouthing the words out loud – *I am the lost one.*

The sadness seemed to descend from his head down into his throat, heart, belly. Sloan let himself feel the shame of realizing that Miami, because it was a state school, was the only one he could afford. Others, Kenyon College, Bucknell in Pennsylvania, had also accepted Henry. But they were more than forty thousand a year, and neither one offered much aid. Miami cost about eleven, and Sloan knew they could not really afford even that.

The mess of the family finances swam in his head. Seventy thousand a year with his new post as editorial page editor. Another two or three thousand for free lance work. Jen's tuition for her doctoral program at City College was now a wash, since she taught freshman writing classes as part of her assistantship. A fifty-thousand dollar no-interest loan from his father allowed them, barely, to meet mortgage, insurance, and car payments. Sloan loved the old, eccentric, chronically drafty house they had bought in Cleveland Heights, but he could never seem to keep free of code violations – peeling paint, detached gutters, outdated wiring – much less improve and spruce up the place the way he and Jen had planned when, lightheaded about owning a rather big, lovable house, they had made the purchase. *Three thousand bucks a year for heat,* Sloan heard himself saying, again, surprisingly, out loud. There was not, Sloan knew, money for Henry's second term tuition. He would talk to his father, go to the bank. There should be – for Bart, for Jen – a vacation somewhere in the summer. Bart's friends all went to basketball camp. Jen had finally had to turn off the water in the downstairs powder room to stop the leaks. Other leaks had discolored the ceiling plaster in the dining room and the den. "One day we will be eating," Jen had said, "entertaining guests and, ka-boom, the ceiling will crash down and kill us." The boys' bikes were rusted. Car tires were balding, neither car serviced in months. The night before the drier shorted out an electrical circuit. Sloan had been working at his lap top on the third floor when the room went suddenly, silently dark.  It felt like the end of the world.

When Jen yelled up the stairwell, "Supper!  Your family would like to eat supper," Sloan was thinking about talking to his father, asking him for an extension of the loan.  He knew his father would say yes, even though the present loan payment was only three hundred dollars a month, and that from any other kind of investment his father would receive well-deserved interest on his savings.  His father lived simply, almost austerely, with outwardly less, and certainly in smaller quarters, than his son.  His father had been gently humorous and kind when Sloan appealed for Help.  For years the head teller at a small branch bank, his father had retired at a salary of $31,000.  His father had sent him to Amherst.

"Suit yourself," Jen called up the stairwell, "We're eating."


Later that night Sloan half reclined in his battered large chair in the corner of the bedroom.  The clunks and whooshes of the plumbing in Bart's bathroom had stilled, and Jen lay asleep across the darkened room, her deep regular respiration somehow contributing to the quiet.

The house felt sweetly at rest.  A shaft of butterscotch lamplight was just sufficient for Sloan to read the remaining pages of Dr. Chandru Lott's essay on the shadow in mid-life.  Again, as when he first looked at the piece during the morning break, the ideas in the text seem to proceed into the center of his understanding without resistance.

His shadow, Sloan read, was simply the rest of him.  It was, in a phrase he reread several times, the *source of his longing.*  Longing.  The word seemed to belong to an operatic, inaccessible past.  People longed, they yearned in romantic poems, in love songs.  But this was not quite right.  Sloan paused to consider the presence of his wife, the breathing, indistinct mound of her across the darkened room.

Sloan longed.  Sitting in his chair in the lamplight, he realized that he longed, even that "longing" was a good word for it.  He longed for the unexpected sparks of communion with his boys when in the course of their odd errands, outings, shooting hoops in the driveway, they would acknowledge the wonder or the humor in something and then, in a somewhat deeper psychic recess, register pleasure that the moment had been shared. Sloan longed for that wonder, for, especially, his boys to know it. He could not bear to think about them being overwhelmed, shamed, afraid – of what? – of their own longing. He did not want them to draw back from the wonder of things, to grow reflexively defensive, to be always on edge, always a little afraid. Sloan thought about projection. He was, he knew, always on edge, always a little afraid – also that this was the last thing anyone was likely to say about him.

Sloan considered Jen and whether he longed, whether he had ever longed, for her. He pictured the surprise of her quick smile when they had met, his fascination with the sharp bones of her cheek and chin – like Henry's. It was a nervous smile, almost a tic, her eyes narrowing in a way that made her look at once delighted and suspicious. Yes, Sloan had longed for her, had sensed her in rooms, in crowds before she would arrive. There had been the exquisite softness of her skin. What words could describe it? Like silk, like satin – but not really right. Like – like *her skin*, like skin if skin could be powder or the softest breeze: without blemish, seemingly without pores, creamy, milky white skin which, through the medium of Sloan's fingertips, had once made him worshipful. Yes, he had longed.

Jen would not hear that she was beautiful or desirable. Slender, small boned, and delicate, she protested, and also felt, that she had been denied the requisite feminine allures of her era. "Don't tell me I'm thin!" she would shriek. "Look! look at me" -- she was standing naked, just out of the shower, her heels together as if under mock inspection. "I have no definition, no muscles. Look! I just hang there on my bones. I'm all white and horrible. I'm a dough girl." She was being funny for Sloan, but he sensed a kind of terror in her self-effacement. To Sloan the very qualities about which she complained, the absence of chiseled contours, defined musculature, any kind of athleticism, were themselves wondrous.  Dancing, she seemed nearly to disappear against the pressure of his embrace, as insubstantial at his chest as the bird skeleton of her delicate bones.  She did not understand that he loved this mystery in her, that her physical being, as when they made love, somehow joined and received his but without any apparent mass or resistance.  Sex with Jen felt to Sloan like dissolving ecstatically into softness itself, an exquisite release into white milkiness, feathers opening into feathers.

Sloan lay the shadow article aside and turned off the standing lamp.  Deeply sad now and surrendering all resistance to this sadness, he was stirred, awake and vulnerable in a new way.  *The source of his longing* was within, a shadowy but irrepressible part of himself.  He wanted it to come out.  He wanted it to come true.

# 2

## BREATHE

"Breathe!" Naomi Wise said to Sloan. Her expression was wondrous, as if she might break into laughter.

"I stop breathing?" Sloan said, but he already knew it. He had felt the constriction in his chest.

"Yes, you stop breathing. And you do it – when?" She looked at Sloan encouragingly.

"When?" Sloan paused to consider. He didn't like this. His mind seemed to void itself of all clear thought. "I don't know. I guess I don't feel myself doing it. What does it look like to you?"

"To me? To me it looks like you are holding onto your breath so you don't have to release what you are really thinking, what you are feeling."

Naomi Wise was struck again by the wonderful, unkempt good looks of the man seated across the little glass table that separated their swivel chairs. There was something strong and appealing in his dishevelment, the way the knot of his tie hung askew below his collar, the loosely rolled sleeves over the bones of his wrists, the good strong hands. Sloan Fox, she said to herself, that is a real Anglo name, a name out of a novel. Sloan Fox, she registered with pleasure, was a handsome man, tallish, angular, trim. Good hair, a reddish-brown, mussed and curled over the sharp tips of his ears, over the back of his collar. She took in the regular cut of his face, bright asking eyes, available, vulnerable. A good face, a good, funny man. Also a boy.

She had not expected his call. Nor, for quite a time, was it at all clear why he felt he needed a consultation. She did not know if he was being casually off-hand or genuinely muddled when, after reintroducing himself, he had asked, "Do you do people?"

"Do people?" she had asked.

"Do individual people, or only groups, the way you worked at the Hyatt?"

"Do you mean, do I have a practice, take private clients? Yes, I have and I do." Even over the telephone something unmeasured and giddy in her laughter delighted Sloan.

There was a substantial pause before Sloan could say, "I think I'd like to be done."

Setting up an appointment was a more elaborate process than he imagined it would be. She was not sure if she had any available hours in the next several weeks. Then when she called back and confirmed that there was a late afternoon opening three weeks later, Sloan was told he would have to confirm the appointment with the secretary of the clinic where she practiced. Her fee, one hundred twenty dollars for an hour-long session, was about twice what he guessed it might be, and he was initially discouraged by the realization that he would not be able to afford many sessions, but the receptionist at the clinic told him the initial consultation and most of any "treatment" to follow would be covered by his *Sun Messenger* health plan.

"What are you looking for in this consultation?" Naomi Wise had asked him.

Sloan took time to consider, to find coherent words to explain that he wanted to feel more of what he felt when he heard her talk about the shadow. He wanted to feel the unfurling of surprising, possibly great inevitabilities. He wanted to approach *the source of his longing.* He was willing to long. He wanted to long without propriety or caution. He wanted, he thought, to confess a little, to explore some of the shadowy, beckoning recesses of imagery and feeling for which there was no polite outlet at home, at the paper, in any kind of company he knew. He wanted, for the first time in his life, to be absolutely frank about sex, about how and where he would really like to live. While it would take several sessions before he could say it clearly to Naomi Wise, Sloan had begun to feel an intimation that there was a world, a possible paradise, tantalizingly at hand, just beyond the sphere that presently confined him.

Sloan had finally telephoned Naomi Wise not because he had reached a point of new clarity about his longing or what he longed for. He telephoned, rather, because he realized he didn't care anymore about clarity. He wanted only to revisit that expansive opening-up feeling, to say yes to longing. Moreover, although he would not have been able to admit any such thing while he was formally in therapy, he wanted to unfurl in the safe, soft presence of a woman, preferably a kind of sorceress or seductress, a lover, an approver, a yes-sayer. Sloan wanted to let go, to disclose himself utterly. To be able to do this, even to try, in the care of a beautiful, welcoming woman felt to Sloan an indescribable relief.

"When you are breathing," Naomi Wise drew a deep resonant breath, closing her eyes as she exhaled, "You are there, you are in the moment, right here, with me. When you hold back breath, when you clench, you are stuck somewhere else in your head, in the past. Do you mind when I tell you to breathe?"

Sloan did not mind. It distracted him to be self-conscious about breathing, but he did want to be, as Naomi Wise had put it, in the moment, fully there, with her.

Sloan was not prepared for how unprotected, how intimate, the consultation would feel. A striking and very appealing woman was seated a few feet in front of him, and Sloan realized he had possibly never experienced such a prolonged spell of sheer looking into another person's eyes. The little room was softly lit. The door was closed.

Naomi said, very deliberately, "Now Sloan, tell me about you. Help me understand who you are."

"About me," Sloan's mind began to race. He pictured himself looking impenetrably dense, a comic oaf. *Who I am.*

"Well, I'm a newspaper writer, news and features – except, I guess now I'm not. I am editorial page editor. I write editorials, opinion pieces. I assign editorials, edit them, edit letters."

"That's very interesting," Naomi said, attending closely. She was not mocking him. "So you are the editorial voice of the *Sun Messenger.*"

"Not exactly. We have staff meetings and decide on editorial takes. I write one nearly every day, but I rarely surprise anybody."

"So there is a kind of party line."

Sloan paused to consider. Was there? "No, not really. We just get a sense of what we're going to stress, and then one of us does it." Then – the words out of his mouth before he knew it – "Why are we, I mean why am I talking about the paper? I work for it, as I said, but it's not really important to me at the moment."

"Let's talk about what's important."

Again Sloan grew quiet. He lost his train of thought. Naomi said, "Breathe."

Sloan inhaled and exhaled slowly and said, "I'm forty-four. I'm married, for twenty-one years. I've got two kids, two boys, fourteen and nineteen. My wife's a graduate student at City College, working on a Ph.D. in English. We life in Cleveland Heights. We –" Sloan looked away.

"We--?"

Sloan had been about to say that while far from destitute, he was feeling pinched for money, but realized this, too, felt perfunctory, beside the point, as if he were killing time.

"I'm forty-four," Sloan said, "and I wake up feeling – in fact, I usually feel – like I'm twenty-four. I can't literally believe I have a son in College. Sometimes I can't believe I've got a house, that I have a job, that I'm married."

"You feel surprised to find yourself where you are?"

"Yeah, a little. I don't know if I'm *surprised.* I'm more frustrated, impatient."

"Impatient for--?"

"Impatient for things to come together, to--"

"Things?"

"For something to come up that carries me away."

"You would like to be carried away."

I would, Sloan thought. That's it exactly. I'd like to be carried way by something irresistible. He fantasized sometimes about a majestic global war and that he was carried off in its unfathomable currents, posted to teeming cities in China, moving about the sere rubble of the Near East, cut off from everything known and familiar. Anonymous, he would feel everything, feel history itself. Or he could be carried away by a cause. He was always moved by appeals to house and feed disaster victims, to succor the urban homeless, minister to the dislocated survivors of Kosovo or Rwanda. He would be effaced, blessedly lost in his work. Carried away. He could not have brought it to consciousness in his first consultation, but Sloan would also like to have been carried away by a woman, by a figure at once sensual and impulsive, reckless and strong. Someone who would not, like Jen, pass every urge and possibility through a filter of timidity and doubt.

"I would like to run away from home," Sloan said at last.

Naomi smiled appreciatively. Her hum of approval hung soothingly in the air.

"But I will not run away from home. I love my kids, I love my wife and – I'm just not done there."

"But something in you wants to break out. Do you ever break out, a little?"

"Do I break out?" Sloan gave out a nervous laugh. Did he? He thought about Friday afternoons, the perceptibly mounting kidding and silliness in the City Room before they headed out at five to Dulaney's for a beer. "A beer" was always three or four, sometimes five. Even now, in the late afternoon hush he could feel the softly lit, beckoning appeal of Dulaney's. Was it "breaking out?" No, there was no breaking, no forcefulness in it. Dulaney's – its glittering sprays of white holiday lights, the surges of chatter and laughter, the welcoming, faintly sweet atmosphere of beer and cigarette smoke, onions on the grill – felt like a gentle summons, a place to thaw out, come to rest. Once, when he had been with the paper for about a year, Sloan realized that drinking beer with his new colleagues had the effect of releasing a surprisingly insistent warmth – love – for them: older and younger, men and women alike, the more of them the better. At the time he thought he now understood and gladly acquiesced in pretending to thank-God-it's-Friday. He wondered a little at how a beer or two could release such an intense, unnamable affection. Later it occurred to him, as it did acutely now in Naomi Wise's consulting room, that the beer did not cause or catalyze the fellowship, but merely granted a kind of permission. The twinkling dark of Dulaney's, the muted roar of its happy-hour, the amber lager, the last trace of chill gone from the glass – yes, Sloan thought, it's a ritual, a sacrament. It is a sacrament of yes-saying, of coming off it, of shedding the work and loving the people. Then an unpleasant, called-to-task feeling, like a blow: Jen. Jen still resented his late Friday arrivals. There would be a single place setting at the deserted table. A terse note. Fridays were often Henry's game nights, and Jen would be cool and unapproachable when Sloan joined her late in the raucous gymnasium stands. "You smell like a brewery," she would say without turning to look at him. Dulaney's, he had told her, was part of the work. "Tell me about it," she would say or, even more icily, "Like hell it is."

"Where did you go?" Naomi asked. "So many things going on in your face?"

Sloan smiled, looked directly into Naomi's inquiring eyes. He would like to have cupped her accepting face between his palms, and drawn her forehead to his.

"I was just thinking about if I ever 'break out.' And I'm not sure I do. A few beers with my friends before I go home on Fridays. I might try to stretch an extra day into an out-of-town trip when I go, but I guess I'm not much of a breaker outer."

"You look disappointed."

He was. He was also becoming agitated at himself. He had come to Naomi Wise because he had wanted to lift some kind of lid – to *break out.* Yet he felt himself sitting with his shoulders slouched forward, feeling vaguely penitential and subdued, resisting, for some reason, the impulse that had urged him on to find Naomi Wise and let himself go.

"I think this is it," Sloan said.

"Is what?"

"Coming here, talking to you. I think this is breaking out."

"Yes, and have you?" Naomi spoke the words with an exaggerated slowness, a hint of mocking. "Are you?"

Sloan felt himself draw back cautiously. "I'm waiting for my moment."

Naomi did not answer. She looked at Sloan, smiled, and waited.

Sloan felt the silence grow until it seemed to envelop both of them.

"Sloan Fox," Naomi said softly, "breathe!"

Without looking at his watch, Sloan knew there was little time left in the session. Why not, he thought. "Let me tell you about New Orleans."

"Tell me."

"Last spring I was in New Orleans, for a press awards convention. It was April, first time for me, never been to New Orleans." Sloan felt a pang of doubt: *why am I doing this?* "Have you ever been to New Orleans?"

"No, tell me about it." Sloan saw Naomi glance at her watch, which she had unclasped and set down on the glass table between them as they had begun.

"Well, I think New Orleans is an amazing place, and I think something happened to me there."

"Something happened?"

"Something new. It felt like I woke up to something, like I was getting a message."

"And what was the message?"

Again his nervous laugh. "I don't know about this – it's going to sound pretty seedy."

"Seedy? Seedy is all right. Tell me."

"O.K.," Sloan reconfigured himself in his chair. O.K., he thought, here goes.

"What did you just do?" She asked Sloan brightly. "Look what you just did. For the first time since we've been talking, you have opened yourself up. You unfolded your arms" – Naomi demonstrated – "and you spread your knees apart and now here you are, looking straight at me, wide open."

"I guess so," Sloan looked at Naomi to see if this required more discussion, but she was alert to him, listening.

"So I found myself in New Orleans, in this new city I'd always kind of heard a lot about. Mardi Gras, Bourbon Street, music, night life, fun, maybe a little sleaze. And," Sloan paused to consider, "it was. It was all of that. I was there three nights, and a bunch of us went out, and each night it got better."

"What got better?"

"The excitement, or the *allure*, got better, got more intense. It'd start with a good Cajun dinner somewhere, and by then we would put together a group and go bar-hopping through the French Quarter, no map, no plan, staying on if we liked the music, just following our noses." Sloan could feel, hear himself growing energized.

"When did it happen?"

"What?"

"The thing that happened, the amazing thing."

"Right." Sloan collected himself. "It's going to be hard to describe. But here goes. Each night we went out was really late. We were out till three or four. But I *never got tired*. I wanted it to keep going, keep happening. Drinks didn't seem to make any difference. I could have had a million drinks. And I was smoking, having a good time smoking, and I don't smoke."

"So it was wonderful staying up late drinking and smoking in an exciting atmosphere."

Sloan knew this wasn't it. "No, I'm making it sound stupid, like a lot of carousing.  It wasn't – no, we *were* kind of carousing, but what happened was the women."

"You met women?"

"We met women wherever we went.  Actually, we looked in at some topless places and nude bars."  Sloan looked at Naomi, "A first for me.  And it started to dawn on me.  These women sitting at the bars in the clubs, all slinky and shiny in black – these women were *incredible*.  I mean there were lots of them and they all had a look."  Sloan wanted to convey this look perfectly.  "They all seemed to be wearing black, slinky, glittery things.  They were all very thin, dark, black women, Creoles, Mexican, Italian – I don't know, except they looked so similar, so striking.  I would walk down a side street, and there would be two, three, a half dozen dark women lounging in front of the bars, smoking."

"Were they prostitutes?"

"I don't know.  I don't think they all could have been prostitutes, not in all those places."

Naomi looked with concern at her watch.  "And the amazing thing?"

"The amazing thing, I think, is that I couldn't get enough of these women.  I felt like I was falling in love with them, not with any particular one, but with all of them, the idea of them.

"On my last night, I left my friends and went back to the hotel, but after a few minutes, I went back out on my own.  I didn't know exactly what I wanted, but I wanted more."

"More night ladies?"

"Yes."

"And did you find them?"

"I did.  I did.  They were everywhere.  They were in the clubs.  They were on the street.  I went back into one of the nude bars by myself, and there were dozens of them.  They come up to you and offer table dances for money and there are private booths for more money.  But when they were moving around, working the floor, I got the feeling they were doing a kind of dance around me and that the dance was all about this new *quality,* this new feeling that had come over me." Sloan looked up at Naomi. "I can feel it now."

"And how does it feel?"

"Exactly the same. Like another world."

Naomi was looking at Sloan intently, but he was not sure what she was thinking.

"So is that a strange story, or what? I didn't take anybody to bed, by the way."

"I am not sure if it is a strange story. It sounds like the beginning of a strange story."

"The beginning." Sloan watched Naomi pick up her watch and refasten it. The session was over.

"One more thing about the women," Sloan said. "Some of them were strippers, and maybe some of them were hookers. There is something obviously sexy about that look for me, but I wasn't feeling sexual, or mainly sexual, about them."

"What were you feeling?"

"I was feeling...you stand for something. You are sending me a message, some kind of irresistible message. I don't think I wanted the women. I think I wanted the message." Sloan had it: "You know what they were like? *Priestesses.* They were like priestesses in a dark and mysterious place."

Naomi smiled with kind regret. "We must stop. We must stop in a dark and mysterious place. But I will tell you something, and I want you to think about it. Sloan Fox, you have some surprises ahead of you."

She looked at Sloan with concern. "Breathe!"

# 3

## SUPPRESSED DESIRE

"**A**nd who is Dr. Naomi Wise at East Shore Psychological Services?" Jen asked, flatly, as Sloan stepped into the kitchen. She sat at the kitchen before a littered crescent of mail and catalogues. Her half-glasses were riding low toward the tip of her nose. Sloan saw no food in preparation on the counter, no pot simmering on the stove.

He looked at his watch and made an exaggerated grimace. "Have I got the right house? I'm due at the Foxes for supper."

"East Shore Psychological Services, Ninth and Lakeside," Jen had not looked up from the billing statement.

"And by the way, Jen darling, *hello*. It's good to see you, and did you have a productive day?"

"What's with the bill?" Jen turned to Sloan, holding the statement before her at arm's length. "What is it?"

"There shouldn't be a bill," Sloan said, "Medical Mutual is supposed to cover it."

"This is *from* Medical Mutual, and it is covered." Now Jen was agitated, sharp. "What is it? 'Three consultations at one hundred twenty dollars per hour'?"

"That's what it is – three consultations at one hundred twenty dollars per hour."

"*What* consultations?  Yours?  For *what?*"

Sloan almost said: it's really nice to be home.  He pictured himself turning away, heading back out into the rainy night, driving off.

"Naomi Wise," he said, unbuttoning his damp raincoat, "is the psychologist who ran the retreat downtown last month.  You remember.  The one who talked about the shadow.  She was terrific, so I decided to talk to her some more.  And so, I did.  I have.  I've seen her four times."

"So you see this Wise woman now, and you're – in therapy?  Talking about your shadow?"  Before she finished speaking, Jen could see the hurt resentment in Sloan's face.  The sarcasm was reflexive; she had overstepped.  Then quietly, in a conciliatory tone, "Were you going to tell me about it?"

Sloan felt his anger begin to dissolve.  "I was going to wait and see if it amounted to anything.  I suppose I could have told you.  I thought there was a chance it would turn out to be stupid."

"And it isn't."

"No, I don't think it is."

"It's nothing to be ashamed of," Jen said in a wispy, girlish voice, playful now.  She felt an urge, but suppressed it, to tease him, to ask him if he was more "in touch with his feelings."  Had he located his dark side, his deep feminine, his – she remembered the word for it – *shadow.*

"So what are you smiling about?" Sloan asked her.  He felt better.  Now Jen knew about the sessions with Naomi, and those times would no longer have to feel so oddly and secretly circumscribed, so discontinuous with the rest of his life.

"I'm smiling because – because maybe you are more interesting than I thought."

"No," Sloan said, stepping past her to hang up his coat, "I've always been really interesting."

In ways she would not have found easy to explain, it excited Jen that her husband had, on his own and unexpectedly, initiated a program of counseling. She warmed to the idea of his vulnerability, even his help-lessness. She was fascinated that he had chosen a woman therapist. The thought of it aroused her a little, yet without jealousy – if anything, she realized, she felt envious of his sequestered, privileged encounters with another woman, a woman he seemed to admire almost reverently, with whom, Jen imagined, he could say or feel anything at all.

She did in fact find Sloan more interesting. He had, all on his own, set out on this guided course, or so she imagined, of interior explora-tion. She felt, although she could not quite bring it to conscious clar-ity, that Sloan's reaching out was a tacit admission that he might not be managing well. He had sought and perhaps needed help, and this comforted Jen. If Sloan was imperfectly meeting life's vicissitudes, she could freely and openly acknowledge the same, which was a calming relief. *Sloan is looking for help,* she told herself, *and from a woman.*

In the days following the disclosure of her husband's therapy, Jen felt altogether more alert. It had been a grim, confining win-ter. Henry's lackluster start at the university and his impenetrable, noodle-y responses to her concern had been a source of insistent, daily unease. Bart, in his way, seemed to mimic his older brother's diffidence, making – except when, maddeningly, Sloan would joke him out of it – only the most general, passive account of his start at the high school. My boys are ciphers, she told herself. They are learning, a little more each day, how to withhold and distance them-selves from their mother, from mother-like people, from all who care and want to know. Who wrote this script for men? Henry and Bart would emerge, she knew, like Sloan one day. They already showed signs of his quirky charm: a distracted, almost dazed air of not quite meeting the situation on its own terms, then some sudden, surprising acuity, a joke or an observation that would strike the heart. There was a subtlety, a kind of genius in Sloan's ability to withdraw into impenetrability. He could stand in a line or sit across from her at the table looking so sleepy, so clueless that it seemed a clear trespass to ask anything of him. And she deferred to him! She let herself draw on his strength, leaned her own often crippling inertia against his. *Was* he quietly strong, she wondered, or some kind of absence onto which she projected the strength and constancy she needed?

Jen sipped cold coffee in her third floor "office." She had not touched Krupansky's research or her own dissertation notes, although she had been up and awake since six. She had instead been musing, concluding that all males claimed the privilege of unavailability. They exited the present and went wherever they went. Sloan did and would continue to do it, and there were going to be two more just like him down the pipeline.

Feeling the descent of powerful fatigue, Jen unzipped the plastic folder containing Dr. Krupansky's research project. It title page, "Syntactical Clues to the Disappearance of the Personal: The Structure of Mind in the Northern Renaissance," had been Xeroxed so many times the darker masses in the letters looked scratched and faded. Two years ago she had been elated that Ted Krupansky had agreed to advise her dissertation. Working as his graduate assistant was considered a plum appointment at City College. The University's Department of English had no national status whatsoever, but Edward Krupansky was a much published and respected Elizabethan scholar. Schooled himself at Yale, he brought, the Provost thought and the graduate students in English wanted to believe, the cachet of Yale's modernism and critical tradition to the City College of Cleveland State University.

Jen would concede that Ted had been nice enough to her. He had given her masses of references and structural tips on her own dissertation proposal – *Edith Wharton and the Negation of Gender* – though far from his own scholastic preserve. He made himself and his office generously available to her and would talk to her freely, but with a detectable lack of intellectual interest, about her thesis. A thickening, graying man of about sixty, Ted Krupansky seemed to Jen to have settled into a permanently bemused professionalism: long tenured, a full professor, his scholastic claims, however finally modest, forever staked. Childless themselves, Dr. and Mrs. Krupansky had graciously included Jen and Sloan in a half dozen social evenings: a wine tasting (Wines of the Hapsburg Empire), a recital of a string trio followed by dessert and coffee, small dinner parties of assorted City College academics. Jen had gone with playful curiosity, willing to find the assembled professors exotic. Sloan had been gracious but, Jen knew, inwardly fitful. After the Wines of the Hapsburg Empire he had been relentless during the car ride home. "Well, we've obviously got to have them all back to our house. What do you think? Should we do the wines of the Nixon Presidency? Wouldn't cost us much, or maybe the peanuts of the Carter era?" Jen had told him to shut up. The jokes belittled a world she wanted to matter. It annoyed her that she wanted it to matter also to Sloan. It annoyed her, moreover, that the Krupanskys had unmistakably *liked* Sloan, made a fuss over him.

Jen fanned through the photocopied material that would be "Syntactical Clues to the Disappearance of the Personal." Even before the new software, her assignment had been numbingly mindless. She had photocopied page after page of Elizabethan prose, beginning with the essays of Francis Bacon, then laboriously determined and classified the length and syntactical type of each sentence. Now she was able to scan the pages directly into her computer, and – click, click, click – the new program would identify and count. While much simpler, Jen realized, the work was even more brainless. She had seen Ted Krupansky's other published articles based on this kind of analysis. There would be an unreadably clotted abstract, then a short thesis statement in similarly vacant sentences, each footnoted, followed by text broken by authoritative-looking graphs and tables. Jen imagined that learned journals in anthropology, perhaps even in chemistry, were filled with similar, indistinguishable articles.

Jen did not mind that Professor Krupansky's work was obscure or highly specialized, but she did not like feeling that it was of no possible human interest or use. She had hoped that her own thesis about Edith

Wharton's fiction touching on a kind of humanity that "transcended" and thus "negated" gender would matter to somebody. This morning she doubted it. She felt heavy in her heart, heavy in her bones. Her City College crowd – Ted, his colleagues, the other doctoral fellows, Lu, Janice, Phip, seemed this morning like a sorry, fussy lot.

Maybe not, Jen said out loud in the empty house. Maybe not. *What's with me?* For an instant Jen felt preposterous, not quite real, seated at her desk in the palely lit attic room. She was frightened by – hated – the feeling that her preoccupation with her dissertation, teaching sections, research – was really a phony aura surrounding nothing, connecting her to nothing and to no one else.

Jen longed to connect. She wanted to teach and be taught by her boys. She wanted to feel the way she had felt when they were babies clinging to her neck, reaching desperately up to her from their cribs. She wanted to connect the way she had when Sloan first overcame her edginess and resistance, when she had been tipsy and fell back naked and amazed into lovemaking.

Now there was a wall, a barrier. She felt cocooned and remote from the other shoppers wheeling their carts through the Stop 'n' Shop. She felt ominously alone parking her car in the University lot. She could feel it, feel crazily isolated in the noisy, lurid chock-a-block gymnasium stands as she sat watching Henry, and now Bart, race up and down the floor with the other players, all of them linked as by an invisible thread to the progress of the ball. Tears welled in Jen's eyes.

Over dinner, Jen could feel herself being needlessly sharp with Sloan. Though they had resolutely refused to set a firm dinner time, Jen had on her own determined that it was six-thirty. By six-thirty Bart was home from practice, and his appetite-destroying raids on chips and sweets could be reasonably resisted. When Sloan arrived, with apologies, at seven, Jen was already edgy.

Over chicken much drier than she wanted it to be, Jen grilled Bart about school, course by course, and received only dull, serviceable replies. Then, with unexpected life he looked up at Sloan and said, "Coach says I can dress varsity for the play-offs."

"Really?" Sloan was elated. "As a freshman? Bart, that's fantastic. How many is he allowed to dress?"

"Fifteen."

"Fifteen! Bart, that's terrific. He's obviously had his eye on you."

"Yeah, maybe." Bart was beaming, his open smile concealing nothing. To Sloan he was radiant, beautiful.

"Does that mean you'll play?" Jen asked.

Bart's smile receded. "Doubtful. Maybe if we're up or down thirty at the end of the game."

"But it's a good thing to dress?" Jen asked uncertainly.

"It's a great thing," Sloan said. "It's an honor. He's one of the top fifteen basketball players in the school, as a freshman. Every other freshman watches the game from the stands."

Jen looked combatively at Sloan, "So he'll be closer."

Sloan felt he was being baited, challenged. He had wanted to celebrate a nice moment for Bart. He addressed his chicken.

Bart asked to be excused, cleared his dishes, and left the kitchen.

"It's a big deal for a freshman," Sloan said quietly.

"Now I know," Jen said. "So why were you late?"

"I had a session."

"A session?"

Sloan knew Jen had understood him, "Yes, a session with Naomi Wise, the psychologist I talk to."

"You could have told me this morning."

"I didn't think I'd be late. Sorry."

"It got you a dry chicken. So how's it going, if you're allowed to tell me."

Sloan did not want to talk about his work with Naomi. Part of his pleasure in the sessions was the relief he felt in not having to be acceptable, admirable, outwardly accountable in any way. That afternoon he had talked with Naomi about sex, how the transporting wonder of it could so quickly and utterly vanish before the weight of routine and responsibility. At one point Sloan had said, "Sometimes I just want to *stay* in that place where sex takes me."

Naomi acknowledged this admission warmly. Sloan heard her lovely hum. She said, "What a beautiful way to put it."

Sloan did not want to violate the sanctity of his sessions with Naomi, nor did he want to establish any expectation on Jen's part that she had access to what transpired. But Sloan knew that his therapy raised inevitable questions for Jen. He knew if their situation were reversed, he would want to know what was at the heart of his wife's concerns.

"It's nothing mysterious," he said, looking up at Jen, trying to remove any edge to his voice. "It's like any good conversation, except with no practical point. A lot of it's about how what you say is related to the way you feel." Sloan felt himself warming to the challenge of explaining. "For instance, she stops me all the time. I'm rambling away and think I've just made a dynamite point about something, and Naomi will stop me and say, 'and how does that make you feel?' It was annoying at first, but now I can see what she's doing. She's trying to get me, as she says, to come down out of my head and into my heart and body." Sloan looked for a sign of derision in Jen's eyes. "She keeps telling me I've got to breathe. I guess I stop breathing, which she says means I'm holding back."

"Do you? Stop breathing."

"I guess I do. I don't know. You know what? I'm just *going* with this. I'm not being analytic or skeptical or anything. I just try to open up, let go, see what happens."

"And what happens?" Jen said with unexpected gentleness.

Sloan gave a quick laugh. "What happens? I don't know, I don't know yet. Maybe the best of it is that, for a minute or two I feel very disoriented, very helpless and out of control. What am I *doing* talking to this stranger in a dark office? My real world, the paper, *you* feel somewhere on Mars. I feel like I really don't know anything. *Anything.* And then there comes a really wonderful awareness, like what I felt for a minute during the Retreat. I see that the world is really a bigger, more mysterious place than I wanted to think it was. The rules and the boundaries restricting me aren't really real. They're mine. I made them, or I accepted them blindly the way a little kid does. The truth is, I can probably do anything."

Jen felt a jolt of anxiety. She believed Sloan could abandon her. "Like what? What could you do?"

"I could bag the *Sun Messenger*. I could go" – Sloan caught himself – "We could go to New Orleans." Sloan wished he had not said this. "We could go to an island. I could write a good book." This was not it. He had veered far from his intent, far from the value of his talks with Naomi.

"Could you let me know a little in advance?" Jen said with a studied lightness. She was ready to withdraw, to clear the table.

Sloan was reading in his reclining chair when Jen emerged naked from the bathroom. He watched her in shadowy light as she rummaged through a bureau drawer for a nightgown. When she came to his chair she was wearing the plum colored satin chemise he had bought her, on a whim, at the airport Victoria's Secret. Their large dormered bedroom was poorly heated, and Sloan, in his sweater and corduroys, could feel the chill. Jen would be cold. Her bedtime routines were usually invariable: bath, teeth, moisturizers, flannel nightgown, and a beeline for her side of the bed.

Tonight she stood behind his chair, gently kneading his shoulders with her delicate fingers.

"Am I in your light?" she asked.

"You are always in my light," Sloan said. "I like your outfit."

"Oh, good." Jen tucked her chin into her neck so she could see the fall of the scooped satin over her breasts, belly, hips. "It's the kind of thing you put on in order to take off."

When they were in bed, when Sloan's body heat had made their place warm and comfortable, his hands guided hers as, sitting upright, she raised the slippery chemise up over her head and arms.

Then she let Sloan fold her softness into him. Held fast, heart to heart, thigh to thigh, she felt him begin to rock her slightly, gently back and forth. She heard a hypnotic hum in the dark air, then realized it was hers. Over the curve of her shoulder, the rim of her breast, softly, almost tickling the blade of her hip, each touch was dreamily, thrillingly anticipated. In the bath, she had been aroused thinking about Sloan. He had surprised her at dinner. Bart left the table and she knew it had gone sour, that she had somehow spoiled it. Then Sloan was different. He had not been clear, but he had been soft – no, not soft. He had been new. She felt again the jolt of fear that he could release himself, take off somewhere. He could admit that he was looking, could say yes to new and unheard of things, say no to what was familiar and certain. This was unfamiliar, terrible, wonderful. Jen believed she could really lose him. Why was this exciting? Because, it came to her pleasingly, they could start again. She could find him again, find him different, bigger, more. Lose him.

Jen guided him unashamedly down to her pleasure. On the threshold of oblivion she silently opened her mouth.

Yes this, Sloan thought. He wanted only this. He realized there was no end to it and that he could have, as he had at this moment, the very thing he desired.

***

The party was to have begun at eight, and at nearly half past, no guests had yet arrived. Naomi made her way to the vestibule, where ghostly orbs of light from the votive candles flickered on the polished marble tiles. Naomi peered through the wavery glass panels at the side of the front door. No one.

Known for being a meticulous planner, she realized now that three or four of the invited couples, associates of hers from the clinic, would not know that she and her husband had kept their family names.

They will be looking for Wise, Naomi thought, and see Weingart on the mailbox.

Naomi had wanted to feel lighthearted, even a little outrageous, about this party. She had recalled such an evening, fantastic in her memory, her parents had hosted in New York when she was six or seven. Guests were to come as their Suppressed Desire. She had not known the meaning of the phrase, but the sound of it enchanted her. The hushed sibilance made it sound unearthly, portentous: *Suppressed Desire*. Naomi remembered the laughter, an impression of theatrically vivid faces, wonderful, surprising exposure of limbs, shoulders, décolletage. Women were sprites bearing real wings, faces sequined. There were gowned princesses and divas, a ballerina, a platinum wigged Mae West. Men were decadent emperors in togas and sandals. There was a scarlet coated Canadian Mounty, a rabbi, a great ox of a man in only a cloth diaper. Her parents' party had been a thrilling, transforming evening for Naomi. The metamorphosis of the adults into exotic other beings struck a deep assurance in her that the wondrous was possible and close at hand. She had known many of the guests in their waking lives. They were her parents' friends. But she also felt in her deepest knowing that in so changing themselves outwardly, they were excitingly alive in a new way; something charged and volatile had been released. She loved this potential in the animated, and now beautiful, adults and believed it would be hers also.

Naomi returned to the kitchen to share her concern about the late arrivals with Nathan. In contrast to the eerily flickering passages and sitting rooms, the kitchen was brilliantly and whitely lit. Caterers, the men in black tie, the women aproned, pulled baking sheets of canopies from the oven, arranging them on garnished platters. Her husband stood, theatrically posed, hands laced behind his back, watching as Chardonnay was decanted into goblets.

Nathan Weingart turned his attention to his wife and said in a voice pitched to win the attention of the caterers, "Ah, yes, Salome! Of the deadly dance."

Nathan, she realized, looked entirely comfortable in his velvet doublet and pantaloons, black tights and buckled shoes. He was Faustus: although only the ancient leather volume tucked into his belt suggested anything of the Medieval scholar. Mainly he looked like a dandy of the court, prosperous, pleased with himself. Smiling broadly, publicly, his silver hair swept back, he looked, Naomi realized, exactly like himself.

"And aren't you beautiful," she said to him. Preoccupied by the late arrival of the guests, Naomi had forgotten for a moment that she too was in costume. Recalling the impression of fairies and gossamer moving through her parents' party, she had wanted to embody a similar figure. She had decided on the biblical Salome and wore a black spandex body suit under a tented series of sheer, spangled veils. She had twisted her hair into a top knot wrapped in a yarmulke-like cap of gold lame. From this cap fell a black, glittering veil.

The door chimes sounded, and Naomi dropped the veil over her face as she moved to greet her guests. Something, it occurred to her, was not right.

The Stockfishes, amiable and uncertain, stood for a moment just inside the front door. Joy Stockfish was a newly appointed family counselor at the clinic. She and her husband, a television weather forecaster, had newly arrived in Cleveland, and Naomi wanted to help get them acquainted.

Naomi noted something brittle, faintly troubled in their smiles of greeting. Then she realized they were not in costume. He wore a blazer and tie, she a sheer silk top and slacks. A bottle of Chardonnay – Naomi pictured the cases stacked on the pantry floor – was awkwardly proffered, and because Naomi was now distractedly preoccupied wondering if, by any chance the invitations, or even some of them, had omitted mention of the Suppressed Desire theme, she forgot to acknowledge the gift.

Naomi threw back her veil, made her eyes go wide. "O.K., I'm stumped. What is your suppressed desire?"

The Stockfishes looked startled, unhappy.

Naomi heard herself laughing. "I'll bet it's not to have to make an idiot of yourself at somebody's loony idea for a party."

Still only bewilderment from the Stockfishes.

When in doubt or trouble, Naomi trusted warmth, openness, the energy at hand. "Trust me," she said, "costumes will be strictly optional."

"Was this a *costume* party?" Joy Stockfish said, raising a hand to her heart.

"Suppressed desire," Naomi said, she hoped warmly, understandingly. "Whatever that means."

"Suppressed *desire*," Joy Stockfish repeated to her husband, still vacantly smiling.

"Not to worry." Naomi laughed again and wondered whether she sounded like a mad woman. "Come have something to drink and meet my crazy husband."

Nathan Weingart, in doublet and pantaloons, met them in the vestibule. Framed dramatically by an archway, he raised his goblet, touched heel to instep, and made a deep bow.

"Joy and Jerry Stockfish," Naomi said, "My husband, Nathan Weingart."

Naomi heard herself talking over their mumbled greetings. "Their suppressed desire, we have decided, is to be normal."

*No*, Naomi realized, hearing her own words. That's insulting! She trailed behind as her husband led the Stockfishes to the small den where a fire had been lit. She heard Joy Stockfish saying, "I had no *idea*."

By nine thirty, fifty or sixty guests – Naomi could not quite tell – had established themselves in the sitting rooms and den. There was a variegated din of talk and laughter, barely audible passages of jazz piano from the sound system. It's a party, Naomi concluded with relief. But it did not bring her hoped for fantasy to life.

Only the Stockfishes and one other couple had failed to wear costumes. A number of the men had done themselves up as professional athletes, their jerseys, football breeches, satin trunks looking inauthentically pristine. There was a Hamlet all in black, a revolutionary in camouflage and head scarf. A couple had come as President Clinton and Monica Lewinski. The wife, slightly heavy, her dark hair stiffly set in the manner of the notorious intern, wore knee pads beneath the skirt of a polka-dot dress. There were two Madonnas and a stunningly wigged Tina Turner.

They are colorful, Naomi mused. Maybe there are not enough people. The sitting room, large, austerely and elegantly appointed, resisted transformation. The house seemed to diminish and subdue the guests. Naomi moved from cluster to cluster, room to room. She had not yet been engaged by anyone. She felt a growing unease. We are all timid, she told herself. Locked up. Then the twinge of an insight she wanted to remember to write down: affluence masquerading as taste – no, better: how affluence and taste subdue and isolate those confined by them. No: how affluence and taste -- how impressiveness -- quiets and shames the body.

Naomi approached the dining room and felt a sharp pang of disapproval. Nathan had unrolled the architect's plans and drawings of their beach house on Edisto Island. They had agreed the dining room would be off limits. She had not wanted the party to become too diffuse. Nathan was bent over the polished surface of the dining table, smoothing the drawings, talking enthusiastically. Clustered respectfully about the table were the Levinsons, Rudins, Demases Haverhills: nurse, football player holding his helmet, a maestro with baton, the great diapered baby, a tart draped in a fluffy boa, over black miniskirt and fishnet stockings. None of them, Naomi thought, feeling the clench of her jaw, owned such houses, could afford to build such a house. She imagined their twinges of envy dissolving into polite disinterest.

Nathan caught sight of his wife and straightened himself. "Naomi, darling, I'm telling them about Edisto."

"An unsuppressed desire," she said. She raised her empty goblet and left the room.

Just before eleven a light supper was served, and it was clear to Naomi that the collective energy had waned hopelessly. Tip Lillienthal, chief of services at the Clinic, arrived late wearing the chains and black leather of a masochist. His presence among the diners was greeted with raucous comment and shrieks from the women. Making his way to the center of the sitting room, he dropped to his knees, joined his palms in supplication, said "Oh, *hurt* me." Another crescendo of surprised laughter as Mimi Lillienthal, also in leather, chained, preposterously pierced, swaggered menacingly up to her husband. She cracked a plastic whip, then her shoulders sagged, and she shook with laughter.

For a second, Naomi felt energized, alert, drawn out of herself. There had been something about Mimi Lillienthal, specifically the shiny, inky mesh of stocking over the flesh of her strong, good legs. A spark of sex, some escaped possibility. An image – images – began crowding into her consciousness. Dark shimmering women, seductresses smoking cigarettes on damp midnight streets, leggy women on barstools. Beckoning, available women, whores – *priestesses.* New Orleans. She saw Sloan Fox's face inclining toward her.

Naomi could feel the tension in her jaw as she beheld the standing and kneeling Lillianthals on the silver blue carpet. She could not laugh. The stylized, cartoon perversity distanced everyone from suppressed desire. And now she was tired, heavy in her legs. She wanted the guests to disperse and go.

At the adjacent marble sink, Nathan quietly gargled and spat tooth paste into the bowl.

"You made a perfect party," he said, eyeing her in the mirror.

"Mmm." Naomi prodded her gums with a red rubberized pick. Perfectly wrong. How easily Nathan said the perfectly wrong thing. His hair was still slicked back, meticulously parted as when he had first dressed for the party. Now he wore a black silk robe drawn loosely together revealing an expanse of sun-tanned chest. With no bodily feeling, with a kind of aversion, Naomi considered the handsome figure of her husband at her side in the mirror. She too wore a black silk robe over her nightgown. Tonight, again, she felt herself resisting the artifice of their standing together at their ablutions, each robed in black silk, gold and porcelain fixtures for each, a black veined porphyry basin for each. Naomi wished she were in bed, in her own bed – no, out in the night air away altogether.

In bed, in the darkness, Naomi opened her eyes. The party had at best been quietly agreeable. Faultlessly catered in their faultlessly appointed house. But Naomi knew; the evening was an airless failure, a betrayal. She let herself feel what she imagined her new colleagues at the clinic felt as they made their way through the house. They were people of modest and ordinary means. There could be no foreseeable bridge to such rooms and pictures and carpets and polished marble. Some people live this way, they would think, numbly distanced, perhaps resentful.

Nearly everyone, she recalled, had been at one time or other summoned to the gleaming dining room table to admire the plans for the house on Edisto. *I did not let myself go with anyone,* Naomi said to herself. By ten o'clock it had been clear. There would be no release, no real hilarity, no boundary crossing, no careless ascent. No one, she realized, had touched her. No arm had come to rest around her shoulder or waist. Even in greeting and saying good-bye to friends, she had not been kissed, kissed on the mouth.

*Forty-six,* Naomi thought, silently mouthing the words. I am forty-six. She pictured herself as Salome: scented and supple in her cat suit and scrim. *Fifty-five. Sixty-five.* The hollow recession of her eyes, the collapse and sag of her breasts. Desiccated. She could not, at the core of her, feel or even imagine feeling the tug of desire.

She pictured the two of them, a stylish woman and a stylish man in matching dressing gowns, framed in the gilt mirror. A pose, an advertisement, Naomi thought, an advertisement for...for unearthly bathrooms, for being better off than everyone else, better off than people with children and failing parents, than people with mortgages and car payments. *Seventy-five.* Old now and idle. And alone. She could hear Nathan's regular, husky respiration. "You made a perfect party."

The rest of her life like a perfect party. Alone.

# 4

## PUT YOURSELF IN YOUR STORY

"Go get 'em, big guy." Sloan said to Bart as the slender boy hauled his bulging back pack over his shoulders and headed out the kitchen door to school.

Sloan felt heavy and agreeably sleepy. Three quarters of his outsized Starbucks mug was filled with warm milky coffee. *The Sun Messenger* Metro Section was spread open over the condiments and butter dish, and his eyes came to rest, again, on his editorial in the morning edition: "CEO Salaries Embarrass Everybody." Easy target, Sloan knew. The paper had that week published the annual income of the city's top bank presidents, developers – revealing that, with stock options and annuities, at least ten men in Cleveland pulled in more than ten million a year. Sloan liked the piece. With an easy target, he knew, the trick was understatement, restraint. He was also pleased, knowing his own tendency to ease, that he had done some research, the results of which had genuinely interested him. He had shown a dramatic – tenfold – gap between bosses' compensation and that of entry level employees over the past ten years. Reading his own published work was always the same for him. He concentrated on the printed words, noting painfully any infelicities in flow and phrasing, until the final effect, the shape, of what he had written registered in his interior.

Then, at that moment, he could not bear to look at it again. His colleagues, even those who liked him least, admired his writing, its surprising compression and clarity. He was thought to be a gifted natural, otherwise easy-going, a flake. Sloan, while actually composing, never felt this way. Topical issues rarely went deep with him, but rendering them with the proper balance, tone, and weight felt excruciatingly important. When he missed, when he reread printed pieces that failed to flow or, worse, sounded false or predictable notes, he felt physically ill. He had no critics, only admirers, at the *Sun Messenger*. Sometimes he wondered where his interior standard had come from. In no other area of his life did he feel at all fastidious. In a deep if unexamined way, he felt mysteriously guided in his writing, and despite self-recriminations, he was grateful for it.

Without greeting him, Jen came into the kitchen. She moved to the coffee machine and patted the Pyrex pitcher, testing it for warmth.

"Bart go?"

"Yes," Sloan said, "he's got something before his first class."

"You're up early."

Sloan knew he wasn't; Jen was down late. She had still not turned to face him, to touch him. He tidied the sections of the paper, and drank down the rest of his tepid coffee.

Slumped comfortably behind the wheel of his little blue Honda, Sloan felt like a bead in the tight strand of morning traffic, a block or two of motion in second gear, then stalled for a light. He didn't mind. He wanted that kind of enclosed time to let the jumble of what he was feeling settle, to come clear. The rhythm of intense communion with Jen followed by bouts of sullen alienation on her part was now a familiar pattern. The sessions with Naomi had released something in him, allowing him to talk more easily and frankly to Jen, to report honestly and with less caution. He could feel this new expansiveness, and sensed that Jen did too, at dinner and especially later, after Bart went to bed. Jen was stimulated by his readiness to talk, but she also resisted it. It was as if some deep but powerful need for parity in their relationship made her dubious about any change or new resolve in him. And he *was* different with her. He heard himself asking more, opining less. He made more out of what she said, took care to draw her out, although she often retreated. More than once she had said, "Are you doing therapy with me?"

Sloan was also working on lowering his resistance to stating what he strongly felt. Once, when Bart had said good night after an exchange of jokey banter, Sloan heard himself say out loud: "I love that kid." Jen had said nothing. Sloan wanted her to confess her own love, to say something unguarded and appreciative. He realized that she did not say such things because she was constitutionally unable to do it. She was funny; she was valued among their friends for being mordant and dry, the sting of her utterances somehow forgivable coming as they did from a diminutive, very pretty woman. But Sloan realized, more with concern than disapproval, that she withheld tenderness because she was afraid, afraid, he believed, of exposure. Down-shifting before a red light, he thought he had it. For Jen, giving away love and deep trust meant losing something she did not believe she could get back; to love, therefore, was to be diminished. He realized also that the insight was not necessarily helpful. *Transformation*, he said to himself, is what matters. What could he do? Not much perhaps: love her, be good to her, be reliable.

It was a puzzle, a wonder to Sloan. He had managed recently to get closer to Jen, especially in sexual communion, than perhaps he had ever been, but then there would be a withdrawal, a calculated distancing on her part, as if in compensation. Nevertheless, he found himself longing at mid-day for bed, for sweet, unbounded deliverance.

Leaving the house, Jen had barely spoken to him. He would tell Naomi. He would ask her: am I making progress, or am I making a mess?

It occurred to Sloan that he had been talking for a long time.  He felt an odd lack of relatedness to Naomi in the dimly lit consulting room, aware only of the crossing and re-crossing of her knees below the hem of a leather skirt.  He looked up into her eyes.  She was unreadable.

"Such a lot of thinking," she said very slowly.  Was she teasing him? "Such a lot of analysis."

"Yes," Sloan said. He felt his earlier enthusiasm and energy begin to recede. "I have been thinking a lot. I think something is going on, mostly good. And it's not just with Jen. It's at the paper, too. It's…it's when I'm with someone now, it feels like I'm really with them, that it's deeper, that it's warmer. I'm honestly more interested in people, and I think they *like* it. People are coming up, seeking me out who never did before." Sloan was aware that he was repeating himself, praising himself.

"Yes, that's what you said." Naomi was slow, cautious. "But do you hear anything peculiar in what you are telling me?  In the way you have been talking about the past week?"

Sloan knew he had talked a lot, in a kind of torrent.  He didn't know what she meant.

"This is why sometimes it is good to have a tape recorder," Naomi said. "Here is what I have been hearing. You have been paying especially close attention to your wife's responses to you. You talk about being passionate with her – in a different way, a good way – in bed, but then afterward she is no different, perhaps even cooler to you. You suggest reasons for this. You analyze her style with people, the effect of her parents." She paused and seemed to study Sloan's face. "All very interesting, all very smart, and I suspect it is true, But do you know what?"

She waited until Sloan responded.

"What?"

"I couldn't find you in what you were saying.  Find *you*.  There was no 'I' in it.  And what I hear in that is that you are far removed." Naomi demonstrated by balling a fist and drawing her other hand over it and raising it over her head. "You are talking from way up here."

Sloan started. He felt anger rising warmly from his gut. If he was being analytical, removed, this was the opposite of what he had been telling her. He was negating the impression he had wanted to create.

"You must put yourself in your story."

"I thought I was." Sloan could hear his own defensiveness. Then, loudly, with an edge he regretted in his voice, "How can I not be in my story? How could there be no 'I'? I'm telling it."

Naomi did not retreat. "You can tell a story, even about yourself without an 'I' in it, Can't you? Isn't that what writers do? When they use the 'third person'?"

"So, I'm not in my story," Sloan said flatly. He felt defeated, irritable. He did not want to have to be self-conscious about how he selected words. For the first time since the sessions began, he wished he had not come.

"Not in the story of relating to Jen. Your story was about how you figured things out, how you think. Look at you!" Naomi let a little gulp of laughter escape. "I have hurt your feelings!"

Sloan tried to look receptive. He told himself: *this is over, no more.*

"Sloan," Naomi said with feeling, "make no mistake about it. You are smart. Your analysis is very perceptive, right on target. But is the cause of Jen's inability to open up to you what you want to understand? Or is it what that means to *you*, how it feels, what you are going to do about it?"

Sloan let himself relax. He inhaled slowly and deeply, exhaled.

"Yes," Naomi smiled warmly, "breathe. I think you see. About your wife's response to you, you are very savvy, very sharp. But about your response to her, you are the uncontested expert. You have all the emotional data." Naomi paused, closed her eyes, as if setting herself to a task. Then she looked intently at Sloan, inclined herself forward to him. "Give me your hands."

Clasping both of his hands, Naomi said, "Sloan Fox, I value everything you say in this office. I value you. I believe I can be of use to you if you let me reflect, literally reflect like a mirror, what is happening with you. When that happens, you will be able to see with complete clarity what is going on inside. It's not always easy. We all want to protect that inside. Everybody hides. One way to hide is to know everyone else's story. But for me to be of any help, I've got to have the 'I' in your story. See?"

Sloan did see. He felt himself almost vibrate with affection for Naomi Wise. He squeezed her hands and released them. They had run well over the hour. "When I was on my way over here, I thought, good, today I'm actually prepared." Sloan rose from the chair and gathered up his jacket. "I think I was looking forward to showing off. What a sensitive, great, thoughtful guy I am."

"But of course you are." Sloan saw something – happiness – in her eyes. "You are."

Sloan was Naomi's last appointment of the day. He waited as she retrieved her coat from the closet, switched off the lights. They walked together to the lobby, pausing at the vacant reception desk.

"Do you think we did anything today?" Naomi asked.

"We must have done something. I always figure things out a few days later, driving to work."

"We've gone too long." Naomi said, "but I want to tell you a story, and I want you to think about it and tell me what it means when I see you next week. This is serious." There was mischief in Naomi's eyes. "So I want you to pay attention."

She began in the practiced, hypnotic manner Sloan had first noticed at the retreat.

"There is a man in this city, and he is very rich and very prominent. He employs thousands of people, and very little happens that matters politically and financially in which he is not a player. He is smart, very powerful. He has not always been a nice man, but" – again the wildness, mischief in her eyes – "he is very sure of himself, and very used to getting his way."

Sloan began calculating, calling to mind such figures in Cleveland. He wanted an image – face, style, voice – to affix to the character

Naomi was sketching. He was also aware of the emergence of another feeling. She had described her man in the most general terms, but there was something intense and admiring in her tone. Jealousy was working in him.

Naomi seemed to be studying him, testing him.

"So this very powerful man, only a little older than you are, gets terrible news. He learns that he has prostate cancer. Very bad. He has to have it out. Nothing can be done. This has been a very active, very virile man. And now that great, central part of his life is gone. He can no longer have sex."

Naomi paused, her eyes widened for dramatic effect. "And so – his life is completely changed. This powerful man, this mover and shaker, loses something. To him it feels like everything."

Naomi touched Sloan's arm at the elbow. "And this is what he did. He still has his big job, his positions, his money. But he has changed. He has become a lover. He loves people, and he makes an art out of making them happy. Not through grand gestures, not through showy philanthropy. He loves individual people. For the first time in his life, people interest him. People who need a mortgage down payment, people who can't pay their bills. His barber, parking lot attendants, young people just starting out. And this man who can't experience sex anymore has become a great friend of lovers. He is," Naomi's laughter erupted, "a *matchmaker*. He is in love with lovers. And this is the point." Naomi slowed deliberately. "He is so happy. He is the happiest man in the city."

Sloan thought he saw something sly in Naomi's face.

"I shouldn't tell you this," she said, "because it's absolutely unprofessional. But I know this man. He is real."

Naomi arched her brows, inviting disbelief. "And will you think about this story?" she said.

At the glass doors, Naomi turned facing Sloan. She said, "I will be *thinking* about you this week, Sloan Fox."

Recreating the moment later, Sloan could recall nothing unnatural, nothing hurried or awkward about Naomi's opening her arms to him for an embrace. Nor had he hesitated to respond. It had been an acknowledgement, more a social than an amorous gesture, but it felt to Sloan full of meaning. His time with Naomi had become important, even central, in his waking life. Holding her, moving a little in the embrace, their relationship now felt embodied. In the days following, the moment recurred insistently in his imagination. He saw the chiseled caps of her knees shifting below the leather skirt. The hug, perceptibly prolonged, with a slight sway in it. He had allowed himself, however subtly, to take the physical measure of her. A little shorter than Jen and, like her, slender, Naomi felt surprisingly substantial against his chest, against the palms of his hands. All week long he pictured her turning at the door, opening her arms to him.

# 5

## CAREFUL OF WHAT WE WISH FOR

S loan swallowed back the last metallic gulp of coffee from the cardboard cup. He had been back to the new machine at the City Desk three times that morning. The size of a small refrigerator and faced with shiny brown plastic, the new appliance had elicited warm approval from the *Sun Messenger* staff. Vertically ordered buttons indicated *coffee, decaf, latte, hot choc, water.* Sloan found the promised variety disappointing; each selection tasted sourly of metal.

The coffee had not stimulated him to action. Less tired than resistant, Sloan had been slow to open the file of clippings from which he was to write his editorial. Over the past week Cooper Morrison had run an investigative series, "Crossing the Line," detailing the sexual impositions of a number of area doctors on their patients. Morrison, who was thought to be the best young reporter on the paper, had worked hard on the series, accessing records from ethics hearings in Columbus, coaxing surprisingly candid disclosures from plaintiffs and others close to the physicians in trouble. At editorial conference meetings, there had been mention of a Pulitzer nomination.

Sloan had read the articles with interest when they appeared. Little review would be required for his editorial. Nor would there be much to the editorial stance, which no one had bothered to discuss at the conference. The tacit assumption among the editors was that doctors diddling patients was a moral outrage, and that it occurred at all was a cry for better monitoring, tighter controls. An editorial on that theme would be, Sloan knew, right-thinking, expected, skimmed if read at all.

More to forestall writing than to uncover any telling facts, Sloan reread Morrison's pieces in the order they were printed, deciding that the undeniable appeal of the series lay in a subtle manipulation of the reader's moral concerns. The first articles detailed the criminal activities of two physicians who prescribed unnecessary addictive substances to female patients who, once dependent, traded sex for prescriptions. Sloan studied the *Sun Messenger* photograph of one of the accused. A near double of former Russian President Boris Yeltsin, he stood at his lawyer's side, face poached and troubled. Sloan noted the home address, an unremarkable neighborhood of tract houses near the lake. The shabby, marginal practice, the wife already proceeding with divorce, the grown children – Sloan felt a welling up of great sadness, also, confusingly, guilt. The final three articles, and the cause of a public stir, disclosed a long-standing sexual relationship between a prominent chief of surgery and one of his former patients. Sloan felt both appreciation and disapproval of Morrison's strategy. He had linked the emotional impact of sordid activities of the sex-for-prescription doctors to the chief of surgery's affair. The facts of the latter made for a scandal, a predictable human-interest story: the high brought low, the weakness of the flesh. The news interest lay clearly in the prominence and distinction of the surgeon. His affair had lasted "intermittently," Morrison had reported, for seven years. His lover, her face attractive and composed in the press photograph, had filed her charges only after the affair was unhappily terminated. Seven years, Sloan mused. He imagined, tried to feel the weight and complexity of such a long-standing, mutually adulterous relationship. It occurred to him that they had fallen in love. Pain from a pinched nerve in her neck had brought her to his care. Her complaint had, apparently, been treated professionally and well. And they fell in love, made love. For a moment Sloan could not locate any feeling of violation. He imagined the mounting power and tenderness in their attraction, their initial surrender. Sloan scanned the concluding three articles a final time and could find no suggestion of manipulation – drugs for sex – on the chief of surgery's part. Sloan knew Morrison; he, like his readers, was drawn insatiably to the fallibility of others. He would leave no equivocal or embarrassing stone unturned. The distinguished surgeon and his patient had fallen in love, adulterously and in violation of standards of conduct established for doctors – but nonetheless in love.

Sloan turned to the bright blue screen of his laptop and set to work.

> Can a doctor and patient fall in love? Not should they, but can they. Of course they can and – problematically – do. It is easy for us to empathize with patients enamored of their doctors. But we reflexively want to scold doctors for such feelings for a patient, even when their medical effectiveness is considerable and undiminished, even when the beloved is an intelligent, consenting adult.
>
> Doctors, we like to complain, lack the human touch. Perhaps we should be careful of what we wish for...

Less reluctantly than usual, Sloan said his farewells, nudging and side-stepping his way out of Dulaney's. The roar of the Friday crowd sounded loud, harsh in his ears.

There was a sectional play-off game at eight, and Sloan looked forward to it, whether or not Bart got to play. Sloan had himself been a player, a high school standout and point guard on fairly good Amherst terms. A basketball game, especially a high school game, was always a diversion.

Driving home with the sloshing traffic at the grey day's end, Sloan was ready for diversion, ready to void all thought beyond the tilting back and forth of rangy boys differentiated only by the contrasting colors of their drooping satin. He loved the game, its fluid quickness, sudden opportunities. He longed for the wild acceleration of pace, the penetration, the deft pass, the shot up and in: the thrilling simultaneity of intention and execution. Playing and now watching basketball radically focused his attention. He instinctively and immediately identified with one team, even when he had no previous stake or interest in either. At a close game's end, the muscles in his stomach would be uncomfortably tight from the accrued tension of watching his team labor to catch up or to stay ahead.

Sloan pulled the Honda into the narrow drive and inched up to the closed garage. It was nearly dark, and fat drops of rain spattered tinnily overhead. He switched off the ignition.

He could see Jen moving about the lighted kitchen. The prospect of their solitary, hurried dinner before the game made him feel tired. He had two beers at Dulaney's, and he wasn't particularly hungry. He could not remember feeling hungry. His days unfolded now in a perceptibly different way. It was as if he were suspended in a medium of continual impatience. He found himself welcoming appointments, meetings, any clearly assigned task that would engage his attention, set him purposefully in action. Time between specific duties, time between arrival home and sleep, once so welcome, made him tense and restless.

In a way he could not think about clearly, Naomi was part of his restlessness. Naomi. Naomi Wise. Consciously unbidden images of her recurred in his reverie, troubled his sleep. The images were like fragments of a film: inclining toward him, *give me your hands*; the crossing and uncrossing of her legs, her knees settling to rest below the leather skirt; turning to him, opening her arms to him like a child; *I'll be thinking about you this week, Sloan Fox.*

*Crush.* Sloan heard himself speak the word out loud. A crush – adolescent word – on Naomi Wise. Then with renewed annoyance Sloan recalled the fussy, hectoring kidding about "transference" at the Krupanskys' party.

The evening had passed agreeably enough, the food and wine especially good. At the point when the other invited couple left to fetch a babysitter, Ted Krupansky pressed Jen and him to stay a while, try some port he had carried home with him from England. Sitting before a refreshed fire and sipping the tiny glasses of port, talk turned to psychoanalysis. Krupansky had read a book making a case that no measurable, provable benefit could be attributed to a century of psychoanalysis. Suddenly, brightly, Jen blurted out, "Somebody better tell Sloan! He's started therapy." Sloan had been surprised, angry to the point of speechlessness that what still felt to him such a personal and private matter had been offered up for discussion with the Krupanskys.

In a measured tone, Sloan explained that he had seen a therapist several times because he was intrigued by her remarks at a retreat called by his paper. Naomi Wise, was not, he explained with an effortful openness, a psychoanalyst. Her training was, he believed in Gestalt and Jungian psychology. Jen, who had drunk several glasses of wine over dinner, continued teasingly. "She tells Sloan he stops breathing." Sloan gave her a look. Ted Krupansky, perhaps reading the discomfort, said something general to the effect that there are as many therapies as there are therapists.

"Sloan's crazy about his," Jen said, "aren't you?"

Sloan felt himself harden angrily to his wife's recklessness.

"She's very interesting," he said. "I'm learning a lot."

"I think my husband's in love with his therapist." Jen said. Her tone was off-hand, teasing. Sloan was incredulous.

"What's not to love?" he quipped back.

"Ah," Ted Krupansky had said, "transference. It's the crucial point in analysis."

*Transference.* Even as Krupansky elaborated on the Freudian meaning of the term, Sloan remembered. Perhaps he had read about it at Amherst. Somehow he had absorbed it; that in analysis the client projects deep personal desires and needs onto the therapist, falls in love. A transference for Naomi Wise. "A trained therapist,"

Krupansky concluded, "knows how to use the transference to help the patient become more fully aware."

"So it's all for the best," Jen said.

On the car ride home, both felt the ache of offense given, offense taken. At length Sloan said, "I hope you'll forgive me if I never discuss anything about my outside life with you again."

"It must be nice to have an outside life."

Sloan had wanted to say: yes, it's nice, it's a life saver. But he checked himself.

"I'm sorry," Jen said softly, sadly.


Heights played desperately and hard but they were overmatched. With a few minutes left in the fourth quarter the team was down sixteen, and they would not close the gap. Sloan tapped Jen on the shoulder and without speaking pointed down to the scorer's table. Bart knelt on one knee waiting to report.

"Isn't it too late?" Jen asked in a bewildered tone.

"Hey," Sloan said, unaccountably happy, "This is a debut."

Both teams had now freely substituted, the victors to preserve their starters for the game to come, the losers to honor subs for a season's contribution. For a minute Bart, all elbows and knees in the company of the older boys, seemed almost comic in the over-intensity of his play. Then he settled down, was impressively alert, moved the ball adroitly. With fifteen seconds showing on the clock, a team mate drove down the foul lane and when a swarm of defenders collapsed around him, scooped a pass back through the mob to Bart who was poised just beyond the three-point arc. In an unbroken motion Bart received the ball, drew it up over his forehead, jumped and flicked a shot which he and his father in the stands knew would pass through the nets. Sloan felt the crowd's squeal of appreciation thrill like cold water down his spine. He clasped Jen's shoulder, drew her to him.

"He's a player."

***

Nathan Weingart thought Naomi would be pleased by the prospect of a long weekend "camping," as he had put it, in the nearly finished house on Edisto Island. He had sprung the surprise over after dinner cappuccino at Sirocco's. "But I can't," she said. "I have clients on Friday."

"Isn't Friday your light day? Couldn't you reschedule? Believe me, darling, Friday is the *only* day I could get both the contractor and the decorator. It was like arranging the Normandy landing." He leaned over the table, covered her hands with his. "Please reschedule. There is no other time to do this. And" – he lowered his voice – "it is going to be warm there, beach weather."

Naomi could not bring herself to return his encouraging smile. She knew he thought she would comply.

"How many appointments have you got?" he asked.

"Two."

"Reschedule. You don't want me to decorate the place. The tickets are booked."

Naomi knew the furnishing must fall to her. She had found the decorator in Charleston. She had convinced herself that her pleasure in what had from the outset seemed a remote, even unnecessary venture, would be to create color and comfort within the dramatic, airy rooms. She pictured the sheen of the hardwood floors, the high white walls, luminous sea and marsh beyond the expanses of glass. Except for the borrowed white sofa-bed and a few kitchen essentials, the house would be empty when they arrived for the weekend. There would be the sharp clean smell of new wood, fresh paint, the sea light creating an atmosphere like gauze. Naomi knew exactly how it would be: like an exile, a convalescence.

"It will be good to get away, to slow down," Nathan said.

Naomi did not want to get away or to slow down. Fixed in the variegated context of her work and friendships, her relationship to her husband was comfortable, agreeable enough. It was certainly the envy of her friends. But when abstracted for any length of time in an unfamiliar setting, time together with Nathan made Naomi feel under-stimulated and anxious. Three days almost exclusively in his company in the isolated beach house – would be lonely. Realizing this made Naomi want to cry.

"What's wrong, darling? You look so sad."

"I'm not sad." Naomi shook her head and made a muttering sound like a horse. She smiled comically. "So we'll go, we'll go." Naomi willed herself to picture fabrics, brightly woven rugs, exotic plants. "And we'll decorate."

Later, lying awake, holding her sheets tight beneath her chin, Naomi mentally rehearsed the rescheduling of her appointments. There was a three o'clock family session with the Durst parents and their bulimic daughter; at five Sloan Fox.

He had wanted the Friday appointment, although he had joked with her about interfering with his "appointment" at Dulaney's. He would graciously accommodate her need to reschedule. He would try to conceal his disappointment.

*And so will I,* Naomi said to herself in the dark. She was disappointed. She had allowed herself to acknowledge her attraction to Sloan, but it was only when Nathan proposed their getaway that she realized exactly how much she looked forward to seeing him. What was it? Something in his posture, his look. There was something pleasingly loose about him: tousled hair, collar loose around his neck, rolled sleeves loose over his wrists. The good ruddy skin drawn tightly back over the bones of his face. He was – touchable. She could paw him, shake him, tickle him. His back had felt wonderfully taut when she had embraced him in farewell. She would like to have run her palms up the ridge of his sides to his shoulders. She could squeeze him. Available – that's what he felt like, sweetly available. He was only a little taller and rangier than Nathan, but he was somehow a far more imposing presence. The way he moved, the way he reconfigured himself in his chair suggested a barely contained impulse to spring, like the beautiful big cats caged in the zoo.

Naomi was wide awake. Thinking about Sloan Fox had made her desirous. She would not like telling him that they could not meet on Friday, but she looked forward to calling him. Naomi stretched her arms high over her head and released a loud yawning exhalation. She was glad, consciously glad that her training allowed her to acknowledge sexual, inappropriate feelings for her clients. The complex of her body/mind was, she had been taught, her instrument for registering the data of another's being. This beautiful feeling, this exciting promise, was part of the truth of Sloan Fox, of what he brought to her. She would use this data, as she used the data of the fatigue she felt when treating depressives.

As Naomi's reflections dissolved into wordless feeling and sleep, her palms circled the warm skin of Sloan Fox's naked back, the nape of his neck. Naked herself now, she nuzzled her cheek under his chin. She was swaying, not a body at all, just warmth and light, light merging into light.

# 6

## ANOTHER LIFE

S loan opened his eyes expecting morning, but the mullioned window gave back only blackness. Propping himself up on an elbow, he peered over the blanketed ridge of his wife at the pink digits glowing from the radio on her night table. 2:45. Why? He gathered himself back into the warmth of the bedding.

Why was he awake? Sloan stared at the smoky ceiling. Last night he was wide awake at four. He wondered whether there was something wrong with him. His sleep had been untroubled; he could remember no dreams. He felt good, warm, faintly aroused.

Jen, jostled a little when he had checked the clock, made an audible sigh and nestled herself into him, her arms tucked against his side, her head finding the crook between his shoulder and chin. Her flannel night dress was rucked up over her waist, and he rested a palm lightly on the exposed base of her spine. The soft skin was dry and warm, and Sloan began reflexively to caress her, his fingertips moving along the delicate nubs of her spine, up over the sharp ridges of her shoulder blades. Jen made her deep, familiar purr. She adjusted her position again so that she rested more on her stomach. She wriggled a little, and with one hand hiked her night gown higher up, exposing more of her back. Sloan's palm moved in wide slow arcs, his mind void of all thought, registering only the progress of his touch:

dips and rises like dunes of powdery sand where rib cage descended to waist then ascended again into the mounds of her buttocks. Jen's purring rose and fell with her respiration.

Sloan warmed in anticipation of their lovemaking. They would feel ravaged, cheated of sleep in the morning, but Sloan was glad now to surrender to the swelling tickle and burn of desire. He lowered himself down along Jen's side, extending his massage to her thighs, her calves, the heels and arches of her feet. His lips, the tip of his nose just grazed the smooth inlet of her waist.

Jen slowly parted her legs, and Sloan was softly kneading the feathery mound of her pubis when she made a breathy groan. He thought it was desire and moved up along her length so that he could clasp her fully to him when, startlingly, he heard her say, in a kind of sob, "No! I don't *want* this." The surprise, the urgency in her cry stilled his hand. Unaware that he was doing it, Sloan stopped breathing.

"What – is anything wrong?"

Jen raised her shoulders a little and with a violent half roll wrenched herself and the bedding away from him. Sloan was aware of her adjusting her nightgown down over her knees. Then she was still. She lay with her back to him, curled into a ball.

"Is something wrong? Did I do something?"

"I just need to *sleep*." The complaint was deep in her throat.

Sloan lay still, his confusion giving way to resentment, a dark ugliness he did not like but which he also welcomed. He thought about quietly getting out of bed, getting dressed, driving off somewhere. He felt capable of the hurtful, irrevocable gesture.

"By all means," he said, "sleep."

Sloan turned on his side, his back to the curled figure of his wife. He knew it was well past three, but he was still wide awake. Thoughts and images crowded into his consciousness. Though it usually commenced sooner after retiring, their lovemaking had invariably begun with soft, un-insistent touches. Then they would guide one another into sleep, or when the touches aroused them, teasingly, gradually, they would make love. No thought, Sloan told himself, no plan, no *permission.* He and Jen rarely talked about sex, either before or afterward. They had married right after college and had over the years without self-consciousness made their way together sexually; their intimacies, Sloan had been sure, were freely given and enjoyed – not won. He did not believe he had ever imposed himself on Jen. He didn't think of himself as sexually aggressive. He liked instead for the sexual urge – mood, spell, whatever it was – to arise unexpectedly and, if circumstances allowed, give himself up to it. He had assumed Jen felt that way also. He had touched her, caressed her back with his palm, and she had responded, snuggled into him, offered the bare skin of her back side, made her sound. Then she had startled him, turned miserably away. Sloan felt his resentment swell. He resolved to withdraw; he would initiate nothing. Then, as the mullioned windows brightened with the greys and greens of first light, Sloan felt an overwhelming sadness, as if there had been a death. No longer fully awake, Sloan felt as if he were crying, yet knew he was not crying.

He awoke suddenly, aware of Jen's hand gently on his neck. He felt himself ascending like a diver from a great dark depth.

"What?" he said, then even more stupidly, "*What?*"

"It's late," Jen said softly. "It's nearly eight." She added, a little hesitantly: "I'm sorry if I was unfriendly. I was very sleepy. You know?"

Sloan remembered. His resolve returned to him.

"No problem," he said. He felt the weight, like a heavy stone, in his breast.


Naomi moved through the empty room to the wall of glass panels. Her bare feet made faint screeches on the polished hardwood, and she felt like a sneak, somehow trespassing in the stark newness of the darkening house.

Out beyond the deck and marsh grass, the declining sun edged the billowing clouds with tints of lavender and green. Naomi touched her forehead to the cold glass and was for a moment lost in the gauzy light. She knew she would feel abstracted and alone on the island; she had not wanted to go.

There had been a long afternoon with Nathan and the designer, leafing through catalogues, laying fabric samples out on the bare floors, sketching furniture arrangements over the architect's floor plan. Decisions had been made. Naomi pictured the vivid cranberry and sun-yellow fabrics she had selected, primitive serrations of the Navajo area rugs, the sea-lit Hopper prints, the lineless white veneer of the kitchen table and chairs, outsized plates in primary colors, the copper bottom cookware – she could see it hanging from the weathered timber beam over the marble-topped cooking island. The pots and utensils would, she knew, feel forever unreal and new.

Naomi gave a little shudder, due less to the hint of evening dampness in the room than to an unease she suddenly felt about the afternoon's purchases. They had virtually furnished the house: beds, bureau, end tables, lamps, coordinated bedding and window treatments, ceramic urns, a low table inlaid as a chess board set with pieces the size of large dolls. All of it would arrive in the weeks ahead and be put in place by Lynn-Marie, the stylish, hawk-faced decorator she had located in Charleston. Naomi imagined Lynn-Marie's long, bony fingers unpacking the shipping crates, laying the gleaming stemware in the drawer, arranging the chess pieces on their lacquered grid. Naomi and Nathan would arrive one weekend to find everything in order, vividly colored, clean, and new. Naomi had retreated to the kitchen to put a kettle on for tea as Nathan and Lynn-Marie began reckoning the cost. Naomi had lapsed into a willed vagueness as she sensed the mounting sum approaching then surpassing a hundred thousand dollars. People – she thought of her parents, friends – bought livable houses for less. The beach house. The "little getaway," as Nathan told their friends in Cleveland, on an island off the coast of South Carolina – "just the basics," he told them "bare bones."

Now the day's purchases – cushions, bedding, framed prints, sideboard, deck chairs – began descending like a bombardment into her reverie.

"*Darling*," Nathan called from somewhere across the house. "*Naomi, Darling.*"

Naomi turned away from the darkening span of sea. Would she ever want to come to this house, sit barefoot in shorts on the cranberry sofa, sipping tea from a bright yellow mug. She saw herself as a figure in one of Lynn-Marie's catalogs. She felt thin, insubstantial, uncomfortably confined. She imagined taking the sun, reclining half naked on the green and white striped chaise they had ordered for the deck, stepping along the narrow sandy path through the marsh to the shore, testing the soupy shallows with a toe. A wall of white sunlight, the force of the heat --*never*, Naomi told herself silently, *I will never want to be here.*

"Darling? Naomi?"

She joined Nathan in the lighted kitchen where he was pouring scotch into two tumblers.

"Ice?" he asked, holding up one of the glasses.

Naomi could see in his smile that Nathan was pleased with himself. He wore the casual clothes of the moneyed islander: new khakis, a polo shirt unbuttoned at the neck. He looked at this moment thoroughly congruent with the house, and Naomi was reminded again of the glossy country living magazines and Lynn-Marie's catalogs.

Nathan handed Naomi her scotch and said "Thank God it's Friday. *Cheers.*"

Naomi held the faintly acrid aftertaste of the whiskey on her tongue. She heard the words, thank God it's Friday, as if from a great distance. Then she realized: *it's only Friday.* She thought about her missed appointments. Sloan Fox. Sloan Fox in his jeans and bagged-out tweed jacket. She tried to picture him moving through the white empty rooms of the new house. What could engage him, she wondered, and decided nothing would. Friday. Only Friday. She recalled that Sloan would be – at that very hour – at Dulaney's with his friends from the paper. She imagined him standing at the bar, his ruddy cheeks illuminated by the muted glitter of bar lights. She could hear his voice, his laughter rising over the din. She had embraced him. She had held onto the embrace in the deserted foyer of the clinic. She saw herself moving to him, catching his eye, surprising him at Dulaney's. Not Dulaney's: New Orleans, the women, the beckoning dark women, blue and pink neon shimmering on the wet pavement.

Naomi raised her glass. "Thank God it's Friday."

Nathan eyed her attentively. Soon he would propose something: dinner out, a moonlight walk on the beach, the Jacuzzi. Naomi wished now that they had come down with friends; she was sure Nathan felt the same. *Only Friday.*

Sloan felt dull, unaccountably sad. He had forgotten how dark the consulting room was.

On the other side of the glass table, Naomi sat, seemingly immovable. He had started to talk about his boys, their reticence, their barely suppressed vulnerability, but he could only tell stories about them, and not even fresh stories. He heard himself rounding off, humorously embellishing his standard anecdotes.

"Your Bart and Henry sound wonderful," Naomi said. Sloan read no warmth in her response; she was waiting. "But I must ask you again. Where are you in these stories of your sons?"

"I guess I'm sitting here, telling them,"

Sloan felt defeated. Naomi had sensed the false note. He had not come to talk about the boys, and at the moment he could not decide what he had come to say. Earlier in the week he had been looking forward to talking about Jen's resistance to him in bed and his new inner resolve to initiate nothing. For six days now he had held fast, determined to offer no spoken or physical endearment. But as soon as he was seated in the consulting room the idea of airing any of this seemed somehow impossible to express. He felt ashamed, diminished. A childish petulance was at work in him, and he knew it; he wanted at the very least to worry Jen, to knock her off balance. He realized he wanted to hurt her and that he could not tell Naomi Wise.

"And your wife – Jen," Naomi said. "She sees these same qualities in the boys?"

Sloan pictured Jen across the table from Henry and Bart, grilling each about his day.

"She gets a little frustrated with them," Sloan said. He could hear warmth, a lack of accusation in his voice. "There's an expression in basketball, a nice expression: let the game come to you. The idea is to wait for your opportunities, not to force things. She has a hard time letting the game – the boys – come to her."

"Maybe you could help her. Help her see how to do it."

Sloan did not want to follow this line of thought. He was working consciously to distance himself from Jen; he was aware of an energizing aggression in what he was doing, and he wanted more of it.

"Maybe," Sloan said dully. "We're pretty different."

"Of course you are," Naomi said. "I am interested in how you are alike."

Alike. Sloan pictured Jen's face: the quick grimacing smile with no light in her eyes. Her delicate, boneless nakedness. Books and documents heaped on the desk in her attic office, the Ph.D., the Krupansky crowd at City College.

"Well," Sloan said. "I suppose we're both white."

Naomi flashed a look of incomprehension; and then her face relaxed in a sad, defeated smile.

"I can feel you battling me today, Sloan Fox. Shall we battle?"

"Battle," Sloan said. "No, I don't think so. He felt a sudden pang of anger. He sat upright, looked straight into Naomi's face. "I think I'm going to go."

Without hesitating, Naomi retrieved her watch from the glass table and clasped it onto her wrist.

"It's about that time," she said quietly.

They walked without speaking to the empty foyer.

"Let's see," Naomi said, "we missed a week, didn't we? Shall we catch up – or should we meet at five on Friday?"

"Next Friday. I don't know." He fixed Naomi with what he imagined was an expressionless look. She stood with her back to the glass door panels, exactly, he realized, where she had stood two weeks ago when she had opened her arms to him.

Sloan stepped past Naomi and opened the door, admitting a blast of cold.

"I'll call you."

# 7

Driving home from the airport where he had put his father on the return flight to Del Ray, Sloan felt a great weight lifting. Everything over the course of the Easter weekend had seemed to carry an unexpected emotional weight. Henry's presence again in the house had been dramatic. In an unassignable way he was not the same boy who left the house in the fall. He seemed physically bigger, more considered in what he said, harder to read. His reticence was no longer annoying, even to Jen; it was as if he had grown into his inwardness and in the process acquired a kind of dignity.

The added presence of Sloan's father had also changed and enlivened the household. The quiet figure of his father at the dining room table aroused a confusing mixture of affection and sadness in Sloan. At seventy-six, his father had grown noticeably smaller, his arms and shoulders more closely gathered into his chest. He had emerged at breakfast on Easter Sunday wearing a newly laundered shirt of deep green flannel and yellow tie. Sloan took in the thatch of white hair over his father's clean, spare face and was overcome with love for him. His father had dressed for them. Sloan let himself acknowledge in unspoken tribute that his deliberate, courteous and resolutely unobtrusive father, however diminished physically, would always be stronger, surer, better than he was.

Jen joked that God was punishing her for her feminist excesses by surrounding her with a house full of men, but she too was touched and invigorated by the added life in the house: the mysterious but undeniable continuity of Fox masculine qualities across the generations.

All weekend something inarticulate but important seemed on the brink of announcement. Green hints of leaf flecked hedges and treetops, and the hazy air was welcoming and warm. More for the novelty than out of any sense of family tradition, the Foxes decided to attend services at St. Peter's Episcopal. Walking the familiar sidewalks, bells pealing overhead, Sloan felt held in the grip of something at once ancient and altogether new. Inside the crowded church he was not prepared for the sweetness of the trumpets, the choir's descants over the hymns. At the service's end, the Rector's "The Lord is risen" was answered thunderously – to Sloan's surprise – by the congregation's "He is risen indeed!" When he caught Jen's eye, he saw that her face was streaked with tears.

And now, driving home from the airport, his father behind him, Henry on the road back to Miami, Sloan felt released. He let down the windows of the Honda and inhaled deeply.

*Let it go*, he said out loud into the slap and baffle of the rushing air – and then he had it. He had been holding on tight to something he did not want at all. He could feel the clench of it in his chest and in his gut. He was holding on, holding in, and there was an angry energy in it. Not making love to Jen, offering nothing, initiating nothing, refusing to feel and to take in her presence – this was the same thing as not calling Naomi for an appointment.

Sloan shouted out loud – *Ayyyyy* – and sustained the tone, glad of the release, pleased at the idea of the sound spilling out through the open window into the din of traffic. He could see that he had been gathering himself in, and not just himself. This was a willful exercise of power. By withholding, he would draw them in. They would wonder at his absence, tentatively seek him out; then they would need him. He would reel them in like fish.

*A game*, Sloan said to himself, *the old game*. He thought of Henry, of how deliberate and unforthcoming he could be: Henry held back because he wanted to be held and he didn't know how. *I want to be held,* Sloan said to himself. *I want to be held and to hold you.* The name, the image, the smell and touch of Naomi Wise arrived at once, like a hunger, crowding everything else out of consciousness. *Give me your hands.* He would call her. He would not wait, and there would be no more indirection. Sloan felt good, totally alert. He looked at the speedometer: seventy-five. Traffic was light on the expressway, but he resisted the impulse to press the pedal to the floor. He clasped and unclasped his hands on the steering wheel. *This is good, this is good,* he thought, the sense of danger and possibility heightening to something like prayer.

The room erupted in laughter, and as it began to recede, Naomi Wise said: "And I didn't think lawyers were going to be any fun."

There was more laughter, and Naomi could feel the effort of maintaining her smile. She was tired, tired behind her eyes, tired in her bones. She had arisen before five in order to drive to the Pittsburgh Marriott where she and Abe Fierstein were to conduct a retreat for The Lawyers Guild of Western Pennsylvania on the theme of Relating to Adversaries.

As soon as she said the words, Naomi was aware that the lawyers were not especially fun. Even before the exercises began, it was clear that the openness and receptivity she had felt in setting up the retreat with the Guild president were not widely shared by the member lawyers. They seemed dubious, cerebral, quick to joke. By pre-arrangement Naomi had set up an improvised deposition in which a young trial lawyer deposed a senior partner. The senior partner was to play the role of a corporate executive accused of sexual harassment. It had been hard to get the sixty lawyers past their joking about the premise. Every clarification and instruction on Naomi's part evoked new howls of laughter. As accused harasser, the senior partner was prepped as to exactly what he had and hadn't done. The interrogating attorney was given a list of outcomes desired by his hypothetical client.

"The deposition should proceed as it normally would," Naomi said, "but with one big difference. Each of you in the course of the interrogation is allowed to say what you are *really* thinking and feeling, regardless of how terrible that might be from the standpoint of your legal objectives. Do you see what I'm saying?"

There was much disruptive banter and laughter.

"In other words," Naomi continued, "if either of you at any point really thinks 'this is such bullshit, why not just come out and say what you mean,' you should *say* it. But when you do, I want you to say it to the group" – Naomi gestured to indicate to the circle of lawyers surrounding the table and chairs of the role players. "When you have made your point, then get back to the deposition."

The surrounding observers were slow to quiet down. Naomi saw Abe Fierstein's expression harden. He had told her earlier while driving east that he had a hard time liking lawyers.

"Come on group," Naomi said. "Listen closely."

For a second, scanning the faces in the observing circle, she wondered whether the women were really being more receptive or whether she merely wanted them to be.

"All right," Naomi said to the standing role-player. "It's your witness."

Naomi closed her eyes and tried to summon up the exhilaration she had felt when she had proposed to the Clinic Board the series of "relational" conferences and retreats for professionals. It had seemed like a good dream, work that would unfurl like a continual pleasure. The one insistent insight that had carried her through graduate studies in social psychology was that formal relationships were always driven by two forces. The first and most obvious was a sum of conscious expectations and protocols: what you were supposed to do as a student or teacher, physician or patient, boss or employee, seller or buyer, partner and partner. The second force, often barely conscious, was the instinctive, feeling-rich drive to satisfaction, discovery, elation, and loving communion. Very intelligent people were especially unaware of the power and dominance of the second, more interior force. Naomi felt she was quick to see it and always warmed to its signs. From the outset her work with private clients had been to take the measure of the emotional agenda operating independently of their stated concerns, then to help them to feel it at work in their lives. Her own awareness of the gap between interior and exterior concerns always preceded the client's by weeks, even years. Some clients resisted the very idea of a purposeful, demanding life below the level of conscious intention. When she had a success, she felt it was due to her ability to project her own vulnerability, her own receptivity to impulse and feeling, her surprising willingness to be unconventional, to be available, not like a therapist at all. Both her colleagues and the clients who worked with her in privileged privacy sensed she was a lively original, perhaps even a professional renegade.

As it happened, there was, to Naomi's relief, some usable substance in the exchanges between the role-players in the mock deposition. The striking contrast between what the players really thought and felt and what they were strategically obligated to say was not lost on them or on those observing.

"Of course it's a game," an ascetic-looking observer in wire-rimmed glasses had commented, "but it's the game a lawyer is expected to play and one a good lawyer plays well. It makes for good practice, and probably for civility in general, that people *don't* always let you know what they're really thinking when they're doing business."

This elicited some laughter and general approval.

"Exactly," Naomi had responded. "Exactly. We really must not blurt out every observation and annoyance that comes into our heads. But when that material surfaces -- that exasperation, that sense of sudden violation, real anger – we need to know it, to acknowledge it. And remember" – Naomi's smile revealed mischief – "that feeling material is personally truer and stronger than what is formally being expressed, stronger than the *business.* And you must not forget this, you lawyers: it has to *go* somewhere, the feeling. You have probably seen how troubling, unacknowledged feeling makes clients you work with irrational. It makes even very smart people crazy, like children.

But that same material makes you crazy, too, only you're less likely to think so in your own case. Instead, you might feel extra righteous, maybe a little obsessed about carrying a point or having your way."

Naomi felt her point crystallize as she viewed the circle of lawyers.

"When people say they don't like lawyers," she asked them quietly, "what is it that they really dislike?"

"Confrontation."

"Being held accountable."

"The fees."

Naomi set her face and scanned the listeners until they quieted.

"What people dislike about lawyers is that they carry out the most emotionally loaded and messy business in a language and in a manner that won't allow any disorder or real feeling at all. Think about it. Think about a husband and wife who have a terrible blow-up and begin divorce proceedings. Think of the volatility, the danger, the sheer craziness of what they are feeling. They each get a lawyer, perhaps you. And the business begins of expressing all the hurt and vengefulness and defensiveness in the language and protocols of the law. Very, very strange. It is like telling two people murderously angry at each other they must from now on communicate only in the language and protocols of cooking. And you know something else? There is a lot of food, there are many meals cooked that way."

By the end of the conference, Naomi sensed that some of the edginess of the Lawyers Guild members had softened. She felt listened to when she spoke. There was little resistance to the group exercises she proposed. As the presiding head of the Guild walked Naomi and Abe Fierstein to her car, he said, "This was good for us."

Naomi wondered. Driving westward to Cleveland in the descending darkness, exhaustion and something hard to name – doubt – seemed to run through her like a current.

# 8

## IT GOES ON FOREVER

The city's fiscal crisis had created a static crackle in the editorial offices of the *Sun Messenger*. There was talk of another default, although Sloan was sure the banks and developers would make a rescue gesture if it came to that. The beleaguered downtown schools were hovering on the brink of state receivership. New and old schools alike had been neglected and stood in need of millions in routine maintenance and repairs. The transience of the students, mostly black, Hispanic and poor, was untrackably fluid. Test scores were abysmally below state minimal standards.

The night before Sloan had watched the mayor on television as he explained what was wrong. Sloan had been moved by the strange, sad honesty of the mayor's approach. He stood, like a teacher, next to an easel supporting a series of charts and diagrams indicating the sources of the city's funds and where they went. Sloan had called Jen to the set. "Watch this," he said, "it's like nothing I've ever seen on television."

Very clearly, very deliberately the mayor described how the hundreds of millions earmarked for the city's schools at the wide end of the funnel in his diagram were reduced to just a trickle per student in real services and instruction. Between the wide mouth and the tiny spout of the funnel, payments to various vendors – bus suppliers, food services, maintenance contractors, consultants, attorneys – could be seen to diminish the flow. The mayor did not say, but Sloan and his fellow editors knew, that each payment for "services" was a privileged contract, a sweet profitable deal for the chosen providers. Without having to raise his voice in accusation or blame, the mayor had shown viewers where the city's revenues really went.

"This is something," Sloan said to Jen. "The man is actually telling the truth."

The editorial should have been easy, but it would not come. Privileged deals had eclipsed civic need; union rules inflating costs had obstructed services to children. There were nameable, even indictable offenders, yet Sloan's editorial would not come. Pointing a righteous finger at the obvious offenders – the political deal makers who arranged the city's contracts with the vendors – would not, Sloan knew, change matters much, although such finger pointing was past due. There was a delicate racial dimension to the trouble as well; many of the deal-makers and the favored vendors were black, and their critics would be countered with cries of racism.

Sloan sat back in his chair and looked dully at his blue computer screen. He felt his capacity for analysis and acuity slow and thicken. Hell with it, he said to himself, hell with it. Then, with real sadness: *the problem is that I am not interested enough.* Sloan wanted to depart the paper, depart the city.

What I am interested in, he said to himself, are my own boys. He pictured Henry in a dingy, oversized lecture hall. Henry was half reclining, inattentive in his seat. Sloan wanted Henry to feel the invigorating novelty of a new world, to be stirred by irresistibly lively and passionate minds. Sloan wanted an Amherst for Henry. And for Bart. More than just a basketball program and endurable classes, more than just the blur of an adolescent march in lock-step, the largely unconscious jumble of style, look, attitude, slouch and non-language, the denial of every threatening intensity.

Sloan addressed his terminal, and his fingers began moving over the keyboard.

> Who can be said to love the children of the city of Cleveland? One hopes their parents do. Some of those parents, we know, are children themselves.

> Who loves these children? Is the question too airy and "soft" – especially in light of such "hard" current realities as the impending fiscal crisis and alleged mismanagement and bad practice on the part of city and school officials?

> When do children thrive? They thrive when they are irrationally loved and fiercely cared for. In the absence of such love, do they ever thrive?

> This is not a soft question. This is the only question.

> Who loves these children?

Sloan edged his chair forward so his knees touched the glass table separating him from Naomi.

"I keep coming back to the realization that I've just turned forty-five, and I don't have a clue about what forty-five is supposed to be like."

"You do keep coming back to it," Naomi said warmly. Reflexively she leaned toward him as he moved forward. "I think you have mentioned your age each time we have met. And happy birthday!"

Sloan felt an urge to reach out and cup Naomi's cheeks in his hands. He wanted to break the flow of talk and touch her.

"What is it?" she asked suddenly.

"What?"

"What just happened there? Your look, everything changed." Naomi demonstrated a kind of feint in his direction, and Sloan could see the delight in her eyes.

Sloan laughed. He felt good.

"I know this is therapy," he said, "but I also know there are some things I just can't tell you."

"Well then I'll never know, will I?"

"O.K.," Sloan said, "down to business."

"Tell me something," Naomi said. "You're enjoying yourself today, aren't you?"

"Yes, I am."

"I can feel it."

"All right," Sloan said, "here's the thing. So I'm forty-five. Everything I kind of expected when I was younger, everything I have read tells me I should be feeling sexually quieter at my age. But I don't, at all."

"And what are you feeling like?"

"I feel like a boy."

"And – do you mind feeling like a boy?"

Sloan paused to consider. "No, not at all. It's not like I'm sitting here as an older, thoughtful person feeling like a boy – 'locating the inner boy.' I *am* a boy."

"Again I'm asking you, how does that feel to you?"

"It feels – great. Fun. Dangerous. Like I could do anything."

"Anything."

"Exactly." Sloan looked straight into Naomi's eyes. She was amused, possibly belittling him. She was very beautiful. "For instance," he said and leaned across the glass table top and cupped her face lightly between his palms. Her cheeks felt silken, exquisite in his hands. He closed his eyes, then drew back in his chair.

"Like that," he said. "I've had an urge to hold your face since we started talking." Naomi's smile was steady, unaltered. "What do you think?" he asked. "Bad form? A violation of therapy rules?"

"What do I think? I'll tell you. I felt – touched. But what I want to know is what *you* think, what it meant to touch my face."

"Meant? I had actually been thinking about touching your face – just like that – for about twenty minutes. I had a feeling that touching you, a gesture like that, would bypass the talking, be truer than talking, go deeper."

"You want to go deeper."

"Yes, and more directly, faster."

"Like?"

"Like" – Sloan laughed – "like a boy."

"Yes, I can see that. But you were saying you didn't feel like a forty-five-year-old man feeling like a boy; that you *are* this boy."

"Yes."

"And do you remember what you were telling me when it occurred to you that you were a boy?"

Sloan suddenly felt dull, barely awake. He could not remember.

"You were telling me you were under the impression that men your age are not supposed to feel so sexual. You used the term 'quieter,' that men your age are thought to be sexually quieter."

"Right."

"But you're not feeling so quiet."

"No."

"And that's not bad."

"No, it's good – but I am wondering if it's normal." Sloan inwardly cringed hearing himself say *normal*.

Naomi laughed. "Got to make a choice, Sloan Fox. You want to feel good or do you want to feel normal?"

"Good."

"I'm glad," Naomi said evenly. "Because normal can take a terrible toll. Good, on the other hand, is life-saving. In my experience, people drive themselves mad worrying about normal, especially in the sexual department where, if you really think about it, there is no normal. Sex and normal are like oil and water. Sex doesn't like normal, and normal certainly doesn't like sex."

Naomi started to laugh, quieted, then erupted helplessly. "I'm sorry," she said, flushed, tears welling at the down-turned corners of her eyes."

"No problem," Sloan said, near laughter himself. "Sex can do that to you every time."

Naomi straightened, composed herself. "Now," she began with effortful evenness, "I am going to tell you something as ponderous and boring as I can in order to recover my mind. There. There now." She looked uncertainly at Sloan, still, he could tell, near laughter.

Sloan stared back at her and – ancient impulse – crossed his eyes.

Trying to hold her laughter, Naomi made a high, sustained whine, like the escape of steam from a kettle. Now she felt she was unable to look at him. Even through the wavy tears of her laughter, he was such a big, open, grinning presence. *You are,* she told herself, *too attractive. And yes, a big happy boy.*

Naomi composed herself. "And you are no help."

"So back to the ponderous, boring stuff you were about to say."

"Yes. As I was *going* to say, there are studies, and I will show them to you next time, showing that sexual desire and performance actually *increase* for many men and women in middle age, and for many of them, the higher level of activity continues into the sixties, seventies, and even eighties. What is confusing is that the majority of people reporting don't experience the surge, only some. But the fact that a significant number of people do is the point, or the encouraging point, not that the average person doesn't. See what I'm saying? The average defines what people think is normal, but only a sad sort of person would *aim* for that kind of normality."

"So if I'm one of the surging types, that's good."

"What do you think?"

"I think it's good, especially since, as you say, normal has so little going for it."

"That's right, I think. I would even go further and say that normal has nothing going for it – because it isn't anything; it's nothing.

Normal is only the attitude most people project onto the facts. It's not a fact itself. It's not real. See what I'm saying?"

Sloan didn't know if he saw. He knew the time was up, and that he felt deeply happy.

*I want it to be May forever,* Sloan reflected as he stopped and started through the homeward traffic. Ascending the steep grade between the city and the suburban heights, he lowered the car windows. The air was soft and sweetly heavy with the afternoon rain, and the rustle and whoosh of breezes through the new greenery seemed to carry him away with them. *Just this,* he thought, *just this forever.* Confusingly, he was both eager and reluctant to arrive home. Something seemed to beckon him, but he could not call it clearly to mind. He would eat his dinner – quickly – with Jen and Bart, and then he would walk the darkening streets of Cleveland Heights. He would walk for miles. He would walk until his legs ached. He would walk and consider Naomi Wise: fragments of her talk, images of her in the darkened consulting room, the crossing and recrossing of her knees below her leather skirt, her shoulders collapsing in laughter, and – always – opening her arms to him in the deserted vestibule. *I will be thinking about you, Sloan Fox. Do you want to feel good or do you want to feel normal? Give me your hands.*

Sloan inched the Honda up to his garage door and switched off the ignition. Again, he felt the unaccountable restlessness. He let himself say the words: *Love. I'm in love.*

As it happened, Sloan was unable to take his long walk after dinner. Jen had asked her freshman writing students at City College to see the new Jane Austen film, and she needed to see it herself. Sloan was only a little reluctant to go. Something in his body was pressing for exertion, for release, but a film was also appealing. Sitting in the mythy dark, he knew he could be drawn deeply into a film story. But Jane Austen? He made an effort to recall *Pride and Prejudice and* what seemed to him the labored, minuscule increments in the progress of Elizabeth Bennett's pursuit of Mr. Darcy. "O.K., sure. Why not?" he had said to Jen. He hoped the leading actress would be beautiful, that the camera would play warmly and intently on her face.

Standing in line inside the lobby of the Arts Cinema, Jen realized she had been mistaken. *Mansfield Park* was coming in a week.

"*Shit,*" Jen said, turning her back to the ticket window. "Now my syllabus is all screwed up."

"You can adjust," Sloan said. "You're all sensible, flexible people."

"Shit anyway. I wanted to see it tonight."

"Well" – Sloan peered over Jen's head and scanned the other attractions about to start. There was a film about a black regiment in the Civil War. Sloan recalled some excited, positive talk about it at *The Sun Messenger.*

"Tell you what," he said. "Let's go in and watch the coming attractions of *Mansfield Park*, then see *Union Blood.*"

"See *what* blood?"

"Trust me, it's a great, great film. You can ask your students to see it in light of Jane Austen."

For a moment Sloan was certain Jen would leave the theatre, but then she said, "What the hell. It's the story of my life. I go out to see Jane Austen and I get a movie about blood."

"I'm not sure it's *about* blood. It's a Civil War movie about a heroic black regiment."

"They're all about blood."

The film was in fact quite bloody, including many unflinching shots of battlefield mayhem and, even for Sloan, an unviewably graphic leg amputation.

Leaving the theatre, Jen said, "I can't believe I actually did that to myself, that I actually *participated* in that – shit."

Sloan threw an arm over Jen's shoulder. He could feel the current of her tension.

"I'm sorry," he said. "But it was shit that happened."

"Spare me."

Sloan guided Jen out of the theater into the street. "Should we get a drink?"

"No. I want to go home and take a huge bath."

They proceeded to the car in silence, Jen brittle and unyielding under Sloan's arm. Driving home, Sloan said, "Do you know what I got out of the film?"

Jen was silent.

"Do you know what I got out of it?"

"No."

"Well," Sloan said evenly, "I'll tell you. For me – and maybe males need the heavy, bloody hand – the movie showed the truth of there being unthinkable, awful things to do which you have to do anyway."

"Awful male things that awful males have to do."

Sloan considered the invitation to quarrel. He could make a case for noble, if terrible, necessity; the cause after all was preservation of national unity and the emancipation of slaves. Jen would, he knew, counter that males created the disunity and slavery in the first place. The prospect of making and countering these points did not interest him; it made him tired.

Sloan reached across to Jen's seat and took her hand. She was unresponsive.

For the second time in only a few hours Sloan guided the Honda along familiar streets toward home. Then his restlessness, irritation, and mounting sense of having lost something essential came together in such a vivid recollection that, without realizing it, Sloan let the car slow to a crawl.

Sloan brought to mind another lush, mild night, but in high summer, perhaps ten years ago when the boys still required a sitter. He and Jen had gone downtown to dinner on the waterfront. There was a steamy, hazy quality to the declining light as they dined. They had drinks before dinner and a bottle of wine with their food, and Jen was playful, relaxed, radiant. Sloan pictured her sitting across from him. She wore loose slacks and a gauzy linen top which exposed a little of her midriff. Uncharacteristically, she had made herself up; lipstick, a faint blush of rouge on her cheeks, some kind of darkening about her eyes. She looked to him wonderfully familiar and at the same time new, like an alluring stranger. She seemed so happy, so perfectly at rest.

Only half aware of himself behind the wheel, lightly clasping his wife's lifeless hand, Sloan could recall the feeling, the rising pleasure in his loins, belly and breast, a kind of combustion which seemed to spill out of his very cells and into the space between himself and Jen. It was an ache. It was, Sloan realized, longing itself, the ecstatic, limitless opening up he had sensed fleetingly when he had first heard Naomi speak. *This is it,* Sloan realized. *This is true.*

Driving home that summer night Sloan had caressed Jen's neck, his fingertips lightly tracing her hairline, the rims of her ear, the delicate curve of her collarbone. She had purred, made her sound, then adjusted her seat so that she was reclining almost horizontally at his side. Sloan was transported. He sneaked a look at Jen and saw that her eyes were closed.

As the car glided through light traffic on the Shoreway, Sloan's free hand found Jen's breasts, the indescribably softness of her belly. Jen unhooked her bra, opened the drawstring of her linen slacks and slid them down below her knees. Sloan touched and stroked her until they were both moving with their desire. Because they were driving, because he was keeping a fixed outer eye on the road, because she had closed both eyes to the waking world and its traffic, because both of them had let themselves pass through a threshold into new territory, there was nothing either of them could imagine that could contain them. They had passed from pleasurable, highly specific sensations into the wide maw of desire itself. Sloan could remember. *I wasn't doing it. I wasn't doing anything.* He felt drawn up into it, alive in its current. Jen – even Jen, Sloan realized – feels this.

Somehow they exited the Shoreway, and finding their way into the parking lot of a deserted mall, they gave themselves up to it, each gesture shameless, reckless, and new for them. Sloan remembered their sweat and the twisted disarray of their clothes. He remembered feeling a kind of wild emergence, as if something unspeakably messy and powerful had finally happened, that sticky with salt and his own seed, he was newly arrived in another world.

"Sloan, is something wrong with you?"

"What?"

"We're barely *moving*."

It was true. Sloan downshifted and accelerated the car.

*But it happened,* Sloan thought. *It happened.* They had that night said yes to everything.

Sloan and Jen entered their darkened house. Sloan straightened up Bart's papers and notebooks on the kitchen table and locked the doors. As he made his way up the stairs, he could hear the muted rush of water filling the tub. In the bathroom Sloan cleaned his teeth while Jen padded about behind him undressing for her bath. He felt sad, a dull weight below his heart as he returned to the bedroom, closing the door behind him. He sat in his chair and tried to pick up the strand of exposition in *Puer Aeternus,* The Jungian study Naomi had asked him to read, but almost at once he felt the tug of sleep. Sloan listened to the slap and slosh of water as Jen moved in the tub. He looked at his watch; it was late.

Sloan undressed and got into bed. Nearly asleep, he was aware of Jen slipping quietly into her place. In the dark she seemed to be far away from him. It occurred to him that they had not spoken since they entered the house.

# 9

## NOT QUITE RIGHT

"**I** just want you to know, you're the best."

Naomi met the eyes of a small, pretty, emaciated-looking woman in black and said, "That's such a nice thing to say. Thank you." Naomi looked for the woman's nametag and saw none. "I don't know your name.

"I'm Amanda, Amanda Black."

*Black in black, and so bony,* Naomi mused to herself.

"You're just the best. This whole day has been so – so freeing."

Naomi tried to match the force of Amanda Black's smile, and after a moment standing there locked in that attitude, Naomi started to laugh. Amanda Black opened her arms wide, and they embraced.

The workshop for women counselors and teachers in Philadelphia's Quaker Schools had been, from the outset, effortless. Naomi had allowed the maximum enrollment of forty to swell to fifty when the conference coordinator made an irresistibly gracious appeal. The fifty women had generously, even piously, welcomed her and the premise of each exercise, and Naomi found herself working to summon up a reserve in order to hold in check what she sensed was a collective tendency to overvalue her. The group's vulnerability, even their warmth, was vaguely aversive to Naomi, and she felt certain there was something valid and necessary in her aversion. *Do I need edginess and resistance,* she asked herself. *Do I need men?* This line of reverie made her want to laugh. She had been close to laughter when Amanda Black had complimented her. And now, disengaging from her embrace, she laughed again. *I do. I need difficult, interesting men.*

That evening the Quaker women treated her to a formal dinner at the conference center. At the conclusion of an elaborate toast made to her and to the benefits of the workshop, Naomi could see tears welled in Amanda Black's eyes and in the eyes of the women seated around her. The conference coordinator presented Naomi with a gift: a necklace of very fine gold chain holding a pendant which spelled SIMPLICITY at the base of her throat. Naomi felt a surge of warmth below her heart. The necklace was exquisite, unusual. She would actually wear it.

Naomi slept well. Flying back to Cleveland the following morning she realized that she was strangely indifferent to going home. Nathan would be in town, would meet her plane, but was then off to San Francisco for ten days of medical meetings. She realized she was indifferent to this, too. Naomi's spirits fell. *It's because I am so comfortable now.* She thought about her day's exertion with the Quaker women. It had been efficient, fluid, predictable. During the breathing and reflecting sessions, several women had wept convulsively. One had had to lie down on her mat, her head held in a colleague's lap for an hour. They had been eager and, Naomi thought, often too quick to see the point of the exercises and questions posed. In her bag were the workshop evaluation forms, the checkmarks unanimously indicating SUPERIOR. With the additional ten women enrolled, Naomi calculated that she would clear more than five thousand dollars for the day. *Too comfortable,* she told herself again. She remembered the delicate, weightless necklace. SIMPLICITY.

Guiding Bart down the steep ramp to the floor level of the Sportsplex, Sloan had an intimation of something very ancient. The columns of fans, thousands of them, flowing through the corridors and down the passages of the vast oval arena suggested majestic movements of troops, ancient legions forming their assigned lines of battle. At the same time Sloan registered an impression of a fantastic future: the flash and spray of overhead lights which made the hardwood court gleam like glass. He felt the garish vibration of the clashing pastel seats, the sweep of sinister black glass enclosing the executive loges, the great trapezoidal mass of the scoreboard overhead, the size of a house, from which images and slogans erupted and vanished. Even before the game began, the ambient roar was deafening, pulsed almost sickeningly with the bass line of amplified rock anthems.

Near mid-court at floor level, just two rows from the sideline – Sloan had been given complimentary tickets unneeded by the Sports Desk – they took their seats. Sloan caught his son's eye and tried to gauge if he was impressed, if he was happy. Bart looked to him somehow frail and diminished, his skin so translucent – so like Jen's – under the powerful lights that Sloan could see a convergence of purple veins at his temple.

On the way downtown they had talked about school and about the game. Cleveland was already out of contention for post-season play, but the Jazz were leading their division, and Sloan and Bart were both curious to watch Jamahl Ferris, the Jazz's volatile and notorious big man, from close range.

The game unfolded agreeably enough, with Cleveland taking and seeming to hold an early lead. But the rhythm of play – steal, fast break, and gratifying score – did not seem to drive the drama of the spectacle. Something more brash, louder, something mechanical and pre-planned seemed to be at work. Sloan sensed it in the jarring amplification of the cavalry bugles, in the enormous televised entreaties to cheer and to hiss. More than once he was aware that although he and his son were sitting only a few feet from the procession of glistening giants as they passed, he was far removed from the living spectacle; that he was instead held fast in an electronic, already scripted event. He stole a look at Bart; again his son looked small, lost.

Something in Sloan's peripheral vision jolted his interior, and he was reflexively on his feet, a protective arm shielding Bart from the commotion directly behind him. In a protracted tousle for a loose ball at mid-court, Jamahl Ferris and a Cleveland defender had forced each other out of bounds and into the seats. One of the falling players had grazed Sloan's back side, and as Sloan turned he saw that in the row in front of him a man and his son had been knocked from their chairs and were huddled on the floor. The boy, who looked about ten, sprang to his feet, and Sloan could see that he was all right. His father rose more gingerly, working and then massaging a shoulder. Ferris had penetrated several rows further into the spectators, and as he made his way back to the floor, his heated, dripping bulk forced Sloan almost to fall sideways onto Bart's chair. As he recovered his balance, Sloan fought an instinctive urge to follow and hit the retreating figure.

"*Fucking cocksucker,*" Jamahl Ferris said, apparently to the official who had awarded possession of the ball to Cleveland. Ferris was standing between the first and second row, his sweating form separating the man and boy he had knocked out of their seats.

"*Cocksucker,*" he said again. The curse felt to Sloan as if it had come from his own mouth. He was about to speak when the man in front of him moved into Ferris and said, "You're a disgrace."

For a moment the giant did not move, and Sloan tried to picture a way to disable him, to hurt him. Two officials and some players penetrated the seats and extended a beckoning hand to Ferris, leading him back onto the court. Then the big man shook free and turned back to the man who had addressed him. Leaning over the spectators in the first row, Ferris said, "What the fuck did you say to me?"

The man moved in front of his son. In his crew neck sweater and khaki pants, he seemed not just much smaller, but an altogether different kind of being than Jamahl Ferris. "I said you're a disgrace."

Ferris's face seemed to register nothing beneath his beaded skull. Then he grimaced and spat a viscous spray onto the boy's father.

A chorus of jeers and comments erupted from the circle of spectators surrounding the exchange. Then the booing began to radiate concentrically outward until the entire Arena was a chorus of angry complaint. Ferris took his defensive position on the court. The outpouring swelled and deepened. A cup of beer, then other litter was thrown onto the floor. The officials called time out, and the teams retreated to their benches. When play resumed, Ferris was not on the court. He had somehow managed to depart the facility.

The remainder of the game was eclipsed for Sloan, Bart, and others in the vicinity by impromptu conferences of sympathetic witnesses and the man who had been jostled and spat upon by Jamahl Ferris. After the game, the man and his son were engulfed by television reporters.

Driving back to Cleveland Heights, Sloan knew he ought to talk to Bart, but he felt a deep resistance. He wanted to sort out his own feelings. He wanted relief from what he realized was shame.

"That was something," he said to Bart. "Big time basketball."

"Real class," Bart said. "What a jerk."

Sloan could tell Bart did not want to talk. He pictured his son reporting to his friends the next day in school. He would be animated. *I couldn't believe it. He was right in front of me. First he wasted this guy and his son and then he said...*

"You know what I think?" Sloan said.

"What?"

"I think I'm sorry we went to the game."

Bart was silent.

Sloan did not say: I am sorry that life is lived this way, that something like a sports outing, a game, has so far lost the power to move or interest anyone that a claptrap of amplified noise and flashing lights are necessary to pump up the dead.

Sloan could not imagine anything that might move his son, that might pierce him with wonder. Sloan wanted to feel that himself. Sloan wanted longing. He wanted to be in communion. He wanted Naomi Wise.

# 10

## FEAR OF ENTRY

As Naomi let herself out of the back hallway into the garden she realized she was tired to the point of clumsiness. She had slept fitfully, descending into a restorative, vivid dream – leaving the country in an exaggerated disguise -- only as the alarm sounded. She fumbled in her bag trying to distinguish by feel the remote control device which opened the garage door from the one that unlocked the Lexus. The birdsong overhead sounded hectoring in Naomi's ears, as if standing there at that hour on the dewy flagstones was a kind of trespass.

It was only seven-thirty, Naomi thought, and it seemed disagreeably early for her to be up and about. She located both remotes and managed to hold one under the arm which carried her purse while aiming the other, like a pistol, at the garage door. Naomi was struck by an idea for an article: the modern penchant for *remote control*. To control, remotely. The reluctance to enter places and open things up without a distanced, reassuring preview. Fear of direct entry.

She remembered it was Friday and experienced the familiar, pleasing jump in her pulse, then the letdown. Friday at five had been Sloan Fox's scheduled hour, but he had made no appointment for the past three weeks. "I don't know about next week," he had said. "I'll call you." There had been no call.

Naomi had been waiting, she realized, as she had waited years ago for boys she thought she loved to call her for a date. Professionally, she knew this was usable data, usable in her transactions with Sloan, should he resume his sessions, and usable in her own inner work. There was something alive and charged with feeling – counter-transference, projection, crush – at work in her, and if she honestly acknowledged the feeling, took it all in, she would be spared from being held in its thrall; she could deliberate and choose.

Yet she felt a sadness much more enveloping and profound than the possible loss of an attractive client should have produced. Naomi had processed such hurt and losses in the past. In Montreal, Andre, her beautiful guitar player, had betrayed her repeatedly with other women before she was strong enough to break off with him. Later, the uncertainty of Todd's calls and arrivals had made her feel un-controllably vulnerable and weak, but not long after they were living together, he lost the power to upset or, finally, even to interest her. Nathan had been wonderfully impressive, but had never evoked doubt or longing in Naomi, which, if she let herself dwell on it, opened her up to an altogether different kind of sadness.

But Sloan Fox. His unbidden image appeared when she first awoke and recurred insistently throughout the day. *What kind of message are you, Sloan Fox?* He represented, she knew, something to do with vitality. The good bones of his face, the urgency in his eyes as he spoke – he was so *present* when he sat across from her. It occurred to her that she had not told him this. Instead, she had emphasized the opposite quality. She had made him aware of his abstracted-ness, his flight into story, the halting of his breath. *My training,* she mused uncomfortably, *my technique.* She had waited, held herself si-lently in check, when she had wanted to amuse and even to admire him. *Technique.* And now she wondered if she had lost him, such a fresh and invigorating presence in her inner life. *There must have been a reason for you.* Naomi pictured herself, from Sloan's perspective, during a consultation. *My energy is all about holding back.* Therapy, she told herself, is about willful restraint. It is conscious non-disclosure.

There could not be, she acknowledged, an ego-free condition, a therapeutic, neutral place free of desire. She had been a valued therapist *because* she let herself be a caring, attractive, surprising presence to her clients. Her strength, it now seemed to her, was in her willingness to let down her professional guard. *My technique has been to abandon technique.* Yet she knew she had been posturing in her sessions with Sloan Fox. Instinctively, he resisted anything formulaic from her, but he had been polite, almost courtly, in his willingness to play along. Naomi could see his face, the lively play behind his eyes. From the moment he greeted her, she was aware of his restlessness, sensed his desire. *You came to me for a reason.* Naomi felt a sudden resolve not to let him go. *You came for me, but you got technique.*

Naomi arrived at the clinic feeling harried and impatient with the morning's schedule of appointments. She made herself coffee and sat down in the quiet darkness of her office. *I miss him.*

Naomi took Sloan Fox's file out of her desk drawer and looked up his work number at *The Sun Messenger. I have no pride or judgment,* she said to herself. She was close to laughter as she entered the digits on the plastic phone.

Naomi listened to an elaborate network of pre-recorded messages before she got a living voice in the *Sun Messenger's* editorial room. Her heart pounded while she waited for Sloan to be paged. Then, surprisingly, his voice –

"I told you never to call me here."

"You *did?*" Naomi felt startled, guilty, then realized that Sloan was joking.

"Well, I was desperate," she said and laughed, she thought, a little shrilly. There was a pause, and then she remembered that she had placed the call and he would want to know why.

"I'm actually calling because it's Friday and –"

"You miss me."

Naomi saw something like a yellow flash of lightning behind her eyes.

"Yes of course I miss you. But I also need to know whether you have any plans to resume the Friday appointment slot, because if *not*, I would like to rearrange some sessions." *Lie. I am a liar. A shameless liar.*

"Right. I guess I have been taking a kind of a breather, haven't I?"

Naomi considered the words – *taking a kind of a breather* – but they made no sense to her.

"But yes," Sloan continued, "I would definitely like to keep going. I've actually been thinking about you a lot."

Naomi thought of saying, *for three weeks?* She decided she liked the ease and assuredness of his telephone manner.

"For the time being, I will hold the Friday afternoon hour. When you know your plans, you can call and let me know."

"I'll do that," Sloan said, "Either today or tomorrow. Promise. It's good to hear your voice."

*Done*, Naomi said to herself. *Deed is done.*


Standing in line with Jen at the Arts Cinema, Sloan sensed Naomi's presence before their eyes met. She and Nathan were five or six places ahead of them when, for some reason, she turned back toward the street. Sloan started when he saw the familiar blond hair straying from its twist, then the dark eyes bright with surprise. Recognizing him, Naomi felt an almost electric shock. Her smile froze, creating an expression unreadable to Sloan, before she turned back to the ticket window.

Jen, having noticed the publicity poster for *Union Blood*, was saying something in an acidic exasperated tone, but Sloan was unable to process the sense of her words. He was preoccupied with Naomi's companion. He was, Sloan thought, a distinguished-looking man, good color, flushed and tanned, a neatly barbered line of dark hair going silver. He looked to be about fifty. *Her husband*, Sloan thought, and remembered that he was called Nathan. Moving forward through the line, Sloan felt an involuntary wave of aggression. He wanted to meet Naomi's husband, charm him, make him laugh, better him.

Naomi could think only of Sloan Fox as she and Nathan took their seats high in the back row of the steeply tiered theatre. At the moment of recognition he had looked especially vivid, the unruly shock of his hair visible high above the heads of the others in line. He had raised a hand, widened his eyes in acknowledgement.

The lights dimmed, and Naomi saw Sloan and his wife – *Jen* -- make their way into a row of seats halfway down the theatre. As Jen took off her pea coat and arranged it over the back of her seat, Naomi noted that she was dark and pretty, a slender woman in a loose sweater and jeans. Naomi recalled that she was a university academic, a doctoral candidate. She would be bright, Naomi mused, bright and probably difficult. Slender and willowy, dark and difficult – it was a type Naomi had always regarded in a resigned way as being somehow superior.

The film, *American Way Out,* had created a lively stir since it was released. It was the latest in a series of highly nuanced treatments of upper middle class life in comfortable American suburbs. It featured three couples, each attractive, distinctive, approaching middle age. As the film explored their working and domestic lives, each principal was revealed to be on the verge of an adulterous relationship. The appeal, Sloan decided, was that the film resolutely declined to disapprove of the affairs; nor were they played for comedy or made to suggest the loss of something essential in the national character. A good deal of the business proceeded as the various partners reflected, while still in bed, on the meaning of what they were doing. It occurred to Sloan that in both the behavior of the characters and in the language they used to interpret it, the film was all about fidelity, asking whether there were higher, more compelling needs than the obligations of monogamy. The answer was not at all obvious; the families of the married partners were portrayed as valuable and substantial. Being a committed spouse was not presented as merely conventional or culturally narrow. Nor was adultery offered up as a panacea. The film explored, often with uncomfortable acuity, the exhilaration and welcome strangeness of transgressing polite boundaries. A considerable tension was created as the characters, without much self-recrimination, opened their lives to new sexual possibilities, without abandoning the practical, ordered, and rather agreeable habits that had defined them previously.

The most excruciating tension in the film lay in the possibility that one of the husbands, a lawyer, might be moving beyond marital infidelity into incest. In a subtle and sensual progression of vignettes, the sexual appeal of the nubile and often provocative girlfriends of the lawyer's teenage daughter became concentrated in the daughter herself. There were signs, shrewdly ambiguous, that the daughter might welcome a forbidden trespass on her father's part.

The resolution of the film was unsatisfying but decidedly realistic. Each couple's domestic arrangement changed drastically, creating an eerie serenity for some of the partners, misery and loss for others.

Leaving the theatre, Sloan kept an eye out for Naomi. He heard Jen say, "Is that the way it is now in Cleveland Heights? I hardly ever get out. Am I missing something?" Then, clearly agitated, she asked Sloan, "What did you think?"

"Hard to say. A lot." Sloan met Jen's eyes. "I think it might be a great film. A great, strange film. Its point, I think, is that affairs are real."

"Of course they're real."

Sloan paused, considered his words. "They've never felt real to me. I wasn't too crazy about the incest tease. That was kind of a reach."

"Affairs used to be kind of a reach."


Naomi was moved and at times overwhelmed by *American Way Out*. So, she sensed, was Nathan. Neither of them spoke or rose to go as the credits spilled in white script over the black screen. From her anonymity in the darkened back row, she watched Sloan and Jen rise, slip into their coats, and make their way up the aisle to the lobby. Sloan extended an arm over Jen's shoulder, and she edged in close to him as he said something in her ear. Naomi felt a hurt pang of envy at the Foxes' easy intimacy. Sloan looked tall and solicitous moving at his wife's side. Naomi wanted that, she realized. She wanted him. She said to herself: *I need to make a mess.*


Sloan lay awake in the dark, summoning up scenes from *American Way Out.* The characters had – very deliberately – stepped out of bounds. A woman telephoned her neighbor, and when he stopped by, she greeted him naked; without speaking, he entered the house. Another woman was obsessed with her friend's husband would drive each evening to the commuter station to watch him get off the train and walk home. Once in a downpour, she pulled over and offered him a lift. The following day, she picked him up again, and they made love in the car. There was a lot of sex in the film, languorous and exploratory, and Sloan had been excited by it. He called to mind images of the couples in bed. There were long spells without dialog, the partners searching each other's eyes as if for confirmation that something momentous had occurred, that something insistent but shadowed – *the shadow,* Sloan remembered, *the unacknowledged truth –* had come irrevocably to life. *It happens,* Sloan realized as he heard the rise and fall of his sleeping wife's respiration. *It is completely possible.* Sloan felt a pleasurable stirring. He was wide awake.

# 11

## AMERICAN WAY OUT

This was different, Sloan realized. It did not feel like therapy at all.

They had begun, first guardedly, then with excited good humor, by sharing their impression of spotting each other at *American Way Out*.

"I was about to come over and say hello, introduce Jen, but then you gave me one of these" – Sloan wheeled around in his swivel chair so that his back was to Naomi.

*Terrific energy today,* Naomi registered appreciatively. His imitation of her turning her back made her laugh.

"I did no such thing."

"You did – oh, yes you did. The cold shoulder, the full snub. You *dissed* me, Dr. Wise."

*Dr. Wise.* Naomi said, "I did not mean to snub you, but you should know that it's an awkward thing, a delicate thing to see a client in public. With his wife, no less, the wife we talk about. A Freudian would have had to leave the theatre and go home. I am not so rigid, but socializing outside our sessions is a tricky business."

"Even a 'hello' or a friendly wave?"

"I could probably have managed a hello or a friendly wave without losing my license. I am sorry if I was rude to you, but I was just so surprised to see you at all."

"It may take time to heal and a lot of support, but I think I'll recover."

"And that was your wife, Jen."

"Yes, the very one."

"She is very pretty."

"Yes, thank you." Sloan wondered if 'thank you' was right. "I'll pass on the compliment."

For what Sloan realized must have been the full length of the consulting hour, he and Naomi talked about *American Way Out.* Sloan felt free of any obligation to be self-conscious, and he was elated. It was like a good talk at Dulaney's, calling up an image or an exchange from the film with special clarity, working to shape its point, accounting for the impression it made. Naomi too let herself rise past purposefulness. He had seen exactly what she had seen in *American Way Out.* At moments they found themselves almost shouting with agreement, awkwardly talking over one another, then slowing down, careful to trade pleasures and puzzlements.

At length Naomi said, "A story, on its surface, about different ways of doing adultery. Of very successful, comfortable, attractive people entering into adultery. Going straight past the boundaries we expect will contain them. So what do you think has made this film so popular – created such a fuss?"

"Just that," Sloan said, "Just what you said. It's about going past expected boundaries. And because you see outwardly respectable, attractive people doing it, it makes a kind of invitation to cut loose and wander."

"Cut loose and wander," Naomi repeated slowly. She smiled appreciatively at Sloan. "That's a wonderful way to put it. But" – Naomi frowned – "It's always been a pleasure to cut loose and wander. Why now, why at this particular moment in American culture, do these very possible-seeming adulteries carry such force? It's not as if affairs, especially suburban American affairs, are any great novelty."

Sloan brought to mind John Updike's *Rabbit* novels, another novel of his, *Couples*. He began to recall similar snatches of such fiction from John Cheever, from *New Yorker* story writers whose names he could not remember. Images of adulterers converging in familiar American settings were now, all at once, swirling together in his imagination, too numerous to name.

"That's a really good point, a good question," Sloan said. *Oh yes,* he thought: "The impulse to sex has always – since the beginning, I'm sure – threatened the social limits and laws trying to hold it back. That's clear. Sex is not only bigger, more urgent than the rules, it came first. So the will-I or won't-I problem has always been there. It's eternal. And when it's *not* there, when fidelity is sweet and easy, something is probably way off. But that's not what I want to say. O.K., we know there's a constant lively tension, at least sometimes, between sex – between desire – and fidelity. Eternal. And since it's always been there, why does a movie about it now – a movie about six deliberate trespasses – create a big stir? The answer must be" – Sloan thrust forward his open palms in a gesture of mock profundity – "That the dark side of the tension, *desire*, is now receiving more light. The difference is not that there is any more or any different kind of feelings about sexual rule-breaking; the difference is that dark desire is now being held up to the light."

"And when it is," Naomi said, "What does it look like?"

"It looks exactly the way it looked in the movie. It looks exactly the way I'll bet it really is. We both saw it. It looked – sometimes funny, like a desperate game. It looked wild. Sometimes it looked incredibly sexy and exciting. I've personally not been there, but I'll bet that's what it's like."

"But it also could make a big mess," Naomi said, not challenging him, but thoughtfully.

"Big messes, yes. Big messes are part of it. But the ecstatic, thrilling bits are part of it, too. The film really doesn't tip its hand, although maybe the incest business was supposed to say: go here and you're also on the way to there."

Naomi was confused by the phrase "tip its hand" and also, she realized, by what moral or psychological message had been conveyed by *American Way Out.* Her deepest impression was of Sloan's energy, of a possibly limitless strength in him. Now she was past analysis or argument. She was a little tired, although not unpleasantly. She wanted time alone, to take the measure of their time together, of the things they had said to each other about the film.

"Speaking of crossing boundaries," Naomi said, clasping and unclasping Sloan's hands, "We have exceeded our time by" – she picked up her watch from the glass table – "forty minutes."

"My fault. I'll pay."

"No, no. Nobody's fault. Nobody pays."

"Ah," Sloan said, rising from his chair, "another powerful theme of *American Way Out.* Do you think?"

When he was by himself, seated in his red chair or driving to or from *The Sun Messenger,* Sloan believed he could tell Jen. He could, somehow, introduce the – what? – waves and rushes of new feeling, his new sense of giddy, thrilling, dangerous *possibility,* at least offer something of the substance and force of what he was feeling into what had become a growing distance between them.

He had not made love to Jen, or even much wanted to, in weeks. What had begun in resentment had trailed off into a kind of objective curiosity about how she would relate to him in the absence of physical communion. At night when she would join him in bed after her bath, she sometimes moved in close to him for an embrace, sometimes not. He was content to hold her quietly until she moved away or drifted into sleep. Weekend mornings, on one or both of which they had liked to make love, Sloan now woke up early, stretched, put on a sweatshirt, shorts, and running shoes and stepped out the back door to the driveway where he shot baskets, sleepily, mindlessly, happily, until Jen or Bart could be seen in the kitchen.

He found his abstinence somehow calming. He was, if anything, more attentive to Jen's movements, the quirks of her conversation. There would be a time, he felt sure, when he could open up and let her know.

And now the table was cleared, and Bart had gone off with friends to the library.

"Do you ever think about that film, *American Way Out?*" Sloan said.

Jen immediately called to mind unbearable images from *Union Blood.* Then she remembered it was the wrong movie. She was confused.

"No. I haven't thought about it. Why? Have you?" Jen remembered: all the affairs, the insistent probing into what felt unviewably private and forbidden. The naked woman behind the screen door greeting her neighbor at bright midday.

"Yes. I keep thinking about it."

"You have affairs on your mind?" Jen was troubled.

"No," Sloan said, catching her edginess, feeling the familiar resistance. "Not affairs. But I do keep thinking about what the movie was trying to do. Which was, I think, trying to break through the surfaces, through the safety, of what people have settled for. That's the feeling I got. The affairs just put it right in your face."

"And?"

"And it makes you think." Sloan wished he had not said *think.* He wished he had said *feel.* He wanted to talk about how the film – how his life now – made him feel.

"Think about what, having an affair?"

Sloan saw that Jen was apprehensive, and he fought back a reflex to withdraw, bring the conversation to a close and leave the table.

"No," he said, looking directly into her eyes. "No, the affairs were the business, but I keep thinking what the business was *about.*"

"What was the business about?"

"It was about the tension between each person's inner life, which, whatever you think about the individual people, was wild, untamed, unfinished –" Sloan could feel himself losing track of his words – "and the life out for show."

Jen paused for a moment to consider and said, "And in every case the wild, untamed side came out and everybody had affairs. Great."

"Jen, tell me the truth. Did you think there was anything great in the film? Any moment? Any image? Anything?"

Jen thought of the door opening to reveal the naked woman behind the screen.

"Great? There was a lot of sex. It was sensational, I guess." Jen remembered the couples' unhurried lovemaking, the scene in which the lovers undressed each other in the car. It was unsettling, arousing; she could feel it now. "But is that great?"

"You tell me. That's what I'm asking – I'm not making an argument."

Jen looked to Sloan bewildered, perhaps resentful.

"O.K.," he continued, "It was sensational, and it was sexy, I thought really sexy. But what I can't get out of my head is that those people just – and we aren't told why – just went ahead with it. They do what we almost never do. They said yes to their desire, to their inner life. They said yes to their longing ..."

"And you think every married couple is longing for sex with somebody else?"

"I don't know." Sloan worked to keep the combativeness out of his tone. "But I do think that every married person – that I – have an inner life and that a lot more is going on there than the outer world wants to allow."

"And—"

"*And* the inner world is real. It's bursting with things. It feels huge. It feels ecstatic sometimes, and the more you open up to it, the more you bring it up to the light, the more amazing it feels. And yes, sex is part of it. Sex is enormous. But I think most of the time sex is mainly unconscious. You get a sexy signal, you're in the familiar situation, and boom, green light, you do it. And it's great, the big O, the release. But I think great as ordinary, unconscious sex is, it's just a fragment, a little clue to what conscious sex can be. To what consciousness itself can be. I think --" Sloan stopped himself.

"What do you think?"

Sloan felt disoriented, unaccountably defeated. The bright lighting fixture overhead, the checked table cloth between them, the stacks of dishes on the counter behind Jen – all of it seemed to distance Sloan from the resolve that only a few moments earlier had felt urgent.

"What do you think," Jen repeated.

"I don't know. I don't know if I can put it into words."

"Maybe you could try dancing."

Sloan saw a clout of white light behind his eyes. He pictured himself slapping Jen's face hard with his open hand. He pictured her startled look, the sting and ring of it in the bright kitchen light.

"No seriously," Jen said. "Tell me what you mean."

"I mean," Sloan said, quietly and evenly, "that there's something inside, and I don't think it's just me, that feels like paradise sometimes. That is paradise. And it's not just sex, although sex is maybe the express route. I'm talking about looking across the dinner table at my father in his green shirt. I'm talking about Bart rising up from the scorer's table to play ball. I'm talking about sweet, wet breezes washing over me through the open car windows when I drive home. I'm talking about" – Sloan could see Naomi's face on the brink of laughter, about to surrender to it – "looking into somebody's eyes and not stopping, going straight inside." Sloan sat up straight, tilted back his head. "I think we're all practically in paradise, or could be if we are willing to live our inner life. That's what I'm sure the clues are all about, those incredible glimpses. I'm sure you have your own. But it's paradise. And it's real."

Jen got up from her chair and turned to the counter. "And that's what you saw in the film, signs of paradise?"

"What I saw in the film was crashing through the surfaces, mixing up normal and forbidden so that the inner life could start to breathe. Not paradise maybe, but the beginning of paradise." Sloan pushed his chair away from the table. "Need help?"

"No, thanks. There's almost nothing."

"I think I'll go up and do a little reading."

For a moment Jen stood still over the sink. Sloan's departure from the room left her feeling fearful and abandoned, suddenly heavy in her legs. His words had struck her like a blow...*those incredible glimpses...I'm sure you have your own.* Working against a fatigue that felt almost like pain, Jen turned on the faucet and began gathering the assorted pots and pans, dishes and silver. Later she would go up to her office and sit but not work. She would call Henry and risk his flat response. She would lie out on her back in the hot bath water. *I will hang on,* she said to herself. *I will keep it together.* She felt the ache and swell of tears rise in her throat and behind her eyes. *Keep what? Keep what together?*

# 12

## NATHAN

Nathan's plane from the west coast arrived early, and Naomi was a little late, so they met not at the gate but in the terminal corridor near the baggage claim escalator.

Naomi spotted her husband before he was aware of her, and as she took in the full image of him walking briskly among the striding throng, it struck her again how pulled together, how complete a figure he was. He wore a black knit shirt and dressy gray slacks, and his loose black raincoat flared behind as he walked, creating a vague impression of a cape or even wings. As their eyes met and he raised an arm to greet her, Naomi noted the good dark plummy color of his cheeks, the dramatic darkness of his hair and brow. Again, always, *like someone out of a movie.*

They embraced and kissed, and Naomi said, "I'm late, I'm sorry."

"I'm early. Don't be sorry."

Naomi was overcome by the familiar scent of Nathan's cologne and for a moment puzzled over its agreeable sweetness, while at the same time finding it aversive. *What is it,* she thought. *Too easy, a too easy pleasure, an intrusion, an intrusion masquerading as a sweetness, yet it is already inside me, already made itself at home.*

"Is anything wrong?" Nathan asked.

"No, no," I'm just remembering how you smell."

"Smell? I hope I smell all right."

"You smell lovely." Naomi slipped an arm inside his open coat and around his waist. "You smell like a lovely garden."

Driving from the airport to Jasmine where Naomi had made reservations for dinner, Nathan talked about his meetings and lectures in a way that was, while in no way evasive, curiously empty to Naomi. What was it? *There are no people in the stories, no particular people. Memorable, likeable people.* Then it occurred to Naomi: *There is nothing funny.*

Naomi blurted out, interrupting him, "Did anything funny happen?" Her voice sounded strange in her ears, desperate.

"Funny?" Nathan paused to consider. "*Funny?*"

"Yes, anything funny – goofy. You were there ten days. Some funny things must have occurred. No?"

"You mean ha-ha funny?" Nathan was perplexed. "Funny, funny, *funny.* Let's see. I'm thinking. And I'm afraid there is – absolutely nothing funny to report. A lot of talks, as I was saying, and meetings, and dinners. Not one funny thing, I'm afraid."

Naomi was sorry she had asked. She exited the expressway and as they neared Jasmine, she began to feel a kind of dread at the prospect of a protracted restaurant meal seated across from her husband. She shook her head, as if to banish the thought.

"You all right, darling?"

"Oh yes. More than all right. Raring to go."

Naomi willed herself not to find fault with Nathan. For in truth, objectively, there was little to fault. He would be cheerful, even after his long flight. He would be genuinely eager to hear her news and her impressions of things. He would appreciate his food. But – there it was – he would appreciate it too much. Make informed inquiries to the waiter, savor mouthfuls, report his responses with a specificity that made Naomi feel unaccountably contrary. *What was it?* He had every right to enjoy his elegant food, but his doing so had the effect of making Naomi want to order quickly and without deliberation, then bolt down whatever arrived, or, more often, to leave most of it uneaten on the plate. It was not, she realized, his enjoyment that irritated her, it was the quality of *enjoying* his enjoyment, of savoring not just the food, but the kind of person he found himself to be at the moment: in that particular darkened nook, at that particular hour, partaking of that particular delicacy, sitting across from—and this is what made Naomi want to negate everything – that particular woman. *Nathan likes to make perfect pictures,* Naomi concluded as the hostess led them to their table. *And I don't want to be trapped in the picture.*

Seated across from one another – exactly as she had pictured it – Naomi felt herself bristling with resistance to even the most appropriate utterances and gestures from Nathan, and she set about compensating, paying what she hoped was not too exaggerated attention to what he said. Realizing she was inclining toward him almost aggressively, she caught herself, made herself relax and leaned back in her chair. *This is work,* she said to herself, *and I will do it.*

His questions of her were what she had expected. Had Lynn-Marie called about any developments on the Edisto house. Had the anatomy engravings he had found for the small study come back from the framers. Was the new yard crew any good. Were the fruit trees in blossom. *All reasonable questions.* Naomi told herself. *But they are about perfect pictures.*

Nathan asked the waiter about the risotto: mushrooms, shallots, and bits of lobster in a red wine sauce, prepared for two.

"What do you think, darling? Would you like to share a risotto?"

It had actually sounded very good to Naomi, and she had eaten practically nothing all day.

"Oh – no, I think no. I think I'll just have a salad, a nice, simple salad, and maybe about five more glasses of wine." Naomi made a little shriek of laughter.

"A tough day with the clients?" Nathan said, somehow, Naomi believed, for the benefit of the waiter.

When the waiter had gone, Naomi leaned across to Nathan and said, "You know something. I love my clients. I've never loved my clients more. Maybe I should be worried I love my clients so much."

"Why worry? Lucky clients."

"I'm not really worried. What would be the point? Although love can be a problem, don't you think? Love's way harder to deal with than intelligence."

Nathan looked confused.

"Speaking of which," Naomi said. "I can't get over *American Way Out*. What was it, two weeks since we saw it. I think I have to see it again. Want to?"

"Mm. Once is enough for me, I think. It made its point."

*"Really?"* Naomi said, she thought too loudly, too aggressively. "Really. Tell me the point."

"The point." Nathan stopped to consider. He joined the tips of his fingers on the white linen tablecloth. The gesture, Naomi thought, was practiced. His brown hands on the table between them were undeniably appealing, but they were something more. They were, she realized, *pretty*.

*"The point,* Nathan said, "is bored Americans acting out."

"Bored?" Naomi said. "Just bored? What about desire? I thought it was all about desire."

"What desire can do to you when you're bored."

"Mm. I guess we all better watch out for boredom. Speaking of which – what about you? Are you ever bored? Were you bored in San Francisco? You said there was nothing funny for ten days. Weren't you bored?"

Naomi could hear her tone becoming hectoring. Nathan looked troubled.

"Not boring?" She asked.

"I don't think I ever felt too bored. At any rate not driven to adultery. Like – as – in the movie."

"As, yes. Here come our salads. What's wrong with me? I really do want a lot more wine."

Over coffee, Nathan excused himself to go to the men's room, and Naomi studied the dark attractive length of him as he made his way out of sight. Relaxed now, even expansive, she had somehow shed the oppressive weight that troubled her when they had sat down to dinner. Four glasses of wine had been transformative. They had ordered a second bottle. *Is my drinking a problem?* Naomi almost laughed out loud. She didn't care. She was comfortable now, comfortable at Jasmine, comfortable with Nathan.

There was so little wrong with him, really. He was so easy. Naomi remembered when the easiness had been an amazement. There had been the bumpy, rancorous estrangement from Todd in Montreal, the showdown and asking him to move out. Still shaken, she had begun dating again, but found it difficult and disorienting. Having adjusted, however imperfectly, to sharing a flat and a bed with an intimate, she seemed afterward to lose confidence in less committed male friendships. There had been a year-long spell in which she met appealing men – most of them boys – and immediately assumed a jokey, familiar intimacy. She sensed that this had overwhelmed some of them, especially the one or two she had rather liked; the others she quickly determined were not for her, and she broke off relations with a haste and awkwardness she did not completely understand. There were a few one-night stands, one of them with a woman, one of her teachers. In these encounters she gave herself permission to step out of bounds, to take something like an objective measure of her desire and of certain highly specific sensations. To her mild surprise, she not only felt untroubled about the purely sexual outings, she rather liked them – not entirely, she decided, for the sexual sensations, which were a curious and mixed lot, but for the liberation she had felt at being able to decide, in no more than the time it took to take a long look into another's eyes, *I can actually do this.* She learned she could give herself that permission, that it was hers to give.

And at the same time she began to realize, in the close and adventuresome company of several other bright young women enrolled in her graduate program, that finding a man who was sexually and otherwise satisfying was at once an exquisite and a dubious undertaking. Something deep within her had assumed that the great, irresistible communion would somehow simply happen, simply unfold. But with every new relationship and with every passing month in which she had to negotiate the responsibilities of being an attractive young woman living independently in a large city, Naomi began to accept the likelihood that she herself would have to shape her amorous future. She would settle on, settle for. Without the guidance of her parents, who were long dead, or other intimate relations, she would, she suspected, follow the example of her friends and try to make a relationship with someone who, in the language they favored, was "interesting."

The evening Nathan Weingart and two other medical residents were invited to join Naomi's seminar on Defining Life, the problem to be addressed was When Does a Human Being Become Human. Naomi's personal assignment had been to scan the philosophic and medical literature and to propose criteria for viability in a foetus. She had liked this work. So much that was subtle and rich and far-reaching came to bear on such a concrete question: when does sheer biological process become a life that matters? Legally, in many parts of the world, life was held to commence and end with breath. This wouldn't do, she thought, because a baby did not breathe until expelled from its mother at term. It seemed monstrous to regard a baby about to be born as not yet human. Medical technology was moving civilized people toward equating reasonable brain function with life. This was better, she thought. She decided to retain the classical definition of life – the capacity to act and to react. She determined that the fetal brain is structured to carry on the functions that make it viable by the third or fourth month, so it was then, she concluded, that a foetus might be considered human. At the time, though pleased with her work, she was concerned that her paper was too confining in its precision, but her position was, she hoped, plausible and interesting.

The evening of the seminar, Naomi suffered a pang of doubt when her professor announced that she had invited guests from the university hospital. One of them – Nathan – was introduced as a resident in neurology, and Naomi at once became anxious that she had misread or misunderstood the technical papers she had scanned.

As it happened, her paper, more extensively researched and more closely reasoned than the others, was warmly praised, and it elicited a lively response. The medical guests had not commented much – mercifully, Naomi felt – when Nathan rose from his chair. She remembered that it was an effortlessly commanding gesture, and the seminar had fallen quiet at once.

"First," he said, "I would like to thank Dr. Nagel for inviting us. I was very impressed with the argument and position taken in this paper. In fact from a scientific standpoint, I could not fault it. And although I don't set up as a philosopher, I think the criterion of brain structure, which is the *organ* of meaning-making, has real merit. But I do have a personal concern about defining human life in this way, especially if this definition became a basis of policy.

"I have done some work in obstetrics and have assisted in abortion procedures. Has any of you seen what a foetus looks like at two-and-a-half months or three months? It's actually quite substantial." Nathan had indicated the approximate size with the thumb and index finger of each hand. "It is very much a living thing, a person in the making. I am saying this, I suppose, only because I would not like to see the day when it was my job, or anybody's job, to terminate such beings because the structure of their brains had not arrived at what policy had determined was properly human.. You see what I'm saying? To actually be there, to do such a thing feels like killing something quite alive and well."

Naomi had been quick to reassure the seminar that she had not thought of her definition being used to justify abortion.

"But if abortions are to be performed at all, for any reason," Professor Nagel had asked, "*Shouldn't* they be justified by some principle like the one Naomi proposed?"

"Don't get me wrong," Nathan had said. He was animated now and, Naomi realized, remarkably good-looking. "I don't have either a definition or a policy to propose. I simply could not bear personally to do the job such a policy might require. You know, don't you, a fetus that is aborted does not arrive dead into your hands. You have to kill it."

Dr. Nagel served coffee and desserts after the seminar, and Naomi was flattered that Nathan sought her out immediately for further discussion. He praised her paper generously and said he hoped he had not seemed overly critical by bringing up his personal experience. Naomi had been touched that her work, a mere class assignment had been taken so seriously. She warmed to the realization that her marshaled thoughts – that she herself – could provoke an earnest response from this movie-star handsome man, this doctor. She had let her gaze drop to his left hand cradling the perimeter of the coffee mug. There was no ring.

Nathan had departed Dr. Nagel's living room with Naomi's full name, a good idea of where she lived, and her assurance that she was listed in the telephone directory. Not long afterwards Naomi and her friends stepped into the breathtakingly frigid winter street and were soon screaming with laughter.

In the months that followed, Naomi felt as if she and Nathan Weingart had somehow merged onto the same smooth highway. Her previous experiences of love had been mainly unsettling: waves of ecstatic possibility alternating with almost unbearable foreboding of imminent loss. Love had made her nervous, hesitant, too quick to laugh and too quick to cry. Breaking off with Todd had seemed to demand that she assume a role she felt fundamentally unsuited for. It wearied her to have to catalog his lapses and shortcomings, to resist his apologies and plans, to be steely and distant. She had wanted him to disappear. She was close to concluding that love was only trouble when she and Nathan began seeing each other. Trouble now, at least trouble with him, became difficult to imagine.

Nathan had not pressed her to do anything or to go anywhere that was at all disagreeable to her, although she more than expected a few jarring episodes. She assumed some disillusionment as they grew more familiar, but none came. He was five years older, which, as she reckoned life stages then, could have been twenty. Like her, he was an only child of cultured Jewish parents who had managed to get out of Europe between the wars. His father, unlike hers, had made a good deal of money in Montreal, first as a jeweler, then as an importer of furniture. Nathan had been sent to good schools, had done well and found his calling early in medical research. As a young woman and as a graduate student, Naomi had felt enthralled to be standing at the threshold of great ideas, systems of thought, periods and movements of art and music. Nathan gave her the impression of having already passed through that threshold. At the time they met, he had acquired a taste for early music, knew how it was structured, the religious chants and folk melodies on which it was based. He knew about the early instruments. He knew the best recordings. The jumpy, melancholy hooting and jingling of these recordings had charmed her when she first heard them in the course of long cozy Sunday afternoons in Nathan's immaculate flat. Unlike anyone else she knew, he had developed the knack of savoring things, savoring food, savoring the look and texture of rooms. His desire seemed to be to savor things with her, so that they would be held in the same kind of thrall. She had wanted this too, and it pleased him. Yet for Naomi, the pleasure in a new cuisine or a new place or in making love to a new man – all the astonishment of a new body – was not in knowing and savoring, but in the thrill of discovery.

Nathan liked to dine out, and he could afford to take her to restaurants she and her friends would never have considered. He also liked to travel and seemed to enjoy, even more than the trips themselves, making careful arrangements in advance. First there had been Winter Carnival in Quebec, then, in bleak early spring, a surreally bright and vernal week in the Caribbean. The following winter they flew to southern California, rented a car, and toured the cliffs along the coastline, down into the white, clean desert beaches of Mexico. Nathan's preparations were invariably faultless, and travel, which had been uncertain for Naomi, seemed to proceed as if in an agreeable dream. It was in the Caribbean, at an almost deserted island resort, that Naomi discovered, with a delicious feeling of abandonment and pleasure, that she liked exposing her body to the sun and air. As a girl she had been two or three times to the seaside in the summer, but never to the south, and the experience of reclining in near nakedness and feeling the insistent radiance on her face, belly, and legs awakened something welcome and newly sexual in her. "Why, Miss Wise," Nathan had said, approaching her chaise where she reclined bare breasted at the water's edge, "You are an island girl."

She had already realized this, that in the naked surrender to sun and the caress of breezes over her midriff, in the slow awakening to days in which she would do nothing but rise, go outdoors, and offer her body up to the warmth and the sparkling aquamarine, she had arrived unexpectedly at a new home. *This is where I belong.* It was not, she knew, the only place she belonged, but this new opening up, this new sensual territory, was a real place of her heart. In the years ahead she would theorize about this. Her theory, helped along by studies in archetypal psychology, was that she was constructed not of a single evolving self, but of a complex of deeply imbedded, simultaneously emerging selves. She was fully conscious, she knew, of her waking, working persona, of how it makes its way through the world – Naomi Wise, the bright girl, the working therapist, the quirky woman, the Jew, the attractive blond, the deceptively effective one. She also felt with the passing years that her shadow was making itself more fully known to her, and it was often an imperious child, a mischief maker, a brazen seductress.

She marveled a little that she had made these discoveries about herself with Nathan, perhaps even because of Nathan, first as her partner and now as her husband. He was not a Tristan to her Isolde, she realized soon after they were together, *but I am Isolde.* She had never battled him, met him boldly as a romantic masculine Other. She had merged with him, shared a trajectory. He had been a quiet, observant, often appreciative witness to her continuing emergence. Sometimes she marveled at this realization. It has been *so cozy, so undeserved.* It had been like their meeting at Professor Nagel's seminar: strangely perfect. "Of course you would end up with the most perfect man in Montreal," her friend Annalise had joked. The joke had upset Naomi at the time, and she would not forget it. She resisted the idea of a perfect man – of a perfection of any kind. She did not want to be savored.

More than two years after they met, when Naomi was nearing the completion of her degree and certification, Nathan proposed marriage. There had been little drama or surprise. Long before, without formally committing themselves, they had talked and speculated about their futures, always as a couple. Nathan's research specialty would almost certainly take him out of Montreal, possibly to Zurich, which Naomi thought would be agreeably exotic, but most probably to one of the big teaching hospitals in the States. Naomi's credentials as a psychologist were portable, and although Montreal felt like a friendly home, she was ready, even eager, to begin again.

In honor of her engagement, her girl friends arranged an elaborate dinner party for her at the most elegant restaurant they knew, La Place Vendome. There had been much hilarity, most of it expressed as mock resentment of Naomi's having landed the Perfect Man, but there was also a quieter, deeper note struck. This was a milestone. Naomi would be the first of the group to marry and move on. Something delicate and youthful was about to be supplanted by a largely unknown, portentous next step. For a moment Naomi had been teary and unable to speak. She had always made friends easily, drawn them quickly into her confidence. Her friendliness had served her well after the death, when she was fifteen, of her mother, and a year later her father. These interesting, funny, uncertain women seated about the long table at La Place Vendome were not only lovable, but important and necessary to her. Hearing the gaggle of their voices, Naomi thought: *You are extra selves,* and for a moment the picture of herself and Nathan quietly cohabiting some elegantly appointed flat in a distant city made her feel cast off and unbearably lonely.

That evening, when the others had departed the restaurant, Annalise said to Naomi, "Do you mind if I tell you something? Something really terrible."

Naomi started. "No, tell me something terrible."

"It's mostly terrible about me."

"Tell me."

"I don't know why, but I just feel I have to say this – admit this. It's – I always thought Nathan was gay."

For a second Naomi could see nothing at all.

"You did? You think he's gay?"

"I mean *no*, I did, but obviously he's not gay. I mean you know. But I thought that. We all did.

"You all did? Why didn't you tell me?" Naomi tried not to sound accusing.

"Well, we didn't want to be jerks about it, and it wasn't like it was a big concern. Maybe it was a way to be jealous that you had found someone. Anyway, if he was, we were sure you knew, that maybe you wanted to be with a gay guy for a while."

"So you thought Nathan was gay."

"Well – he was so smooth, so *dapper*. I'm sure it's just a huge stereotype. A beautiful, carefully dressed, trim and fit guy who likes music and art – you just rarely see straight guys like that. At least in my little world."

"Well, I have never thought about Nathan being gay, not even for a second. And I practically live with him."

Naomi fought back the urge to convince Annalise of Nathan's virility. She was tempted to discuss specifically how he was in bed, recount intimate talks they had had about sex, but the prospect made her feel weak and ashamed. She had, in truth, never considered that Nathan was anything other than heterosexual. As Annalise tried to steer the conversation onto other matters, Naomi's mind ran riot in pursuit of subtle or missed signs of Nathan's homosexuality. She had never detected any special intensity in his relations with male friends or colleagues. He was noticeably stylish and meticulous in his turn-out, but Naomi had never found this effeminate. Then, too, they had talked, she believed openly, about their past relationships; nothing unusual had been disclosed. Naomi had confessed her own impulsive ventures into lesbian sex, to which Nathan had been attentive and, it seemed to her, untroubled. That revelation would certainly have been an unthreatening invitation to admit any similar inclination on his part.

That night, when they were in bed, Naomi raised herself up on an elbow and asked him, "Have you ever had sex with a man?"

"No, I never have."

"Have you ever wanted to?"

"Not really."

"Even when you were a little boy?"

"No, not at all. Not that I can remember. Why?"

"No reason. I just realized today that I had never asked."

Annalise's confession and what it aroused in her had thereafter altered Naomi's view of Nathan. Their sex, like their friendship, had seemed wonderfully easy, unchallenging, unhurried. Nathan had made her realize that Todd and most of her other lovers had been, she now believed, rather rough with her. Nathan, by contrast, was not without ardor, but his desire did not feel urgent. It was as if he were both participant and thoughtful witness to their sexual play. Occasionally she wanted more from him; wanted him to be, if not exactly brutal, more animal-like, more carried away. She would have liked to carry him away, to excite him, shock him. Before Annalise's disclosure, she had assumed that most women felt that way from time to time; and if not most women, she was content to acknowledge those feelings in herself.

For a time after they were married she had felt grateful that Nathan, while not opposed to having children, had not really pressed her to decide. She herself was confusingly ambivalent about having babies. She – one of her selves – had assumed children would be part of her married condition. Just as often she dreaded the prospect of having even one. Especially just one. She sensed at once some highly localized unfinished business about the loss of her parents while she was still in school. There was still an ominous blackness to that time in her life, and somehow, when she could be at all lucid about it, having a baby represented having another self which would be some day abandoned and bereft.

When she was in her early thirties, Naomi decided to resolve the ambivalence by letting fate decide. She stopped taking the pill. A year passed, then several years, and there was no conception. Her obstetrician, who was also her good friend, pronounced her perfectly healthy and fertile. Then, when Nathan had himself examined, they learned that his sperm count was extremely low and that conception through ordinary intercourse was chancy at best.

They talked about adoption, but for some reason this called up the dark orphan syndrome for Naomi. Artificial insemination had also been discussed, and now she could not even recall the reasons for their reticence. At length they tacitly decided to go on as before, with no elevated hopes for conception. There were children, they consoled themselves, in each of their practices. They would take special care to serve children and to be good to them.

She had been, so far as she knew, especially good to children. But now, in her mid-forties, the fact of her childlessness could make her feel strangely insubstantial, that she was not quite valid. At such moments every concrete reminder of her material existence, the weight and complexity of their home, their cars in the drive, the ornaments and photographs arranged on the shelves of her office, were expressions of a shameful imposture. She felt this also about her looks, which to her seemed to carry the promise of an attractive girl, not a woman. She could feel that both men and women were reflexively drawn to her, yet not really to her but to a stalled, prior self. Since she and Nathan had moved to Cleveland, this realization had become more insistent, but even as she resisted it, she felt herself being helplessly assumed into a stillborn and ever more mocking perfection.

Because she was feeling a little dull and heavy from the wine at dinner, Naomi let Nathan drive home from Jasmine. As they progressed from light to light through the deserted intersections, she found herself fighting back sleep in order to pose a question. It was so simple, and it was so important, but she felt drugged trying to find the words.

"Nathan," she said, "Would you say that you are happy?"

"Am I happy?" As Nathan paused to consider his reply, Naomi sank into sleep.

When she awoke, she recognized the familiar network of suburban streets. They were near the house.

"And what about you," Nathan was saying, "Are you happy?"

"Oh," Naomi said, sitting up, "I don't know. But I think I am on the brink of being happy."

# 13

## AT SEA

*All right, I'm going,* Jen said to herself, gathering up the conference materials to show Sloan.

She made her way down from her study to their bedroom and saw that he was asleep, his head tilted back in apparent discomfort against the back of his red chair. He awoke as she approached.

"I didn't mean to wake you."

"No, it's good that I woke up, so I can go to sleep." It occurred to him, dully, that he had made no sense. He had meant to say "to bed."

"I need to talk to you about something. There's a conference on Edith Wharton in Boston, at B.U., and I think I should go. All the big people are doing papers, and I should probably find out if somebody has written my thesis."

"So you want to go to Boston?" Sloan felt thick and stupid with sleep.

"The conference is in Boston. The department will pay for my registration and transportation. I can drive with the Krupanskys and maybe stay with Mary Beth. So it won't really cost anything."

It had registered to Sloan only that she wanted to go to Boston. Then he thought of a question.

"When?"

"In about two weeks. The conference itself is from June fifteenth to the twentieth. We'd drive up the day before, maybe sightsee and relax a day after. It'd be about a week."

"And you want to go."

"I should go."

"Well," Sloan searched for something to say. "Maybe it will be nice."

Sloan wondered whether it was unfeeling on his part not to object. The idea of her going east for a week reminded him that he had not made or suggested any vacation plans of his own. He had more than two weeks coming but for some reason resisted thinking about how he would use his time off. Last summer he had stayed home. A pleasure vacation, even a weekend getaway, had seemed ill-advised given the challenge of meeting Henry's first tuition payment in August. He had stayed close to the house, painted the trim around the windows, took the boys downtown to some ball games.

"So Bart and I will batch it?"

"Actually, the Staleys called, and Bart's invited to go up with them to their lake till the end of June."

"Does he want to go?"

"I think he does, but you can ask him."

The photograph was still on the refrigerator: Bart in his swim trunks shivering with goosebumps on the Staley's float. Last summer Dave and Jerry Staley had taught him to water ski, and Bart had come home to them asking if there was any way they could get a power boat.

"That's nice of the Staleys," Sloan said.

"So," Jen said, waving the registration form in front of her, "I guess I'll send this in."

"Right." Sloan knew that there was something expected of him, something he ought to say. "And I'll keep my solitary vigil here, returning at day's end to the tomb-like silence."

"If you want," Jen said with an edge in her voice. She wondered if she was being teased. "Or you could go somewhere yourself. You have time coming, don't you?"

"Indeed I do. What do you think, should I take the Concorde to Paris or stay home and get the gutters up to code?"

"The gutters."

"Yes, I suppose that would better advance the family program."

The corners of Jen's mouth dropped, and her eyes narrowed. Now she felt mocked, somehow disapproved of. She was about to go back upstairs when Sloan said, "Or I could go with you to Boston."

Jen hesitated. "Do you want to?"

"Why not? I could bring a fresh perspective to the Edith Wharton discussions. I could go down to ye olde waterfront and walk the Liberty Trail. I could pierce my eyebrows and tongue and hang around Harvard Square with the runaways. I could –"

"Do you want to," said Jen in an irritated tone. "Because if you do, I need to call Mary Beth and the Krupanskys. That'll be five of us in the car."

"No, that's all right. I was kidding. I will not be a specter at your feast. I'll hold the fort – or figure out something to fill my days."

"All right," Jen said, "I'm going."


Sloan's sessions with Naomi had been altogether different since their animated discussion of *American Way Out*. He was less hesitant, quicker to formulate, quicker to joke. He had, he realized, assumed a role in the earlier sessions, that of a client in therapy, a person confused and possibly damaged, at best someone with grave concerns and questions he could not sort out without assistance. Sloan had played this role, he felt, in an awkward, hang-dog manner. He had expressed this awkwardness in his posture, restlessly crossing and uncrossing his arms, leaning back then lunging forward in his chair. Like a beginning stage actor, he had not known what to do with his hands.

Now he was at ease, hyper-alert in her presence. His urge to touch her was now almost constant, to clasp both of her shoulders to emphasize a point. He remembered cupping her cheeks in his hands, the way she occasionally took his hands in hers. By a process so subtly gradual that he could not tell exactly when it happened, he had come to think about his desire for her openly and consciously, without guilt. He was in love with Naomi Wise. She was now an abiding presence with him. Sometimes he was aware that he seemed to be breathing her in and breathing her out. He knew also that he wanted more of her, more from her.

"And so, Sloan Fox," she said, "how have you been?" Naomi unfastened her watch and placed it on the glass table between them.

"I've been – exactly the same since last time, which is feeling pretty much at sea."

"And how does it feel to be at sea."

"Not bad, not bad at all. It's not *lost* at sea and worried or miserable. It's at sea not having a clue what's coming next – although remind me, when there are about ten minutes left, that I want to talk about one thing that's happening next. Anyway, I'm at sea in the best possible way. I feel like something enormous is about to break"

"Something is about to be broken?"

"No, not broken – to break, to break free, to break into being."

"What do you think it will be?"

"I think it will be – ecstatic. I can see myself standing in a new place. I can feel myself being totally in love, that feeling of being on the verge of sex, which can feel more overwhelming than sex itself."

"Because sex runs its course and dies."

"No, I don't think so. It doesn't die. It *rests*."

"Tell me about the new place you see yourself standing."

"I don't know if I can. But I think there are stages – *steps* – to get there, and I'll tell you one."

"Tell me."

"O.K." *Here I go.* "You know when we saw *American Way Out*, on the same night? I had the strangest feeling that we went to the movies together, that we were watching it together."

"Yes, I know that."

"That was good, I liked that."

Naomi waited.

"I want to do more of that." Sloan looked hard into Naomi's eyes. "I would like to go to the movies with you."

"You'd like to take me to the movies?" Naomi felt an involuntary widening of her smile, a warming in her belly.

"Yes."

"Any movie in particular?"

"No. Anything that looked good."

"So you want to take me out on a *date...*"

"Yes."

"I see." *A boundary issue. Here it is.* "And how could we do that? How could a therapist and a client go on a date to the movies? A married therapist and a married client?"

"This is how it would go. I would call you up on the phone. I would have looked in the paper to see what was playing. Then I would ask you to go and whether you wanted me to pick you up or whether you wanted to meet me there. Afterwards we'd go down the street for –"

"Sloan –"

"A drink and talk."

"That is not what I meant by how." Naomi concentrated on steadying herself, retreating from the bantering mood. "How would it be appropriate for us to go out together socially?"

"There you've got me. I can't think how it would be. But I can see doing it. Is this a problem now? Am I allowed to be inappropriate in therapy?"

"I suppose you are, within limits, provided I'm not. But being inappropriate outside in the world is a different matter."

"You know the rules here, and I don't. But I can't see the point in not being honest. I think these sessions are great, but my real interest is not in how I'm getting through my days. My real interest is in you, not in how you are helping me to understand myself. My real interest in you is the way you are, in being with you."

Naomi felt constricted, unable to respond. Knowing that a boundary was being crossed did not help. She did not, she realized, know what to do. *I am just going to feel this, go straight through it.* Sloan was waiting for her to speak.

"And what are we going to do about that?" *Lame,* she thought, *feeble.* She could hear the distance, the falseness in her tone.

"I think we should start by going to the movies."

"Sloan Fox, we *can't* go to the movies!" The force in what she said made Naomi feel better.

"But think," Sloan said, inclining toward her. "We already have. We were at the movies together when we saw *American Way Out.* I felt I was with you as intimately as I have felt with any date. Did you? Tell me the truth."

"I was aware of you all during the film."

"So we already did it. We went to the movies together. Would it ease your mind if we did that again? We could each go to the same movie, arrive separately and sit in different seats. Strange way to behave, but we'd be appropriate then, wouldn't we be?"

"Yes, that would be a strange way to behave."

"Tell me, am I breaking the therapy rules here, by wanting to be with you as a person, not a client?"

"I don't think you're breaking the therapy rules by talking about it."

"So we can talk about it, and maybe later you'll tell me about my *transference,* which I already know, and you will ask me how I feel about it, which I already know. But is it ever allowed to be what you are feeling, to live it?"

Again Naomi was overcome by a feeling of helplessness. Sloan's directness had disarmed her, his words made perfect, persuasive sense, and she could not think, or remember, how to respond professionally. Her training had been clear that when she felt distressed or resourceless in an encounter, she should use that data, that it was good information. *But how can I use this?*

"Let me ask you this, Naomi," Sloan continued. "How do you feel about me? No. Do you ever, when I'm not here, think about me as a person, not as a client? Do you remember me, wonder what I'm doing? Do you look forward to our sessions just – just for the company?"

"Yes." Naomi closed her eyes. "Yes to all those questions. Since we are being honest."

Sloan struggled to find words. He wanted to say *thank you*.

"Well, just in case you don't already know, I have been carrying you around with me every second."

Naomi felt a sweet weakness descending. "The day I called you at the newspaper," she said, "It was because I missed you and was afraid you were not coming anymore."

"You know what I was doing? I was walking through my motions like a zombie, driving myself crazy wondering how I was going to keep coming every week without – exploding. I was telling myself I'll wait for a sign."

"And the sign came."

"So," Sloan took a deep breath. "Where are we?"

"I think I am supposed to say that."

"O.K. You say it."

"Do you know what?" Naomi picked up her watch. "We've passed the ten-minutes-left mark. "There was something you wanted to tell me. Something else."

Sloan had known he would startle Naomi with his announcement. He had almost looked forward to it, but now he felt mired in doubt and guilt. More had been said than he could integrate, and this made the space between them, the very office, seem clouded, held in a kind of uncertain motion. He had made a dark and deceptive plan. He had slipped away from the *Sun Messenger* at lunch and booked his flight and room.

"Remember when I said something was about to break? Break out? It's going to happen next week, I think, on the fifteenth. I'm going down to New Orleans for a few days, by myself."

"What will you do there?" Naomi felt an unpleasant tug. It was jealousy.

"I have no plans. I'm just going. Maybe it's the shadow calling. It's funny, this morning I was so excited about it I felt I was coming out of my skin. Then just now I started feeling sleazy."

"Sleazy because --?"

"Because it's a secret. Because my family will be out of town, and nobody knows I'm going. Sloan looked straight into Naomi's eyes. "Because I want you to come down and join me."

*Come down.* Naomi started to speak, but for a moment the words stopped in her throat. The idea of New Orleans brought up only the dark women of the night Sloan had talked about. She saw herself walking among dark women, one of them.

"I've never been to New Orleans," she said weakly.

Sloan reached for the notebook in the pocket of his jacket, tore out a page and wrote something down. "This," he said, "is the name of my hotel. The days I'll be there, and the times of my flights. It'll be hot, a little off season, and there are lots of rooms."

Sloan lay the slip on the glass table.

Naomi felt lost, already guilty.

"You want me to fly down to see you in New Orleans."

"Yes, I do."

"And you know that it is a crazy thing to do."

"Yes."

"Sloan Fox, I should have known. Even at that seminar downtown at the hotel. There was something about you." Naomi sat up straight. "Come, time's up. We have to go."

She picked up her watch from the glass table and fastened it around her wrist. Then she picked up the slip of paper and seemed to study it.

In the vestibule at the door she gave Sloan a troubled look and said, "Would you please give me a hug, crazy man?"

Sloan held her lightly to him, resting his chin over the top of her head. There was a sweet, clean smell from her scalp. For a moment he shifted his weight from foot to foot, gently rocking her.

Into his lapel Naomi said, "And what did you think we would do in New Orleans?"

"You know. Go to the movies."

# 14

---

## NIGHT BLOOMING JASMINE

---

I t felt like a dream, the solitary ride to the airport on the Rapid Transit, the wait among strangers at the gate, the cocooned, gentle jostling of the flight, which had somehow seemed to take only minutes.

There had been a strange ease to everything. A brief chat with the new Travel editor at the *Sun Messenger* had landed him a free lance assignment, and there was interest from the Sunday Magazine in a related piece. Carl Soderland, the Magazine editor, had told Sloan to find out the latest about the termites. "The whole city," he had said, "is being eaten away from the bottom. They can't stop it – it's like retribution." The trip now looked as if it would cost him nothing. "Lucky you," Jen had said when he told her. "Is that going to be interesting, investigating termites?"

Because he had been there twice and because of the intensity of his night memories, Sloan had imagined that he knew the city. But by lamplight in the cab moving westward through Metairie past the universities, the surroundings looked altogether unfamiliar.

His hotel was The Elysian Fields, a name he thought exotic and fanciful until he realized it was situated on Elysian Fields Avenue. It was an agreeable old building. The late morning air when Sloan stepped out of the cab was humid and still, heavy with a musky scent of earth and pine. Under a colorless sky, the awnings sagged with the damp. Gray clapboard with a darker grey trim, the structure, Sloan guessed, might have been a substantial residence, haphazardly expanded over the years. A pillared porch ran the length of the building's façade, and it was deep enough to obscure the doorway and parlor windows. The Elysian Fields at the moment looked to Sloan as if it were finding its weight hard to bear. Then he remembered the termites. He pictured uncountable millions of them, white and gelatinous, quivering at work in the soggy joists under the porch.

Inside, the musky scent seemed more concentrated, as if captured and held. The dark wings of a ceiling fan whirred and flopped over the reception parlor. Sloan's stomach jumped, and he was aware of his heart quickening. If Naomi came, she would enter this parlor, register at this counter. She would breathe in this heavy air. Sloan drew out his pleasantries with the stylish young Asian woman who checked him in. He would find out everything he could about the Elysian Fields. He would learn what he could about the termites.

His room was on the top floor, large and furnished with an odd assortment of outsized pieces. A canopy over the bed was supported by carved spindles. The window shades were drawn to the level of ancient-looking air conditioner which whirred and rumbled unevenly. The room was mercifully cool.

Sloan looked at his watch. Still well before noon. Since rising that morning in the empty house, time had seemed reluctant to pass. Sloan expected to be tired, but he was alert, wide awake. He unpacked and perched at the edge of the bed. Still not noon. It occurred to him that he had no plans and absolutely nothing to do.

He had not expected to see Naomi at the gate, but he had looked for her. Several airlines offered New Orleans flights. She could arrive at any time, on any day.

Sloan eyed the phone on the bedside table, and his stomach jumped again. The amber message light glowed and darkened. Sloan pressed the retrieval button and heard the prerecorded female voice say "you have no new messages."

Sloan rang the front desk and asked, "Has a Doctor Naomi Wise checked into the hotel?" He was aware of a ringing in his ears. "Let me check." The receptionist said, "No, I don't have a doctor – oh, but I have a, yes, Naomi Wise. Would you like me to connect you?" Sloan said yes and heard the ringing rise to a scream, then Naomi's voice.

"Yes?"

"Yes indeed."

There was a pause, and then Naomi said "You know we are both crazy."

"Speak for yourself. I'm a hard working reporter investigating termites."

"You're – what?"

"Never mind. But you can be a big help. Why not meet me in the lobby in five minutes."

"All right."

"No. I take that back. Make it one minute. I'll be wearing a green shirt."

Sloan listened to the low music of her laughter.

"Certifiably crazy."

Sloan rose to his feet and stretched his arms high over his head. In the bathroom he leaned close to the mirror. His eyes looked swollen and tired. He splashed his face with cold water, looked again at his startled reflection.

As he stepped out into the hallway, he caught sight of Naomi's hair as she descended the central stair case. *On my floor.* He caught up with her on the landing below. When she turned to him, Sloan started. Her cheeks were flushed. She wore a black halter-top and linen slacks. Sun glasses were perched in her hair like a tiara. She looked different. *What was it? Off-duty. Younger.* Then he had it. *She looks like sex.*

"Look at you," he said.

"Look at me?" she said, and Sloan watched her lips draw slowly back from her teeth.

They embraced, and Sloan ran his hands over the bones of her back and shoulders. Then he held her away from him and looked into her eyes.

"You are the most beautiful woman who ever lived."

"It must be the heat."

"Are you suffering?"

"No, I'm thriving. I bloom in tropical heat." She could hear Nathan saying: *you are an island girl.* "Except that when I feel this kind of air, I always want to be naked."

Sloan drew her back into him. "I know a place."

"Are there beaches?" Naomi said, trying to picture one.

"Another place," Sloan said, guiding her back up the stairs.


As they would reconstruct it afterwards, their lovemaking had been kind of a sacrament, or perhaps its antithesis, a rapt ascent together into a new realm of abandonment and sensation. A communion. All of it, too, had been shot through with solemnity and grief. In full unblinking consciousness they had decided to forsake beloved others, others to whom they were promised and committed, others who had kept their commitments to them. Forever and irrevocably, Sloan and Naomi had departed the ranks of the faithful. Each of them experienced the paradox of feeling they had been assumed up into something irresistible while at the same time being in command: helpless yet wholly responsible. Their love was illicit, and they had been deliberate in taking up the weight of its wrongness. Neither of them, they confessed to each other that first day, had been unfaithful before. Nor had they every believed they would be.

Sloan stood back as Naomi pulled the black top over her head, unfastened and stepped out of her slacks. In her nakedness she seemed, though slight and delicately formed, more substantial, her breasts fuller, than he had imagined. "My god" he said. "You are perfect."

For her part, Naomi realized that she had wanted to be naked like this, for Sloan, for somebody, for a long time. There had been an intimation in the Caribbean years before with Nathan, but it had been indistinct. Now it was clear, welling up inside her so insistently that she was trembling with it. It occurred to her that to have this, to go ahead with this, might be to die, and that perhaps dying would not matter.

As they lay down together and began their tentative seeking and touching, Sloan felt himself held in the tingling thrall of the opposites, that in these lay the greatness, the truth of it. Aching to move with his desire, to clasp her so tightly to the length of him that they might pass into one another and become one, he held her delicately away, willing himself to be still, to let only his fingertips carry his wonder. Erect, swollen, his pleasure close to pain, he wanted nevertheless to prolong their exploring and play, to be suspended in that unbearable pitch of feeling forever. He had been tender with Jen, and he knew the reckless burn of lust, but the enormity of this, this feeling of sustained, elevated communion was new; yet, in some ancient or infantile way, sweetly familiar. Sloan knew he could abase himself, that doing so would in some way be worshipful. He wanted to worship her. He wanted her to feel everything.

"Come inside me." She was saying. "Come inside me." She sat up, took him into her mouth and made him wet, then lay back and parted herself for him to enter. Holding himself over her, wanting to spare her delicious softness from his weight, he saw that she was impossibly small, a miniature, and he felt hopelessly too big. Slowly easing himself inside her, he stared down, as if from a great height, at the rosy blush in her cheeks, her throat, the lovely delicate expanse between her collarbone and breasts.

"Naomi, love, love – am I too much? Am I hurting you?"

As she continued to move beneath him working him gradually further into her, Naomi looked up into Sloan's eyes, and he realized that she was no longer seeing. Nor was her smile her own. It was a look he had seen somewhere, perhaps in a painting or a film: an archaic smile. Faintly mocking, knowing better, knowing everything. With dumb wonder, Sloan felt Naomi recede from him. Her eyes were not taking him in and seemed to have turned witchily within. Then the sly, wise smile widened lazily, and Naomi moaned.

"No, you are not hurting me. Are you ever not hurting me."

Sloan tilted back his hand, closed his eyes, and gave himself up to his pleasure. He felt as if he were spilling himself, emptying himself into Naomi. Startled by what he thought was a convulsion of laughter, he opened his eyes and saw that she was sobbing. He lowered himself quietly down over her and nestled his face close to her ear.

"Are you all right?"

"Oh, *yes*, I'm all right. Oh yes, yes, yes, yes, yes."

Naomi freed her arms and wrapped them round his neck and said. "Sloan, do you *know*? Please know. Promise me you know."

Sloan moved away a little so he could see her face.

"I know."

Thinking about it later, it seemed to Sloan that perhaps other people experienced what he did making love to Naomi, but he doubted it. He had known familiar sweetness with Jen and had sometimes felt genuinely transported, but he could not recall having sex with her twice on the same night. But on that day in June at the Elysian Fields he and Naomi had made love intermittently and at close intervals from midday until nightfall.

It occurred to Naomi that she had never until then made love enough. "It was what I always wanted, and I didn't even know it. I'm depraved aren't I?"

"Absolutely not. Because then I'd be depraved too."

"I don't mind being depraved," Naomi said. "I really don't, provided you don't."

Sloan gathered Naomi into his arms and rocked her gently.

"Forget depraved. It's just the way we are. It's a gift."

Naomi closed her eyes and said, "You're a gift."

When the clock on the bedside table said nine fifteen, Sloan got up from under the canopy and raised a window shade. Street lamps cast a dull yellow tint on the leaves of the trees lining the street. It was dark.

"We better go out and find some place to eat." Sloan said, "Or else we'll disappear."

Waiting in the reception parlor for Naomi to come down, Sloan felt as if he had awakened from a profound night and was now entering another one.

It always disoriented him to be newly arrived in a faraway city. Apart from some coffee and juice on the plane, he had eaten nothing that day. He was a little lightheaded, but not tired. Nor did he feel enervated by having made love for hours. For a moment the quietly lit parlor and even his presence in it seemed thin and insubstantial, as if part of a thought or memory. In that moment, too, the fact that he had actually flown south, that he had spent a day in bed with Naomi, felt incompletely established, that he might be drawn back at once into a more substantial waking state, as if from a fantasy or a dream. The reception clerk smiled at him without speaking.

Naomi joined Sloan in the parlor, and he saw the she was striking, somehow transformed. She wore the black top but over a long loose skirt of a crinkly black fabric. Her hair was swept severely back from her forehead and temples, and she had reddened her lips, darkly accented her eyes. Sloan took both of her hands.

"Did I tell you I think you are beautiful."

"Yes," said Naomi, "you have. I think you have set a record for telling a woman she is beautiful on a single day."

"And the day isn't over."

"The day actually is."

Sloan laughed. "You're right, where do they go?"

The clerk at reception recommended they dine at the Harlequin on Toulouse. It was in the French quarter and probably in walking distance, but since it was dark he suggested they take a cab.

"Are the streets around here pretty safe?"

The clerk stopped to consider before meeting Sloan's gaze. "Sometimes. Most of the time they are. But you never really know in New Orleans."

In the taxi Sloan felt happy and expansive. That night and for the foreseeable future there were no confining expectations or obligations. The hour did not matter. They could go and do as they pleased. There would be consequences, he knew, and they were likely to be wrenching beyond his imagining, but he had made and carried out this plan. He had already made love to Naomi. He was holding her to him as they made their sheltered way through the streets of an exotic city. The murmurs of their talk seemed to hover in close around their heads, and Sloan felt that not just the cab, but the spangled world outside was holding them fast.

The taxi nosed into the curb in front of the Harlequin. Sloan realized he had paid not attention to how they had made their way there from the hotel. The glowing neon of the harlequin masks in the windows flanking the entrance were the only indication of commercial life on that stretch of Toulouse. The darkened residences looked forbidding and closed off behind their railings.

Inside Sloan had an impression of an old and eccentric warren of rooms and passages. There was piano music, and muted talk, and when his eyes adjusted to the candlelight he saw that all the tables in sight were occupied.

The concierge said he could seat them right away if they didn't mind the terrace.

"Do we mind the terrace?" He asked Naomi.

"We don't."

They were led out through glass doors to an inner courtyard of mossy wood. Candles flickering under green tinted globes of glass cast a faint light onto the undersides of foliage suspended over the enclosure.

"A grotto," Naomi said.

"The bower of bliss," Sloan said, the phrase surfacing from a murky depth. A poem, he thought, a phrase from an ancient poem.

They ordered vodka and lime, and the waiter left them alone. Their eyes met in the quiet, and Naomi began to laugh. They clasped hands over the table, and Sloan felt the stirring of his desire. He released her hands and stood abruptly in his place.

"Miss Wise," he said. "I just have to do this."

Sloan moved around the table to Naomi's side where he bent low to kiss her. Naomi made a low, lovely hum.

Sloan seated himself and sat up straight. "I had to do it."

Now, for the first time since their meeting, talk seemed to come easily. Naomi told him about her decision to come – that, really, she knew she would come when he had proposed it. She told him how she had been ready for this, without really knowing it, for a long time, that it was time for her to make a mess.

"And I'm your mess?"

"You are. You are my mess. We are each other's messes." Saying this, Naomi felt the alternating descents and raptures of the afternoon in bed coming to rest. She was wonderfully wide awake. Happy.

They seemed to sense it at the same time, although there had been hints of it since they stepped into the night air: bursts of a sweetly-scented, almost overwhelming perfume.

"What *is it?*" Naomi asked as the waiter set down their drinks.

He sniffed and considered. "It is two things, madam. It is magnolias" – he pointed to ghostly blossoms nesting like plump creamy birds in the dark greenery – "and it is night blooming jasmine."

*Night blooming jasmine.* The words released something like a current along her spine. *That is the name for it, for what this is. Night blooming jasmine.*

"If it's too much for you, I can look for a table inside."

"It is too much for me," Naomi said, "and I will stay right here."

The waiter had not quite stepped out of the courtyard when Naomi said with great force, "I *love* you, Sloan. I completely love you."

Sloan touched his glass to Naomi's.

"To mess."

Waiting in the deserted vestibule of the Harlequin for their cab, Sloan felt a great peacefulness descend. He gathered Naomi into him, guiding her head gently to his collar. It seemed to him that an unworldly epoch had passed since they had met on the landing of the hotel staircase.

"Sleepy?" he said.

"Beyond sleepy."

The cab ride back to the hotel disoriented Sloan. He made an effort to note turns and landmarks so that they might return on foot, but he soon lost track. When the cab slowed to a stop in front of the Elysian Fields, Naomi was asleep.

# 15

## THE VOODOO MUSEUM

At dawn – the rosy digits on Sloan's bedside clock showed 5:40 – they awoke, or half awoke, and without reflection made love. They did not speak.

At eleven Sloan opened his eyes to the day. He was aware of slivers of silver light lining the drawn shades, the dark groaning of the ceiling fan overhead. Then he recognized the room, that he was in New Orleans. Naomi had left the bed, and he could hear the insistent hiss of the bathroom shower. He tried to picture the French Quarter streets by daylight, streets he and Naomi would walk without aim or care. Sloan sat up in the bed. What was it? He could feel the tension along his jaw. He was smiling.

The young Asian woman at the reception desk seemed to Sloan knowing and unaccountably eager as she gave them walking directions to the French Quarter.

"Do you think," Sloan asked Naomi, as they stepped out into the steamy daylight, "that we are giving off some quality to the public?"

"The public?"

"The girl at the desk, for instance. She was talking to me as if she had known us for years, as if we were great friends."

Naomi considered for a moment and said, "I am sure we give off a quality. How could we not?"

"What do you think it says, the quality?"

"It says … surrender. It says just jumped off the cliff. It says – you know exactly what it says."

"You're right. I do."

On Dauphine Street between St. Peter and St. Ann, Sloan stopped a tall man in a linen suit and asked if there was a café nearby. They had come down too late for the complimentary breakfast at the Elysian Fields.

For a moment the man stared at Sloan without speaking. Then he approached them and inclined his moist coffee-colored face close to Sloan's.

"A café you're looking for? They's cafes on every street this way."

Sloan peered past the man's intrusive head and saw awnings and sidewalk tables farther down the street. He was about to say thanks when the man, now taking the measure of Naomi, said, "You a wagering man?"

"A wagering man?"

"A betting man."

Sloan felt invigorated by the unexpected question. "Not professionally, no. But I've made a wager from time to time."

"From time to time." The man paused and looked sharply away. Then: "Well, I've got a wager for you." Pointing to Naomi's sandals, he said. "Twenty bucks says I can tell you exactly where you got those shoes."

Naomi thought suddenly: *a kiosk at the airport on St. Martin's.*

"Twenty bucks if you can tell me where she got those shoes?" Sloan considered. "O.K., it's a deal. Where?"

The man met Sloan's eyes with an intensity approaching anger.

"I'll tell you where. She got those shoes – right on her *feet.*"

For a second Sloan did not see the joke, then Naomi laughed and he did.

"Cost you twenty bucks," the man said. Agitated now, he glanced over his shoulder then back at Sloan.

Sloan pulled a wad of bills from his pants pocket, peeled off a twenty, and handed it over. For no reason he could determine, he was elated. He said, "You're a good man."

For a moment the man regarded him suspiciously, then touched his lapel and said, "Good morning to you both. Cafes right down the street."

Settled at their table under the awning, Sloan and Naomi lost track of time. They drank iced coffees with croissants, then bloody Marys. Naomi ordered an elaborate salad, which they barely touched. Sloan tried to find words to describe the quality of their time together.

"I keep trying to relate this to reality, but it's impossible. There's no bridge to my ordinary life. There's no connection."

"I think of it differently," Naomi said. "I start in a different place. For me, this is reality. Everything else is sensible, most of it probably necessary. An endurable blur. But what sense does it make to say that the most intense feeling –completely connecting – isn't real?"

"Why –" Sloan almost stopped himself – "is there a kind of sadness mixed up in it? Do you know what I mean?"

"Sadness. Yes, definitely. I suppose it's because so much has to die."

Sloan paid the bill, and they began listlessly walking the streets of the French Quarter. Most of the bars and clubs were closed, and despite the hiss of traffic, there was a forlorn out-of-season quality to the streets.

"Here we go," said Sloan, stopping at a faded marquee announcing The Voodoo Museum. It too looked as if it might be closed, but the doorknob turned in his hand, and they proceeded into a dark entranceway where they paid for admission tickets.

For a moment, Sloan's eyes could not adjust to the darkness. There was an impression of glowing coals, which turned out to be colored bulbs deeply recessed behind glassed-in exhibits. Moving to these, Sloan saw that they contained mottled snakes, some coiled, others extended. Sloan watched one of the snakes close its jaws over the head of a mouse, its pink rump and tiny hind legs still quivering. Sloan could see no labels on the exhibits, which seemed haphazardly carpentered into the walls. In one glass box a dead bird, a crow, lay stiff on its side, a dull black eye open.

Naomi moved in close to Sloan but did not speak. Though the maze of dark rooms was cool to the point of being chilly, Sloan felt the onset of an almost drugged sleepiness.

Sloan guided Naomi further down a dark passage to another dimly-lit room of exhibits. Live cats slunk about in the shadows. Stuffed cats and owls were arranged in recesses and on perches protruding from the black walls. The atmosphere was musty and pungent of animal excrescence.

From a still more remote chamber Sloan heard drumming and what sounded like guttural chanting. It occurred to him that there were no other visitors, at least none standing, moving through the exhibits. There were, however, men and women seated along the baseboards. They appeared in the indistinct light to be black. They were barefoot, and Sloan had the impression of street people. The men wore bulbous knitted caps pulled down close to their eyes which, when they met Sloan's, looked sullen and resentful.

Sloan suddenly felt repulsed, impatient.

"Let's go," he said close to Naomi's ear

"In a minute. I want to see who is chanting."

Naomi led the way through another narrow passage, its walls textured with crude black dolls fashioned from scorched-looking wood.

The passage opened into a windowless room with reddish-black damask walls. A few barefoot men and women were seated about the periphery. At the far end of the room some kind of enactment or ritual was being carried out against the backdrop of an altar lit with snarls of tiny colored lights. Sloan and Naomi moved a few steps toward the figures at the altar but stopped, uncertain whether the ceremony was intended for public viewing.

A few feet from the altar an African-looking woman with her head wrapped in patterned cloth stood holding a swaddled baby. She was being addressed by a short, wiry black man with matted grey hair and beard. Although diminutive, the man commanded attention. The front of his embroidered tunic was spattered and stained, and he fixed an imploring look on the woman holding the child as he chanted from the back of his throat what sounded to Sloan like:

On-yee, on-yee, ononda-lee

On-yee, buckle(?)

On-yee.

The chanting celebrant moved close to the woman, clapped his hands on her shoulders and growled. Then he cupped both palms over the infant's skull and made a similar growl. Backing in staggering steps toward the altar, still chanting and growling, he dipped his fingers in a succession of small ceramic bowls and inserted pinches of what looked like powders and herbs into his mouth. Then he took hold of the neck of a liquor bottle – Sloan saw that it was Baccardi rum – threw back his head and took a deep draught. His cheeks bulging with the mix, and working his face in a circular motion, he returned to the woman holding the child, thrust his head up close to hers and, with an expulsive grunt, spat a pasty spray into her face. Taking another slug from the Baccardi bottle, he worked the liquor in his mouth and then spat onto the baby's head.

Sloan was aware of a sharp treble pitch, like the scream of a boiling kettle, which seemed to fill in all the space up the room. At the moment he realized the sustained cry was coming from the woman holding the child, he felt Naomi's presence fall away from him.

She had dropped to her knees, and as Sloan knelt down to see if she was all right, she leaned forward on her hands, lowering her head to the floor.

"Are you O.K?" he said. Without looking up, she raised a hand to gesture him away from her.

"I'm – just let me be for a second. I'm – I think I am going to be sick."

Sloan could feel the mounting of her nausea. He took a long breath and rose to his feet. The priest or celebrant had turned away from the wailing woman and faced the altar. His chants were being picked up, mumblingly, by the people seated along the walls.

On-yee, on-yee, onunda-lee

On-yee, buckle

On-yee

Still on her hands and knees, Naomi was swaying slightly. Stepping over her, Sloan put a hand firmly under each arm and lifted her to a standing position.

"We're going, love. Easy does it. You're going to be all right."

Sloan draped Naomi's arm over his shoulder. Wrapping his own arm around her waist, he guided her out of the Voodoo Museum. She was able to walk, but felt the need to close her eyes as they passed the gaping-mouthed dolls, the stuffed and slinking cats, the owls, the snakes.

The din in their ears did not quiet until they were outside in the white humid heat of Dumaine Street.

"How're you doing? You O.K.?" Sloan asked and looked with concern at Naomi whose eyes were still closed.

"I'm fine. I'm going to be fine. Please, let's keep walking." Naomi opened her eyes. She withdrew her hand from Sloan's, and they walked for a while in silence.

At length Naomi said, "Oh dear." Then, "My god."

"Are you O.K.? Tell me."

"I'm fine. I'm going to be fine. How could I be so – arrogant, so *stupid*. To go into that world and think I was all separated and safe, like an observer, like a tourist."

Sloan wanted to ask Naomi exactly what she had felt, but he was unsure of how to phrase the question.

"Tell me what happened."

"I don't think I can. I almost lost it, almost lost everything." Feeling now that she could look at Sloan, she turned to him and said, "The only way to live in this world is to live in it with your spirit wide open. No armor. No clenching. No protection. Totally exposed."

Sloan looked bewildered.

"What happened to me?" Naomi continued. "What happened was – you saw those people in there, right? The ones sitting around on the floor? Their spirits weren't sitting around on the floor. Their spirits were – on the loose, on the warpath, and they wanted me."

Sloan did not know what to say.

"Sorry about the Voodoo Museum."

"Don't be sorry. We're here for a reason. We were there for a reason."


Back at the Elysian Fields Naomi said she wanted to rest for a while before dinner and left him to go to her own room.

Alone now, Sloan drew the shades against the white glare of the declining afternoon. He was both tired and agitated as he sat in the half light under the groaning ceiling fan. He had not been apart from Naomi since her arrival. Now, although only a few doorways down the hall, she seemed unnaturally detached from him. He pictured her reclining under a single sheet, turned away. He felt the void of her absence as a disturbing kind of energy.

Sloan began to think about Jen and the boys, the empty house. He could see Jen rising at first light from her futon in Mary Beth's spare room. He saw her moving through the bright pedestrian traffic of Cambridge. She would be peripheral and attentive among the Edith Wharton scholars. Sloan imagined her standing among the conferees. She would be wearing her layers of wrinkly linen and holding a glass of white wine. He tried to picture Bart among the Staleys at their cabin in Ontario. He would be out on the lake, up on water skis or, water beading on his slender brown arms, waiting for his turn. Henry. He saw Henry rousing himself late from his bed, his eyes still puffed with sleep. He would be heading on foot to Campus Pizza for his delivery assignments. While he knew he must be projecting his own inner condition, Sloan could not help imagining that Jen and the boys were, in their different settings, distracted and troubled. They would be trying not to think about him, purposefully turning their thoughts away. For an instant he was certain they knew, that they must know, not that he was with Naomi, but that he had withdrawn.

Sloan descended sickeningly into a busy darkness of doubt and recrimination. Helplessly, he began reconstructing his liaison with Naomi from the perspective of someone, of Carl Soderland, at *The Sun Messenger.* For a long moment, his stomach fluttering with unease, he let himself name, acknowledge the worst: *fling, tryst, affair.* Predictable, ordinary. But not insubstantial, not laughable, not throw away. The reality was heavy, Sloan realized, roiling and alive. Its presence would be profoundly permanent; what was lost, irretrievable. Like the moaning fan overhead, these realizations felt recurrent, inevitable.

As the dinner hour approached, Sloan felt too muddled and tentative to seek out somewhere new to dine. He telephoned the Harlequin and made a reservation for a table on the terrace.

When Naomi, delicate and striking in a black slip dress, joined him in the hotel lobby, Sloan began to feel better. Her return to his side served somehow to inflate him. The agonizing descent, he decided, was the result of trying to take the measure of this experience of Naomi but without Naomi in it. With her, seeing her, breathing in her scent, he felt more expansive, big enough to contain both his doubts and mounting desire.

There was still some pearly light overhead and a scattering of other diners when they were seated, at the same table, on the terrace of the Harlequin. By the time darkness descended fully, Sloan felt he was awakening into the previous evening. He felt enchanted, drugged, unwilling to look away from Naomi's face.

They drank vodka and lime, putting off ordering food for as long as they could. Sloan tested himself, trying to feel something of the edginess, of the dark descent he had felt earlier but could not.  As the sweetened vodka took its warming effect, something taut behind his eyes and descending down into his heart softened and dissolved.  He felt charged with desire, and he longed to swim out of himself, over and into Naomi's beckoning presence across the table.  Sloan took Naomi's hands in his.

"We should dance."

"There is no music."

"There is night-blooming jasmine.  We could dance to night-blooming jasmine."

"We can dance," Naomi said, inclining her shoulders toward Sloan.  "I want to dance.  I want you to take me to your mysterious places."

*Your mysterious places.* Sloan felt a flaring of desire.  The women, the glittering dark women, and Naomi.

Neither Sloan nor Naomi had an appetite for their salads and blackened fish when they arrived.  As on the night before, Sloan was visited by an agreeable realization that there was no fixed or limiting obligation ahead of them.  He let his mind wander to their sessions in therapy, the glass mound of Naomi's watch face reminding him of the pressing minutes, speeding him to a halting summation and departure.

Tonight, breathing in the irregular eruptions of night-blooming jasmine, working, now, through a second bottle of wine, there seemed to be no imaginable terminus to their thrall.  There were declarations of their wonder at being together.  There were declarations of love.  Late evening lay ahead of them, then midnight, then all the unearthly hours of early morning.  There was, at last, time.

Although aware he had had a lot to drink, Sloan felt wonderfully clear-headed, as though he were suspended in a fragrant medium of dark liquid air.  When it was nearing midnight and the other diners had left them alone on the terrace, Sloan rose from his seat and with a deliberate courtliness moved to the back of Naomi's chair to assist her.  When she did not rise, he dropped his hands lightly to

her shoulders.  Her skin felt like powder, like silk against his palm.
Lightly he caressed the length of her arms to her fingertips.  Then he
traced the line of her jaw, the delicate ridge of her collarbone.

"Make love to me."

Naomi took his hands and clasped them to her breasts.  She tilted
her head back and looked up into his eyes.

"All right.  Yes.  But first take me to your places.  To your women."


Arm in arm, Sloan and Naomi made their way along an ill-lit
stretch of Toulouse in the direction of the blinking lights of the clubs
ahead.  On Bourbon Street amplified music emanating from the
open bars and strip joints and flashing arcades combined to a kind
of roar.  They passed guffawing clusters of glassy eyed college boys,
dark suited men still wearing convention name tags over their breast
pockets. Sloan drew Naomi in close under his arm.

"So what's this all about?" Naomi said.

"It's about prowling."

"There are hardly any women," But as she said it, three laughing
girls spilled out of a club doorway just in front of them.  Naomi saw
that their hair was teased out stiffly.  The girl just ahead of them wore
a knitted top cropped to expose a stripe of midriff above her skirt.
The dark outline of a rosy butterfly was tattooed just above her hip.

Under a blinking marquee spelling GENTLEMAN'S CLUB,
Naomi detached herself from Sloan and studied the glassed display
by the door.  A series of identical posters labeled VIXEN revealed the
head and shoulders and breasts of a blonde woman of indeterminate
age.  Crimped tendrils of silvery blond hair fell away from a darkly
rooted part.  Naomi looked hard into her colorfully accented eyes.

Sloan stood over Naomi's shoulder.  "Someone you know?"

"No," said Naomi absently.  "This is Vixen.  Do you think she is a
priestess?"

Sloan was about to say no when an unshaven barker in a tuxedo
approached them and said, "Show's about to start.  Would you folks

care to come inside?" He looked Naomi up and down, Sloan thought insolently. "*Couples* shows, we have *table* dances, try our *champagne* room."

Sloan guided Naomi silently away through the blare and neon of Bourbon Street. Wanting vaguely to restore darkness and quiet, he turned down a side street and began to walk back in what he thought was the direction of the Harlequin. They passed a bar in front of which three women were smoking cigarettes under the awning. As they passed, Sloan thought he detected the distinctive bite of pot in the air. Then he seemed to remember.

Abruptly turning onto an even darker street, Sloan stopped before a black glass doorway, dully framed from the inside by a string of tiny colored lights. At eye level Sloan read BLUE ROOM in chipped gold paint.

"Are you game?" he said softly to Naomi.

"Game for what?"

"Priestesses."

"Priestesses, yes."

Inside, the darkness was at first so complete that Sloan was aware only of the texture of dark, carpet-like fabric and the pulsing, clicking cadence of highly processed music of a genre --techno? Euro? – he was past being able to identify.

As Sloan paid a cover charge, the concierge, his face a ghostly melon suspended over his black clothes, asked, "You been here before?"

"I think so," Sloan said. "Are ladies welcome?"

"Ladies always welcome."

Sloan edged Naomi past a partition of dark fabric into a cavernous room dimly lit with slender columns of powdery light shining down onto a polished bar from cylinders of blue glass. Sloan could make out the figure of a naked woman, two women, moving between the shafts of light. They gyrated lazily, swaying and stretching, in no apparent relation to the insistent rhythm of the music.

Sloan could make out silhouettes of figures seated at tables on which tiny white wicks flickered in globes of blue glass. Sloan and

Naomi haltingly made their way to an unoccupied table a few feet away from the bar.

Sloan realized he was leg-weary and was grateful to be sitting down in the welcoming dark. Drinks arrived, vodka and lime, and they positioned their chairs so that they could watch the dancers up on the bar.

He had found it, Sloan realized. He had been here before. The pleasing anonymity, the machine gun cadence of the recorded music, the adjustment of his vision to the filtered blue light seemed both to lull and heighten his awareness. The women were exactly as he remembered: dark, willowy, the sheen of their flesh shadowed blue-black as they moved between the shafts of light.

Sloan saw that Naomi was transfixed by the women dancing. They were languorous, distracted, occasionally bending at the waist to receive folded bills offered by men at the bar. The bills were pressed between their bunched breasts, slipped beneath their garter belts. With a few alluring variations, the dancing women looked the same: dark skin, dark eyes, dark hair. They moved with an expressive slowness, as if they were tired or drugged. The women were slender, and their attenuation was emphasized by impossibly high heels. The heels, stockings, and satiny bikini briefs thonged between the mounds of their buttocks seemed to Sloan to amplify their nakedness. Between their sauntering turns beneath the lights, the women moved along the bar and among the tables soliciting private dances. These were offered, to Naomi's dazed astonishment, between the parted knees of a seated customer. *Private dancers.* Naomi could not precisely take in what the private dancers did, and she was reluctant to trespass visually to her right and left, but she had the impression that the lithe women somehow, like pythons, enveloped the men seated before them.

Sloan ordered more vodka and lime and said, "What do you think?"

"I am not thinking."

"Had enough?"

"No. I haven't."

149

Sloan sat back and watched the dark women moving through their trance-like gestures on the bar, working the bar stools, the tables. Twice, a dancer stopped, leaned across to Naomi and Sloan and asked if either of them would like a dance. Sloan had thanked them and declined. He was about to decline a third time, when Naomi spoke up.

"*No.* I mean yes. I would like a dance. How does it work and how much is it?"

The dancer, Sloan realized, was exquisite, long coffee-colored limbs, high cheekbones, her hair gathered into dozens of tight braids. Her breasts were slightly pendulous and surprisingly full in relation to her slender frame. There was something low and teasing in her voice.

"It is twenty dollars for a table dance. Fifty dollars for a private dance in the V.I.P. lounge. A hundred dollars for three dances in the V.I.P. lounge." She laughed. "And up and up and up from there." Sloan heard something else, something British, in her voice.

"Yes, I want that," Naomi said.

"You want what? Which?"

"A private dance and up and up."

Sloan began to speak, but felt slow, stupefied.

Naomi touched his arm. "Can we pay? Have we got money?"

Sloan retrieved the rolled wad of bills from his pants pockets and tried, in the dim light, to count them. They were all twenties from the bank machines. He counted fifteen – *three hundred dollars* – and there seemed to be more.

"We can pay." He handed Naomi the bills.

"Follow me," the girl said and took Naomi's hand.

"Aren't you coming?" Naomi asked Sloan. She turned to the girl. "Is he allowed?"

"Of course he may."

*He may.* Again, the lilt, the singing in her voice. Sloan followed Naomi and the girl to a candle-lit alcove which they entered by pushing through strings of shiny black beads.

Due either to the amount he had had to drink or to the sheer novelty of the circumstance – possibly even the overwhelming intensity of his feelings – Sloan retained only one lucid image of their time together in the V.I.P. lounge of the Blue Room. Naomi had said, "May I touch you?" Then – something was lost – Naomi was on her feet, her arms raised above her head, as the girl helped her out of her dress. The two women stood facing one another, Naomi decidedly shorter, blond wisps of hair falling away from her clip. Fingertips nestling lightly on one another's bare shoulders, the women stared into each other's eyes, a look, it seemed to Sloan, of startled recognition.

# 16

## SLOAN NEVER IMAGINED, NAOMI NEVER IMAGINED

S loan never imagined he could lose everything. He had at times, faced with some some new, seemingly unmeetable financial obligation, fantasized darkly about losing his job and being unable to find another, losing the house, living day to day in a desperate panic. He imagined himself feeling worthless and ashamed in the presence of Jen and the boys. Those spells, however, were infrequent, and even as he entertained them, he was steadied by a deeper awareness that they were not quite real, that they were summoned up, like certain dream images, to shame and punish himself. There was, too, an element of excitement in those reveries.

Now that he was really adrift, negotiating his daily way minute by minute, decision by decision, there was nothing like excitement at work. He felt strangely sedated, aware of observing himself as if from a distance, passive and deliberate. The misery he felt in anticipation of confessing his trip to New Orleans with Naomi did not seem to abate in any way afterward, although his most excruciating exchanges with Jen were mediated by a kind of numbing fog.

"You *what--?*" Jen had said. "You fucking *what--?*"

Sloan felt guilty about being unable to summon up what he believed was a suitable—or at least clearly readable-- pitch of feeling in response to her. In straightforward terms, if clumsily, he explained to Jen that he'd not been himself for quite a while, and now realized that he had fallen in love with Naomi Wise, and terrible as that was and as bad as he felt about betraying her and the confusion and worry he was sure the boys were going to experience, he didn't think his feelings for Naomi were a mistake. This and other honest admissions, he knew, were cruelly hurtful, and it was sickening to inflict that cruelty. But he could think of no gentler way of telling Jen what happened without lying, without withholding what she would insist on knowing, perhaps even more aggravatingly, later.

"I'm not saying this is right," he said to Jen. "I am not saying you disappointed me, that you are not enough. It's just," he struggled to find the right words, "it's just something that happened to me—like something that was maybe *supposed* to happen."

"It was *supposed* to happen," Jen repeated, enraged, incredulous. "Your *destiny*." She was standing up. Sloan thought she was about to strike him. Jen began to speak but the shaking of her lower jaw stopped her. Then she said, "You are a worthless piece of *shit*."

That night in what felt to Sloan like a bit of stock business from a romantic comedy, he brought his toothbrush down from the upstairs bathroom, gathered Henry's sleeping bag from the closet, and slept the night on the living room sofa. Neither he nor Jen had mentioned anything to Bart in the course of their brief, nearly wordless evening meal. In the morning as Sloan was about to go out to his car, Jen appeared in the kitchen and asked him what he was planning to do. The question confused him.

"Where are you going to *live*?" Jen said.

Sloan paused to consider. He had not thought about it. He had so far spoken only with Naomi about their new, altered condition, and most of their talk had been about what they were feeling, the decisive weight of it, and the looming necessity of telling their partners. Incredibly, it occurred to Sloan as he stood by the kitchen door staring intently into Jen's imploring eyes, neither he nor Naomi had talked in practical terms about what either of them would do next, where they would go, how they would live.

"I don't really know," he said.

"Just so you know that here is not an option. God, you're a mess."


Sloan never imagined the free-falling, unattached feeling that now permeated his days. He was aware of it as he dissolved into sleep, and he was immediately aware of it on waking: a vague but pervasive sense that he was now a fallen, damaged man. He had been a husband, a faithful husband, but now he was not. He had been, he was sure, a real, credible father, a father *figure*, to Henry and Bart, but now he sensed that he had become, or would soon become, diminished in their eyes, a far less substantial, less reliable presence. His own father had been a steady, loving, at times quietly suffering provider, but Sloan could no longer imagine being regarded as such by his boys. He would become a problem for them, a disappointment. Moreover, he understood that his estimation in their eyes would necessarily be colored by the hurt and loss and outrage Jen would bring to any consideration of him at home. He believed he knew his boys well enough to know that they would try to minimize their now troubled domestic situation, that they would avoid thinking about him as much as possible. He could picture his increasingly intermittent presence in their lives as a strain. He could imagine them dreading his company.

Sloan never imagined how much his general well-being, the unreflective sense that he belonged in the world, rested on embodying a clear set of culturally understood qualities. Husband. Father. Neighbor. Decent guy. He felt none of those things now, and yet their loss produced nothing like guilt. He felt, instead, detached, unrelated to everyone with whom he had been familiar before. He felt a new distance from even his closest friends and associates at the paper. Their familiar greetings, questions and responses seemed alien to him, and he was aware of himself filtering their language and attitude for signs that they knew anything of his altered condition. There was a new caution, a guardedness in his response to what people said to him. Moving among streams of pedestrians on the street outside *The Sun Messenger* or standing in line at the Stop 'N Shop check-out line, Sloan felt marked out, unassimilable.

He found himself craving the company of a new kind of person, an intimate who had himself, or herself, strayed adulterously. He would have liked to listen to such a person discourse at length about everything that happened. If Naomi had not been his lover, if she had been as before, he would have rushed to her office to unburden himself. He would have eagerly sought out her reactions, studied her face for signs of recognition and, just possibly, her approval. He searched the library for books he believed would open up his condition. He reread *Madame Bovary*. He sought out memoirs of literary adulterers. He checked out several glossily illustrated books about Spencer Tracy and Katherine Hepburn.

Sloan never imagined "the news"-- volatile developments in the Near East, the impending likelihood of devastating acts of terror, increasingly clear signs that critical sectors of the economy were collapsing or on the verge—could matter so little to him The facts ordered themselves in the old way, but they struck no chord of feeling. More local developments, whether involving prominent persons or consequential events, seemed even less substantial, so that determining subjects for his editorials and writing them had become, he felt, increasingly capricious. Editorials were written in an informed, persuasive voice, and though he took care to be well informed on matters of civic concern, he found it difficult to summon up any kind of persuasive attitude. He suspected, even in the face of damning evidence, that parties seemingly in the wrong, exploitative landlords, public figures on the take, officials performing badly, anybody embarrassed by illicit or unconventional sex, were probably not fully understood, and even if they were, if their crimes and short cuts and impulses were indisputably reprehensible, the perpetrators, being who they were and how they were situated, could probably not have done otherwise.

Sloan's editorials began to shift tone and stance. He was aware of himself composing them with a new depth of care. His obligation to anyone who read them, he decided, was to *open up* the subject under consideration to a wider, perhaps unfamiliar perspective. Sloan wanted readers to see behind the obvious and familiar foibles documented in the paper's news pages. To the extent he could in an editorial of three hundred to six-hundred words, he wanted to raise the possibility in readers' minds that greater, deeper forces than newspapers ever acknowledge might be driving events and that aligning oneself with these forces, not railing against them, was the best bet for living fully. The mistake, the recurring mistake was to armor oneself with unconsidered assumptions, to assume a posture of impatient certainty in a world in which no such thing is remotely possible. Sloan's colleagues at the Sun-Messenger for the most part passed favorably on these editorials, complimenting him from time to time that they were "well written." Sloan, who also edited the letters-to-the-editor and op-ed pages, noted with interest that fewer readers wrote to take issue with his recent editorials—or to praise them—while his personal correspondence with readers had become almost unmanageable. Sloan found many of these personal letters touching in their admissions, and almost all of them raised questions he could not begin to answer.

Sloan had carried out most of his married life worrying with lesser and greater intensity about meeting his financial obligations, but he never imagined being without all means. His first night away from Jen and the house he dined with Naomi at a quiet Italian restaurant a few doors down from the Sun Messenger offices. After coffee, they moved to the bar and sipped cognac and soda until ten when Naomi had promised Nathan they could talk further about their situation.

"What does he want?" Sloan asked.

"He wants," Naomi paused. "Mainly, I think he wants to feel better, for everything that just happened to make sense, even if it's terrible and sad. I think he wants time. I think he wants to feel that if he can talk to me in our old nice way, I won't really be different from the way he needs to think about me, and that maybe there is really nothing wrong."

"So what doesn't he get?"

"Me. What I did. The way I am."

"Does he want you to stay with him?"

"I'm sure he does."

"Could you?"

"No." Naomi looked hard at Sloan, bobbing her head a little for emphasis. "No. I knew I was leaving Nathan, ending our marriage, when I decided to go to New Orleans. Going away with you was the end of my wondering about my life with him, not the beginning."

"So what will you talk about? Is he miserable? Is he angry?"

"He's not angry, or at least not angry in a way anyone would ever call angry. In his very deliberate Nathan way, he may be miserable. But he mainly wants to be thoughtful and slow about what seems to be happening so fast. Last night, he suggested we should see someone, a therapist."

"And--?"

"It's a perfectly reasonable thing to suggest, and it is certainly what I would suggest to anyone who came to me with my story, but I think tonight my job is to explain nicely why counseling would not improve or change our situation—although it may well be a good thing for Nathan to see a therapist, and I'll bet he will."

"But not you. Do therapists see therapists?"

"Oh yes, probably more than other people do. But not me—two reasons. First, I would only see a therapist if I was confused about what I had done. I am not confused. I know exactly. I deliberated quite a bit in advance and chose to do what I did. And did it. Second,"—Naomi looked as if she might laugh—"I'm pretty sure I don't believe in therapy any more."

"Better not tell your patients."

"I won't have to. I have already begun to advise my clients that I am ending my practice, and this week I will tell my associates at the clinic."

Sloan felt a pang of concern for what he was sure would be a wrenching loss for Naomi. He sensed it would be awkward at the bar, but he wanted to hold her.

"Why end your practice, love? You're really good at it. I'm speaking as a client."

Naomi smiled. "I told you. I don't believe in it anymore. In the biggest sense, in the sense of *curing* people, changing them from worse to better, I don't believe in it. I honestly don't. And besides, I have violated the strictest, clearest professional standards of therapist-client relations, and if I didn't quit they could and should haul me up on charges and banish me from the profession."

"So," Sloan said, choosing his words, "you are leaving your profession because of me."

"Absolutely," Naomi said, smiling wonderfully. "You have ruined me for psychological therapy, and I am very grateful to you."

Sloan rose from his stool and held Naomi to him. There was a scent like jasmine in her hair as he kissed the top of her head.

"Night blooming jasmine," he said.

"What?"

"Nothing. A good memory. But, um, Mrs. Wise, I think we better figure out how to earn some money and how we are going to live."

The thought of money—the looming swirl of her salary, her accounts, her accounts with Nathan, their houses, their possessions—was deadening to Naomi .

"Money," she said, "is not our problem."

"Good to hear," Sloan said, "Because I've got enough money in my wallet, after I pay this tab, for maybe a day and a half at the Days Inn off the interstate ramp. After that, it's hand-to-mouth."

"Then I better take care of this," Naomi said, picking up the bar bill and opening her purse.

"I'll get the next one," Sloan said. "The Days Inn is pretty grim, I 'm afraid, or I would invite you for some further discussion after you are done with Nathan." Sloan was joking, but he wanted her to come to him, to lose himself in their lovemaking.

"So I'm not invited?"

"You are permanently, eternally invited to stay with me anywhere, even the Days Inn, but I have a feeling your shower set up is going to be better at home."

"You can't even imagine," Naomi said. "So I should shower first?"

Sloan unlocked the door of his severe little room in the Days Inn.

Even before he switched on the light he was met by a faint but insistent aroma, which he recognized as stale cigarette smoke, although he had booked a non-smoking room. The slightly acrid tang, like the harsh yellow of the walls, seemed to match his present condition precisely, a jarring announcement of discontinuity with all previous expectations, especially any expectation of comfort or pleasure. Exactly the kind of room, he thought, in which not to belong.

Sloan switched off the light, eased out of his shoes without untying them and lay out on the bed. At this hour, at home with Jen and the boys, in that very different darkness, he would have let the clicks and knocks and hisses of the old house lull him into a reverie in which, until surrendering to sleep, he would configure himself in the larger world, as a character, himself, in the continuing, highly particular story of his life. But on this night he could find no such perspective, nothing continuous with his prior story. He commanded no words, summoned no memories, even the agreeable memory of dining with Naomi, chatting with her at the quiet bar. Eyes closed, still aware of the pungency in the air, feeling for some reason enormous in recline, too big for the bed, he more sensed than recalled that Naomi might come to him-- *Am I not invited?*—and lay awake, waiting.

Years later, long after he had assumed an altogether different manner of living, Sloan attributed his safe passage through what had seemed like bottomless uncertainty to the fact that he had not resisted it. He had made no compromises, sought no temporary safe haven. He never grabbed the lifeline of reconnecting to Jen, improvising some endurable accommodation. He made no semblance of amends. Nor could he have named what sustained him as he proceeded through what seemed little more than a fog of reflexive transactions. He had felt no real pain or anything like fear. There had been a kind of curiosity, bordering on resolve, about arriving into some altogether altered condition. He allowed himself to imagine it would be some kind of illness, even death.

Through all of it his primary waking reality had been Naomi. Outwardly, he was aware of meeting his practical obligations as effectively as he had in the past. He spent some evenings and whole weekends with Bart, and occasionally with Bart and Henry. He listened to what they said to him, answered without reserve the few questions they had of him. On warm summer nights, they shot baskets and worked their way into pick-up games at the Rec Center. Still numb from sleep, they played golf early on Sunday mornings, watching their putts make sloshing trails across greens still heavy with dew. They went to action movies and sat baking in bleacher seats watching the Indians. They ate hamburgers and spaghetti at familiar haunts.

There were unvarying office routines, meetings, banter, coffee, blocking out and filling in his editorials, a beer or two at Dulaney's, expectations and deadlines duly met but carrying little force of feeling. All of it felt to Sloan like a single atmospheric substance he was able to arrange, as one might arrange cloud, around the charged, beckoning presence of Naomi. His attraction to her never diminished or steadied. It seemed only to mount. It mounted even in her sustained presence. Beneath the measured, even laconic outward demeanor he was sure he projected, his desire to reconnect with Naomi when out of her presence for even an hour could feel unbearable. He would tell her—eagerly, happily—*it never changes, it never goes away.* In these words and in other, similar words Sloan and Naomi testified to their mutual condition nearly every time they made love.

As he had in New Orleans, as he did the full duration of his night's stay at the Days Inn, Sloan gave himself up entirely to Naomi in their love-making. His desire was endlessly renewable. He had never imagined such sex was physically possible. It was not that Naomi was insatiable, nor was she in any way aggressive or needy. She was, he kept discovering, entirely reciprocal, as animal as he was when moved by stirrings of lust, then, by turns, playful, tender, unhurried. There was no question of agreement, permission or consent. Their unspoken understanding was that they were joined—held fast—in a condition of mutual desire beyond all practical or social consideration. Sufficiently removed from others, doors closed behind them, they embraced, undressed, and made love until, often together, they would dissolve into a few hours of dreamless, deeply restorative sleep, then awake to the delicious, arousing touch of the other.

Up and about, apart from Naomi, Sloan could summon no trace of jealousy or concern about her whereabouts or whims. He did not doubt her attraction to him. He was certain she felt as he did: that their communion was elemental. There could be no better, more satisfying alternative. Knowing this, Sloan felt no need of any promises or spoken reassurances. As they proceeded through whatever practical business might be at hand in the giddily mounting anticipation that they would soon be making love, they exchanged fewer and fewer words, a surrender which, had Sloan tried to describe it, was an acknowledgement that they were entering what felt like sacred territory. To describe this, categorize it, attempt to contain it with mere language would be to diminish and falsify it and thus—unthinkably—to risk its loss.

Open ended time with Naomi was new territory for Sloan. There was a surprising, languorous quality to her company. Until New Orleans, he had only experienced her as her client in therapy. Out of bed, their time in New Orleans had been spent primarily in restaurants and cafes, in which he felt he could have lingered indefinitely, bantering aimlessly, taking her in, holding her gaze. Watching a film, listening to music, focused activity of any kind would have been distracting. He had wanted only her attentive presence. Now there was time, more time. There was the prospect of all of their days together. Sloan began to imagine relaxing in her presence. He took increasing pleasure in indeterminate outings, walks with no specific destination in mind. He looked forward to the merest of errands, happy to join her for a trip to the pharmacy for dental floss, to the video store to return a disc.

At her side on these outings, Sloan was overcome with agreeable new impressions. He had not imagined Naomi would be so shrewd and efficient in practical matters, that she was, for instance, a decisive shopper, a rather fast, skillful driver, an accomplished and imaginative cook. He was pleasantly aware that she could be quiet in his company but not at all disengaged. He had been struck before by her unexpected observations, her ability to cast ordinary experiences in unusual light, but now that they were free to explore experiences beyond what might arise in therapy, he realized that she processed ordinary experience in a way altogether new to him. Her vocabulary and range of cultural reference were extensive, but she conveyed nothing of the self-conscious intellectual. He found her very funny, believing at first that his heightened arousal in her presence simply found release in jokes and banter, but the more time they spent together, the more he realized that she had an exceptional eye and ear for people's oddities and quirks and a comedic gift for recounting stories and anecdotes. More than anything else, Sloan was struck by the fact that despite her distinctly stylish manner of meeting the world, Naomi was almost completely free of conventional restraint.

She was not merely willing, but eager, to make love. Sloan sensed it in the way she approached him from the other side of a street, in an enlivening flash in her eyes, an infusion of energy in her talk when they were dining or sitting at a bar. He could see it in the slightest movement, in the relaxing of her shoulders, the crossing of her legs. She welcomed his embraces, his touch. Driving together in the car, one hand on the wheel, the other caressing her open palm, Sloan felt her desire mount, and with it his, to a pitch that silenced their talk.

Naomi's clothes held Sloan in inarticulate fascination. He could identify no obvious feature in the way she turned herself out that signaled availability or desire. She dressed stylishly and simply, favoring silky, seemingly weightless fabrics the fall of which defined her breasts and shoulders in a way that immediately aroused him. She rarely wore a bra or stockings and thus always seemed, and often was, especially available to his touch.

When they went out for the evening there was a moist sheen to her face and throat, a dark new complexity to her eyes. She liked outsized, delicately cascading earrings of metals worked to a lacey fineness. Even before they moved in together, Sloan had taken almost prayerful pleasure in watching Naomi make up her face and dress for an evening out. In all there were not many garments: panties, a silk top, a dark skirt. Dressed—and for the duration of their time out—Naomi seemed to Sloan giddily, teasingly close to the nakedness which he knew was her deepest comfort and ease.

Making love, Sloan would ask, "Do other people know about this? Do other people have this?" For Sloan it was a serious question. Naomi lay back, considering, then her smile that still looked to Sloan as if she were about to laugh: "I don't really know—but-- don't you hope so?"

Within ten days of confessing their infidelities to their respective spouses, Sloan and Naomi moved into a third floor apartment in the city. The building rested on an escarpment overlooking University Circle's complex of hospitals, museums, and schools. The neighborhood was, Sloan realized, no more than a five minute drive from the house he had lived in for fifteen years, but the prospects and feel of the place were entirely discontinuous; he could as well have been in another city, another country.

When the broker first walked them through the unfurnished rooms, the high ceilings, newly painted white walls, and the sheen of the varnished floors gave Sloan an impression of airy vastness. An oblong living room overlooking the street extended back to a marble counter, dining space and kitchen. A passage to one side of the kitchen led back to two bedrooms and a bath. Appliances, plumbing and fixtures looked to be new. Sloan turned on the taps and for a moment watched the flow of clear water. He flushed the toilet. Naomi stood before the bank of windows in the back bedroom overlooking a complexity of spires, rooftops and smokestacks below. Sloan joined her at the window and took her hand.

"There is absolutely nothing wrong with this place," he said.

"No, nothing."

"And we can afford it?" Sloan was pretty sure the listing had indicated $1300 a month.

"Yes," Naomi said, then, looking behind them to see that the broker was out of hearing, "It's *nothing.*"

"Well, that's a relief," Sloan said. He was still somewhat unsettled by Naomi's revelation of her assets, sums in savings, securities— *properties*—the likes of which he had no experience. The sole source of his income, a monthly check from the *Sun Messenger* was deposited directly into his and Jen's joint account, and he had not attempted to draw on it since leaving the house.

Sloan looked directly into Naomi's eyes. "There is no reason not to take this place, is there?"

"No reason at all."

Sloan was aware of an internal disturbance, not altogether unpleasant: *this is it, it's starting, this is real.*

"But let's keep it like this," he said, feeling suddenly energized—happy. "Let's have all this light. Maybe we can put almost nothing in it. Maybe a bed, some place to sit, a few plates—towels."

Naomi laughed. "That sounds just right. A towel for each of us."

They signed the lease and moved in that evening. Sloan drove to the Wal-Mart and bought an air mattress, a double sleeping bag, two towels, two stools, two settings of stainless steel silverware, two tumblers, two wine glasses, two sets of dishes, a set of four kitchen knives, a frying pan and sauce pan. While he was in the store, Naomi went to Whole Foods and bought a roasted chicken, a sack of basmati rice, olive oil, an assortment of spices, a gallon of cranberry juice, a dozen eggs, a loaf of sour dough bread, two bottles of chardonnay, a carton of vanilla ice cream, a container of fresh raspberries, black tea, butter, milk, and a wedge of havarti cheese sprinkled with dill.

Not once in the course of the ten days he stayed at the Days Inn and then at a succession of friends' spare rooms did Sloan imagine that he might feel comfortably, much less pleasurably, situated. But the apartment above University Circle lifted his spirits as no prior residence had ever done. Its white walls and high ceilings seemed to hold the light, creating in the mornings and late afternoons a vaporous, milky atmosphere. True to their initial impulse, they kept the rooms nearly empty, although Naomi arranged to have a good bed, some occasional seating, lamps and an oriental carpet trucked over from her house. Sloan bought an inexpensive disc player at Circuit City, and he and Naomi were startled at its surprising resonance in the sparely furnished rooms.

At his desk in the editorial office Sloan found himself accelerating daily routines against the possibility of leaving early and returning to the apartment. Waking in the morning light of the back bedroom, he was playfully slow to leave the bed. He and Jen had for years risen separately, the routines of feeding children and preparing them for school eclipsing all other business. There had been little talk.

Sloan and Naomi awoke and made love, then shared remembered fragments of dreams, forecasted the day. On weekends, Sloan put on a robe, clumped downstairs for *The Sun Messenger* and *The New York Times*, and got back into bed. They read and chatted over the papers until Naomi got up to make tea late in the morning. At first, the agreeable progression of these mornings aroused in Sloan a twinge of panic, an uneasy sense that he could not possibly deserve such ease. He had been long practiced, he came to realize, in edgy defensiveness, a readiness to parry Jen's critical barbs. And there had been plenty to worry about, money, the house, the boys' finding their way. He found himself frequently on the brink of reassuming the old weight and agitation. Thoughts of Jen and the boys, angry, confused and abandoned at home, would arise in punishing flashes, insisting, speaking in a *voice*, a voice like Jen's, deriding him for even considering the possibility of ease, comfort, pleasure.

High aloft in the apartment with Naomi, Sloan was able to resist the beckoning oppression. This new quality of being in the world, although still half dream to Sloan, was, he determined, real. *If this is wrong,* he thought, *what right could possibly win my higher allegiance? How could it be right to deny this? This is where rightness comes from, what rightness is made of.*

On their first Saturday morning in bed in the apartment Naomi said to him, "Look out the windows. We are on top of the world. We have an aerie." Sloan had joked, "An aerie on Erie." But he knew what she meant, what she felt.

# 17

## SUMMONS TO RELAX

Sloan knew Jen well enough not to expect anything more than her vituperation. There had been a few incursions back into the house, preceded by phone calls, to retrieve clothing and other belongings, and there were sometimes a few minutes' of mutual proximity as Sloan picked up or dropped off the boys. On those occasions he found her looks of revulsion and terse, dismissive comments awkwardly theatrical, and he was determined not to answer her in kind.

As he was settling into his desk work one morning at the paper, the receptionist buzzed through on the intercom to tell him that someone whose name Sloan did not recognize was waiting to see him. Sloan told her to send him in. The young man who parted the glass doors and strode briskly to his desk looked to be in his twenties. He wore a shiny, ill-fitting grey suit, and his hair was moussed upwards over his temples, the two sides coming together to form the approximate shape of an overturned canoe. Sloan could not place the face. As he rose to greet the approaching figure, the young man extracted a business envelope from his coat pocket and held it out to Sloan.

"You Sloan Fox?" the young man asked. Sloan said yes and took the envelope.

"Summons."

"Summons for what?"

The young man had already turned to go. "You have a nice day," he said on his way out.

The letter contained four or five pages of a paper stock so substantial the dark type face was recessed deeply into the vellum. Below an imposing letterhead indicating Vitak and Hervey, Attorneys at Law, was a heading, SUMMONS, stating with what seemed to Sloan ponderous officiousness that the writer, Bela Vitak, had been retained by Jennifer Fox to initiate proceedings in divorce and thus a number of conditions must be met "immediately and unequivocally." Under a following heading, URGENT ORDERS, was a highly repetitive enumeration of transactions he was apparently now forbidden to make, including "undisclosed" withdrawals from his bank accounts, closing his bank accounts, opening new bank accounts, selling or renting his house, altering the terms of his mortgage, using the residence as equity in borrowing new money, altering or ceasing payments on either of the vehicles financed and registered in his name, removing or selling belongings, tools, appliances or other portable property associated with his residence.

Sloan sat back and reread the letter slowly. The summons, beginning with its jarring delivery by the young courier, succeeded in conveying a kind of ominous aggression, even though none of the specified cautions and measures seemed to bear on anything that might actually trouble him. He had given no thought to secreting away money or possessions. He had not felt any need to hoard or even lay claim to anything in his prior life. The guilt and remorse he felt for leaving and hurting Jen was unqualified. If a court, civil or celestial, decreed that he should in consequence of leaving his wife go penniless and comfortless for the rest of his life, he would not have been surprised, nor would he complain. The house, he realized with a liberating clarity, had never felt like *his* house, or even *their* house; it was just the house they had arranged to live in and pay for. Nor, really, did he regard his *Sun Messenger* salary as his. He felt responsible for the quality of his work, the time spent on the job, but the compensation for it felt more as though it belonged to Jen and the boys, if only because they clearly needed it.

Why then, Sloan wondered, did the summons feel so malignant, like such a violation? He had known, although he avoided thinking about it, that he would have to consult a lawyer at some point about his altered life. He also knew it was possible that he did not really understand the summons and its urgent orders.

Naomi turned out to be unexpectedly helpful in this regard. Her continuing relationship with Nathan bore no resemblance to Sloan's and Jen's. She and Nathan continued to talk amicably and productively about practical matters. They had already agreed that they would seek, with legal guidance, an uncontested "dissolution" of their marriage, rather than a court-mediated divorce. She and Nathan had together met with a lawyer Nathan had found, and the lawyer had quietly and clearly explained how dissolutions proceeded. He explained that un-contested dissolutions could be heard and granted in a few months, provided the divorcing parties were in agreement on the distribution of property and assets. Technically, he told them, each was entitled to exactly half of their joint holdings. Although both Naomi and Nathan had been comfortably set up before they married, Nathan's wealth had at the time been considerably more than hers, as had his earnings over the course of their life together. Naomi thought it was only fair to acknowledge this and to leave the marriage with only what she had brought to it. In that case, the attorney had said, there seemed little obstacle to proceeding other than inventorying their property and preparing the necessary documents. Since there was no foresee-able point of contention between them, Naomi asked the lawyer if he might represent them both, but was told it could not be legally done in Ohio. He recommended a number of attorneys for her to consider, all of whom he said he could work with agreeably. Naomi contacted the first name on the list, a woman, and, when they met, she concurred entirely with everything Nathan's lawyer had said.

Naomi next called her lawyer to ask if she might recommend one for Sloan. Again a number of names were proposed, and when Sloan called the first number, he reached Tom Wiseman, of Wiseman and Wiseman Partners, and he immediately liked the sound of his voice on the phone. In the course of their first consultation, Tom Wiseman laughed out loud when Sloan showed him his summons.

"I *guess* your wife is angry," he said. "Bela Vitak is….the ultimate *shark.*"

"Yes," Sloan said, "she is very angry."

Wiseman laughed again. "Bela *Vitak.* I mean, I'm not trying to worry you, because, from what you've told me, they can't hurt you. For one thing, you haven't really got anything, except the equity in the house and your salary, and from what you tell me you are willing to give it all to her—which, by the way, however generous or guilty you are feeling, that is not the way to go. But anyway, you don't seem interested in holding onto anything, so there's nothing much for them to get out of you—which makes me wonder why Vitak took this on. He's not going to get much, and he's normally a pretty high roller."

"Will Jen have to pay him a lot of money?" Sloan asked.

"Don't see how she can. She doesn't seem to have anything either. That's what I mean. I can't figure out what Vitak gets out of taking her on."

"She can be an appealing woman," Sloan offered.

Wiseman looked confused. Then he said, "The best thing you can do right now is relax and not panic about anything. Whatever bad feelings are rattling around out there, this is a low stakes, uncomplicated divorce. If you two were fighting over custody terms for the younger boy, that would be one thing, but it looks like you're not. So there's only your property, and it's not much, and it's not complicated. Ohio's a "no-fault" divorce state, which means each of you is entitled to half of your joint worth. Until you divide it up, each of you owns half of the other one's underwear. So the only real job is to decide who gets what and write it down. That can be messy when the parties want things the other one wants, but that doesn't seem to be the case with you. Am I missing something?"

"No, that's how it is," Sloan said.

"O.K. So just remember to relax." Wiseman held up the summons and rattled the pages. "You could be getting more stuff like this in the mail, maybe even phone calls with tough talk about filing dates and money transfers and this and that. Thing to remember is-- don't get worked up. Don't even respond except to say that you'll refer the matter to your lawyer, me. Since there's nothing really for them to gain here in the material department, the only satisfaction your wife can get is to make your life miserable and—excuse me—scare the shit out of you. My advice—don't give her that pleasure. And don't let Vitak get to you. *Relax*."

# 18

## THREE MESSAGES

S loan's first weeks with Naomi in the aerie above University Circle were at once unsettling and invigorating. At day's end when they walked down the narrow bricked streets into Little Italy to dine, Sloan felt as if he could have been living in another country. Apart from certain effortful stretches at *The Sun Messenger*, he was aware as never before in his life that his time was his own, that it was his to shape, which made him feel not so much lazy as languorous. He read quietly for hours. He found himself transfixed by light, upon waking by the spectacular irradiation of the city's rooftops beyond the bedroom windows, in late afternoon by the butterscotch gleam in the hardwood of the living room floor.

It was, he was certain, the ease of Naomi's company that was responsible for this new restfulness, her capacity when they were together to infuse the surrounding space with vaguely arousing possibility, yet never crowding him. He was always so glad to see her when he returned home from *The Sun Messenger* or when he heard her ascending steps on the stairs after an hour's errand. Neither of them pressed the other to go out, to look after impending business, to act, to move. It was a positive pleasure, Sloan found, to deliberate together, with little urgency, about what they would do next — which restaurant, whether to browse a farmers' market, stop in at a gallery opening, take a hike, drive southward out of the city with no destination. The dreamy calm in which these plans and excursions were undertaken was due, he realized, to the fact that it was always equally enjoyable to stay home, improvise a meal, let the apartment darken about them, make love to new music.

Of course there was, more for Sloan than for Naomi, a measure of dissonance and uncertainty. Henry worked his pizza delivery job in Oxford and went weeks without a visit home, but Sloan saw Bart every weekend and on the odd week day evening. He was concerned about both of them, about what sometimes looked like diminished drive and spark, especially in Henry. Tom Wiseman had been correct in predicting frequent, jarring letters and calls from Jen's attorney, Bela Vitak, but Sloan had succeeded overall in not responding to either the hectoring tone or the substance of what was demanded, instead passing on the papers and referring the calls to Wiseman.

When Sloan picked up and dropped off Bart at the house, he sensed that despite her icy contempt, Jen was studying him for some sign that Vitak's salvos had registered. Sloan never mentioned them. In his minimal gestures at communicating—hellos, good-byes, the briefest indications of where he and Bart were headed or where they had been—he struck the friendliest tone he felt she could bear. This sustained non-communion was for Sloan fairly continuous with the tense dynamics of their previous life at home. Jen's relentless barbs, as aggravatingly as they had worn on him, were also, he knew, an indirect, perhaps even desperate effort to reach him. His defensive rejoinders or, very occasionally, angry outbursts had served in a strange way to calm her down. His worst behavior—sarcasm, shutting down in silence—seemed to confirm her expectation that he would fail her, that in time the worst would happen. She seemed relieved and even energized by their most bitter exchanges.

He knew that Jen wanted nothing more now than for Vitak's threats and accusations to undo him. He knew she would have been fortified by some expression of complaint, fear, worry, or even rage on his part. But because he did not feel it, because in so many ways he felt elevated and lucky in his new condition, he could not satisfy this expectation, or hope, of Jen's. Yet, through all his saving preoccupation with Naomi and his pleasure in their life together, he was never entirely free of an awareness that his unbroken condition was to Jen an ever deepening wound, a realization that aroused in him both sadness and tenderness.

It had started as a kind of joke between them. Naomi and Sloan would be talking aimlessly and agreeably about something of no great consequence, and one of them would pause, fix the other with a hard stare, and say, "So—what are we going to *do* with our lives?" A day might pass or even several, but the question would arise again, and each of them felt a mounting force in the asking. Only later would they see a clear pattern in the three events that propelled them into an altogether unimagined future together.

The first of these was their encounter with the furious man at the Target store. They had gone inside together so Naomi could replenish their dishwashing and laundry supplies. As Sloan browsed aimlessly near the check out counters, he was aware of a sudden sickening tension in the air. He couldn't place it at first, not sure if it was arising from within or somewhere in the store. Then it was unmistakable. It was noise. Somebody—a man—was shouting angrily: *And don't think I'm going to...for a GOD DAMNED fucking MINUTE...EVER AGAIN going to...* The voice was high, wavering, out of control. Sloan turned and saw that it was coming from the lunch counter beyond the registers. Feeling his gut tensing, he moved to the sound. He remembered the feeling, in the blurring speed of tight basketball games, when an elbow would strike a temple or the swipe of a hand would meet face instead of ball, and then, triggered by no more than a flash of white light, jerseys grabbed, fists flying. *Fuck you, asshole!*

Sloan moved past displays toward the lunch counter. The shouting man sat on a stool at the counter next to a boy Sloan guessed to be about ten or eleven. Elaborate ice cream dishes—Sloan could see pastel scoops and the curved arcs of banana under swizzles of whipped cream—stood uneaten in front of them. The boy was hunched forward, his head tucked down almost to the level of the counter. The man, half turned to the boy, had lowered his voice for a moment but then it flared again. *Anything you want…Anything you FUCKING want, but you know what, buddy?* The man gave the boy a jarring nudge with his upper arm. *You fucking HEAR me? It's not going to happen with me. I haven't fucking GOT it, you understand? Your mother's got it. She got it all. So maybe she can fill up the fucking house with video games and EVERY SINGLE PIECE OF SHIT you want, but it's not happening with me.* The man paused, and Sloan could hear the boy say something softly, perhaps just a snuffle. Then the man's voice rose again, *Yeah, CRY. CRY YOUR HEAD OFF, because it's not going to change a fucking thing. You got me buddy, you got me for the whole fucking weekend. Just you and me. Great, isn't it?* The man nudged the boy again, hard enough that he had to reposition himself on the stool. He was crying. Sloan was of aware of Naomi silently at his side. He was about to speak to her when the man's voice erupted again. *So what now—you're not going to EAT that? You're just gonna let it sit there? Well, here's news for you. In MY WORLD that costs money. MY fucking money, what's left of it, and you're gonna eat that, god damn it. You hear me?* Then piercingly loud: *Do you FUCKING HEAR ME?*

Naomi had just begun to speak when Sloan moved to the counter. He had no clear plan. He wanted the man to stop his abusive talk. He wanted the boy to stop hearing it.

Sloan sat down on a stool two down from the man and stared ahead. There appeared to be no one else in the dining area, either customer or server. Sloan made a show of looking around for someone to serve him. He caught the man's eye and asked if there was a waitress. The man answered with an indeterminate gesture, a sweep of his hand that might have said, *look around.* Sloan was struck by something in the man's face, something almost cringing, which might have been shame at having been witnessed, perhaps anger, or sadness.

Sloan managed to hold the man's stare, aware that he risked provoking him further.

"You okay?" he asked.

There was a silence, and Sloan had to make himself breathe.

Sloan said, "Sounds like you're having a tough time."

Something shifted in the man's features, but Sloan could not read the change. Sloan said, "I've had some days like that."

The man turned away toward the boy but then he looked back at Sloan and said, "I just got a little pissed off at my boy here. I've got him for the weekend, and he seems to think he's got it better at his mother's place."

"I know a little about that, too," Sloan said. "I only get my boys at the weekend."

A waitress in uniform appeared. She looked uneasily at the man and his son before taking Sloan's order for coffee. He guessed she had gone off to find help.

In what sounded to Sloan like a self- consciously unexpressive tone, the man asked his son if he was going to eat his ice cream. Sloan heard a mumbled, "Not really hungry," but then watched as the boy slowly dipped his spoon into a soft, glistening pool.

Sloan drank a few sips of sour coffee and left his money on top of the check. As he rose to go he said to the man, "Hope things look up. You have a good weekend."

Naomi was waiting for him at the spot where he left her.

"Oh my *god,*" she said. Sloan thought she might be about to cry.

"Guy's having a bad day," he said.

"His boy is having a worse day," she said.

"Mmmm."

Naomi said, "That boy is *not* going to be all right."

Sloan said, "You've got to hope he will."

"But he *won't be.*" Naomi's eyes were now rimmed with tears. "He won't *ever* be."

That was the first thing.

The next thing was a mid-July outing to the city zoo. Naomi revealed that in all her years in Cleveland, she had never been to the zoo, had never once thought of going. Sloan paused to consider. He had been to the zoo. There were hazy images of a childhood excursion or two, a sense memory of the humid stink of the reptile house. He and Jen had taken the boys when they were ten and six. It had been a bitterly cold day in late March, and although the zoo had opened to the public, the lot was nearly empty, and inside the grounds looked unready and forlorn. They may have enjoyed themselves. Sloan could not recall. He did remember all of them laughing out loud when Jen pointed out the flamingos. Six or seven of them were standing in an outdoor pen before a pool of black water, and their pink stick legs were shivering and knocking wildly in the cold. "It's *Cleveland*," Jen had called out. "Someone should have told you."

The zoo when Naomi and Sloan passed through the gates was bright with sunshine, the force of the heat on their faces relieved periodically by gusty breezes. The lot had been more than half filled with school buses, and throngs of children who looked to Sloan to be of elementary school age shrieked and babbled along the exhibit pathways.

Just a few yards inside the grounds, Sloan and Naomi paused to observe two elephants nodding and striking the dusty earth distractedly with their front hooves. In seconds Naomi and Sloan were surrounded by dozens of children, all, Sloan noticed, African American, their bright tee shirts, the vivid swirls of their sneakers, the red and yellow ties around the girls' pigtails combining to festive, chattering effect.

Sloan leaned into Naomi and said, "Do you get the feeling we're too big for the zoo?"

Naomi slid an arm around Sloan's waist and whispered up into his ear. "You may be too big for the zoo, but I am just right for the zoo." Sloan looked into her eyes. She was smiling wonderfully.

Not that same swarm of children but others seemed to envelop them wherever they came to rest. The frantic acrobatics of the arboreal monkeys thrilled the children to the point of screaming hilarity. But it was in the simulated Rain Forest, under the bright glass dome over the misted fronds and blooms of the butterfly exhibit that Naomi was overcome.

The children who now enveloped them at the level of hip and waist were all girls. They wore uniforms of plaid skirts and white blouses. Sloan saw on the tee shirts of the attending adults that these were students from Sisters Mary and Martha Prep, a new inner city outreach school for children of indigent parents. *The Sun Messenger* had run an extensive feature on the school, and Sloan mentioned it approvingly in an editorial he had titled "The Profits of Non-Profits."

Sloan tapped the little girl in front of him on the shoulder and asked her, "Do you like your school?"

The girl's expression clouded and then cleared. Her smile revealed a wide gap of missing front teeth.

"Yes!"

"What do you like about it?"

"I like—the *ZOO!*"

Sloan said, "Sounds like a good school to me," but his words were lost in a chorus of shrieking agreement of the other girls: "I like school too," "I like *GOING* to school," "I take the *BUS!*"

As the girls chimed in, Naomi embraced Sloan loosely. In a louder voice Sloan said, "Do you like going to school in the *summer?*"

"*Yes!*"

"I like going to school *every day.*"

"In the *BUS!*"

Sloan realized he may have been distracting the girls from their intended researches, so he said, "Have you guys seen any butterflies?" He felt the soundless quivering of Naomi laughing at his side.

Walking later to the parking lot, aware of the oppressive force of the sun but happy, Sloan said, "How old are we now, and what's our I.Q.?"

"I don't have an I.Q. any more."

"Children will do that to you."

"I *love* those children. They were the best things in the zoo. I love *every single one* of those children. If it weren't a crime, I would steal a bunch of them and take them home." Naomi looked up into Sloan's eyes. "Aren't they the *best* people?"

Then it occurred to Sloan— he was certain— that when he had felt Naomi's quivering at his side while they were bantering with the little girls from St. Mary and Martha's, she was not laughing. She was crying.

That was the second thing.


The third thing occurred weeks later, in August, when the sweltering morning heat convinced them to drive an hour east to the Mentor Headlands beach on Lake Erie. They could feel the faint sting of the hot sand through the rubber soles of their flip-flops as they hauled their blankets and cooler past the throngs of family bathers to a relatively remote cleft between low dunes. The heat was relieved by a steady offshore breeze.

Without speaking they laid out their blankets and towels, weighting the corners with stones, and went straight to the water. The water was a little brackish, a dull greenish brown where the waves broke near the shore. Together they swam past the soupy shallows thirty or forty yards out where the water temperature was just cool enough to relive the heat.

Treading water, Sloan said to Naomi, "Feels good, doesn't it?"

Naomi said, "It feels better."

They took the sun together through the glaring heat of midafternoon, periodically refreshing themselves with a swim. As the dinner hour approached, they watched the families furl their beach umbrellas, gather their children and their toys, and head off to the parking lots. The breeze remained steady, an they could feel the pin pricks of the day's sun on their faces.

"This is a perfectly good beach, a perfectly good endless body of water," Sloan said. "Why don't we come here all the time?"

Naomi considered for a moment and said, "It's an imperfectly good beach."

Sloan was about to answer when she said, "No. It is not even an imperfectly good beach or an imperfectly good body of water."

"What do you think its main problem is?"

Again Naomi paused to consider. "It's just a deep, strong impression. First, look at it, closely. Look at the sand. See"—she gathered up a handful—"it's not all sand. There's all this dirt mixed in with it. I think that's what makes it so hot."

Sloan could see what she meant. It wasn't quite sand, not like Florida sand or Michigan sand. It looked a little grimy, and he could see where their feet had left smudged streaks on the blanket.

Naomi continued. "And the water. It was nice to swim and cool off, but the water isn't right either. It's not sparkling blue and green. It doesn't look or feel very clean, does it, especially close to the shore. And it has a faint smell, don't you think—nothing rotten or putrid, but something a little *off*-?"

"*Stop!* I'm starting to feel pretty terrible about being at the beach."

Naomi laughed. "Don't feel terrible. It's nice enough being here, but it's not...it's not the *real* beach."

Sloan was about to say *let's go to the real beach* when Naomi said, "We could never be naked here."

That was the third thing.

Negril, Jamaica

# 19

## JEN

Thunder rumbled intermittently overhead, and the atmosphere outside the permanently open windows of Buster's battered Lada was heavy with the coming rain. In the passenger seat Sloan absorbed the bumps and lurches as the ancient public cab eased down the rutted earthen road from the cliffs to the roundabout. As they neared the mottled terracotta façade of the Hi-Lo, Buster stopped the car to admit a broad-bottomed Jamaican woman and her two small children.

"Let see," Buster said, turning around uncomfortably in his seat, "How we all fit in."

Three Jamaican men, day-workers on their way to patch the pool at Cole's Cozee Cabins, sat shoulder to shoulder in the back seat. Their faces looked dully troubled, but they made no move to accommodate the additional passengers. Eyeing the low-slung tiled roof of the post office beyond the Hi-Lo, Sloan jimmied open the passenger side door and stepped down out of the cab.

"Here you go, ma'am," he said, gesturing to indicate the vacant seat.

"Oh, God bless you." the woman said, gathering up her children.

Sloan probed down into the pocket of his shorts and from the wad of bills and coins extracted a fifty J note and handed it to Buster through the window.

"You don't have to get out da cab, mon," Buster said. "We make a place."

"It's O.K., Buster," Sloan said, "I'm just going to the post office."

"You want da change?"

"No, we're all set."

Buster put the Lada in gear, ground forward for a few yards, then stopped. Poking his head out the window, he called back to Sloan, "You wait for me at da post office. Gone to rain, mon. I'll take you back da house."

Sloan waved him on. Gusts were hissing and rattling in the palm branches overhead, and he felt good to be stretching his legs.

Inside, the Negril Post Office was sourly redolent of stale smoke and perspiration. Sloan extracted the letters from both boxes he rented and began discarding the fliers and public notices. Naomi had several official-looking letters, probably Mission business, from the states and Kingston. The letters addressed to him were mostly payments for advertising copy in *This Island,* and -- Sloan gladdened reflexively – there was a check for his last National Public Radio piece. There was also a personal letter, very fat, from the states. Sloan recognized Jen's distinctive angular script. She had, he noticed, reinforced the envelope's seal with Scotch tape.

Sloan bunched Naomi's and his personal mail into the pocket of his shorts and stepped outside under the post office awning where he paused to breathe in the fresher air. There was another muted tremor of thunder. Sloan scanned the alternating patches of blue and billowing grey overhead and determined there would be time to walk to Haddie's café on the beach where he could relax and read Jen's letter.

There were still puddles from yesterday's rains on the berm of the roundabout, and the rubber soles of Sloan's sandals slapped wetly on the spidery cracks in the macadam as he made his way over the bridge to the beach walk.

It was not yet noon when he ducked under the low eaves of Haddie's open-air cafe. Out toward the horizon, the grey waves were roiling and irregular. Most of the beach chairs were abandoned, but a slender and darkly tanned woman – Sloan guessed European – was poised next to the volleyball net chatting, topless, with Fletcher the carpenter. A blond child, a girl of perhaps five or six, presumably the woman's daughter, shrieked and giggled as she darted back and forth between the two talking figures and the shelter of the café.

"Mornin', mistah Fox," said Haddie, looking up from the bar sink, "Is good too see you."

"Good morning," Sloan said. "It looks like Fletcher is making another friend."

Haddie laughed, a series of high staccato *hah's*. "That Fletcher," he said, "he never guess tired his ladies."

Sloan considered the slender brown back of the woman talking to Fletcher. "She looks like a good friend."

Haddie laughed again. Bending over the sink behind the bar, he continued to mumble inaudibly. Looking out toward the water, Sloan was struck by the iridescent green strip of the woman's bikini bottom. She was inclined earnestly toward Fletcher's face, resting close to hers against the near standard of the volleyball net.

Sloan started to order a Red Stripe, but decided instead on iced coffee.

"Tell me something, Haddie," he said. "Does Fletcher ever have any luck with these women?"

Haddie stood upright at the sink. "Any luck? Wit da women? You mean he take dem to bed?"

"Yes, does he?"

"I think Fletcher jess talk to da women, you know? Fletcher, he not a young mon."

Sloan considered the shirtless figure of Fletcher inclined against the volleyball post. Trim, his dark, almost plum-colored skin gathered tightly about the nicely defined muscles of his abdomen, he was nodding earnestly in response to the slender woman.

"How old is he?"

"Fletcher, he at least old as me, and I'm sixty."

*Sixty.* Sloan was astonished. "You're sixty?" he asked, "Haddie I thought you were about thirty-five."

"No, mon, I'm old. So is old Fletcher. Is why he like to talk to da ladies stead of work on da houses."

Sloan took his iced coffee down to the end of the bar, rattled the ice cubes with his spoon, and pulled the letters from out of his pocket. Putting the others aside on the bar, he considered again the special heft of the envelope from Jen. It might be past clippings, he thought, from Bart's games. With a relexive twinge of dread, he reread the return address in Cleveland Heights, then, as he tore into the envelope, it began to rain.

Sept. 15

*Dear Sloan,*

*Before my memory fails me, I have to tell you about tonight.*

*Henry, my star lodger, did two noteworthy things. (1) he planned, executed, cooked for, and cleared up after a dinner party here for four. (2) He asked my advice on how to prepare marinara sauce, how to cook pasta, how to prepare and dress a salad.*

*Yes, the same Henry of once epic silences, the Henry happy to eat cold week-old pizza out of cartons, the Henry known to eat dry cereal for supper. But perhaps you know this new Henry since he was there with you all summer – perhaps you even witnessed or inspired the transformation. But let me tell you it was news to me. Not that, seriously, Henry has been anything but a doll lately, even before Negril. These days his routine is to get up (on time!) shower, coat and tie himself, then walk, or I give him a lift, to the Rapid Transit stop. Long days at the agency, which he seems to find absorbing. He thinks he's about to get his first solo account, a mainstream pop station, and this feels huge to him. Don't let me belittle it – is huge. But this is* Henry! *Henry of the dreamy inertia, the afternoon riser. And there he goes, a willowy (and I have a feeling, in his world, rather dishy) semblance of a young working person. He might be a little more wrinkly and mismatched than most, but he is unmistakably on task. And maybe he's not more wrinkly. My window onto the world is so small.*

*So off he goes by eight to Slazenger and McManus Advertising, and he returns usually by six or seven but just to shed his jacket and tie and head out to the Brewery Pub on Taylor Road, where apparently every unmarried twenty-something on the east side hangs out, sipping and nibbling, eyeing, shooting pool, and chatting up until closing time, which is a couple hours past my personal closing time, so Bart and I exchange only glancing hey's and how's it goings when H. is departing or arriving. But there is something sturdy and healthy about it, a feeling that he is in quite a lively little groove. And despite his hours at the pub, he doesn't seem to be staggering with drink when he comes home, or really ever. I suppose if he wanted to go mad with hedonism, he would have done it with you this summer working at that loony Cliff Hangar place. Is it as crazy as it sounds? H. says it is the American kids who get loaded and then swing out over the cliffs on ropes and plop into the sea. Is it really like that? H. tells me: "Mom, you can do anything in Jamaica." Can you? Do you. Did he? Don't they get hurt or killed getting stoned or loaded and then jumping off cliffs into the ocean?*

*Where was I? Henry's party. It was just the best. The reason for it, I now see, is that there is a girl he likes, Julia. Julia is another regular at the pub, and, I now know, she is a paralegal who is studying by night to be a complete legal. Sloan – this is Henry's first take-home girl! And she's a complete doll. Tiny, wiry, with a wonderful pixie face, big eyes, a big funny mouth. Her hair is cropped off like a boy's and is smushed up every which way, but it is, beyond my powers of relating, becoming. Very sharp, Julia. Very funny. Not shy with me, but not smart-alecky either. Just real and funny, and her eyes follow H. worshipfully as he moves about the kitchen.*

*The idea, he told me, was to get Julia to come over for a nice dinner, but that would have to involve at least one other decorative couple which was, handily, Desmond and his girl Carrie, whom Julia likes well enough and H. didn't have to worry about.*

*So here is the evening.*

*Henry comes homes at 4:30, early. He calls me down from my eerie, and by the time I enter the kitchen he's got cans of diced tomatoes, bulbs of garlic, little packets of fresh basil leaves, olive oil, a huge bag of mixed greens, boxes of rigatoni and chicken breasts laid out on the counter. For some reason all of this, and the impending enterprise of transforming it into a meal, seems wondrous, a complete novelty, even to me. And in some ways it is a novelty, since old Henry, either out of innocence or because he was feeling flush, spurned the prepackaged chicken and got specially trimmed cuts from the butcher, a specific kind of chicken he somehow knew about, Bell and Evans, reputed to be treated pretty well, allowed to run around a little before slaughter.*

*"You've got to buy free range," Henry tells his old mother, whose eyes, permanently fixed on the dollars per pound tags, have never wandered in the direction of the butcher's station. And I <u>like</u> it, like the idea that for Henry the Giant Eagle, and maybe the whole commercial world, is tangled with moral considerations.*

*He wants to know the most basic things. What pans do what, what goes in first, how do you know when pasta is done. We start with the sauce, dicing onions and simmering them in some olive oil at the bottom of a pan. Henry studies me intently as I peel some garlic cloves by rolling them around in my special rubber cylinder. Then I show him how to use the garlic press (an incredible, heavy, sculpturally beautiful one from Williams Sonoma), and after his first squeeze and the sight of the little mushy ends of garlic extruding from the press, H. says, "Cooking is amazing."*

*A little bit by little bit, juggling this and that, dancing from pan to pan, Henry has it going, the tomatoes cooking down into the bubbling sauce, the humanely treated chicken breasts sizzling in a shallow soup of lemon and wine, the pasta water starting to gurgle on the back burner. H. Surveys the busy stove, stirs this, licks a spoon, likes what he sees. Then he steps back and like a dervish sets a fancy table for four in the dining room. He wants more candles than I can find holders for, so we do some goofy improvising. The downstairs is starting to smell persuasive, and I am hungry myself. Henry uncorks two bottles of wine so, he tells me, they can breathe.*

*While he is upstairs changing his shirt, Julia arrives with Carrie and Desmond. I give them some wine and we are having a nice lively time already when H. comes down all shiny and glad. Because he is especially nervous about it, I agree to hang around until the pasta is ready and I show him how to drain it in the colander under the cold water. I've arranged to have dinner out with Angie and the Krupanskys, but watch in the kitchen with my coat on as H. dresses the plates and glides them out to his guests. He is radiant, he thanks me, and gives me a big hug. This is Henry, Sloan! Henry. In the car I cried and cried and when I got to the restaurant, I had to stay in the car until I could stop. I don't believe I have ever been happier or could be happier in my life. Can you understand this? There was H., an absolutely bone-deep beautiful person, all, completely all, I could ever want him to be.*

*Perhaps you are thinking: it's been a long time coming, this happiness. For other people it might be an abiding condition. Who knows, maybe it is for you. For me it is so new. And it is more than just Henry. There has been a nice gradual coming together of things lately. After years of feeling certain that my academic stuff was going to wind up a pointless dud, I slide into a tenure track job at City College, due of course to no initiative or special brilliance on my part, but to the unearned kindness of Ted and the other war horses in the department. Ted's cover note on my contract said, "We are so lucky." I have now arrived at a point where I can imagine he might mean it, which for me is new mental territory. I still battle the old demons, and tomorrow morning they may convince me of my shallowness and fraudulence, but there's a good chance they won't. I find that I can talk back to them now. I am sure you have felt the same thing, or at least something like it. Maybe when you realized This Island was going to be more than weekly listings with enough paid advertising to get you by. By the way, if I haven't told you sufficiently, I really like your column. H. Brought back a dozen issues from this summer, and I have been through them all. I hear you loud and clear in every one of them. I think I like the funny ones best, but you succeed in sounding a note of urgency and concern about the civic issues. A+ for instance on scolding the authorities for looking after sanitation and water quality for the tourists, while the locals are getting sick. If I were a Jamaican, I would be a passionate fan of This Island. But you don't need to hear this from me. My schedule at the University has been diabolically set up so that I can almost never listen to your NPR spots, but the bits I do hear are fine, and even when I was working so hard to hate you, some dissenting little pocket of objectivity had to agree that you were in top form. So let me say it (imagine a loud ringing voice): Congratulations,*

*Sloan! You are making a mark in the big real world, and even better, it's a good mark. That said, I probably don't have to tell you that when Bart – of all people – first told me you were on the radio and that he had heard you and you were "really great" (almost two years ago?), the demons rallied and made a tremendous jealous rage. Bugger, rat, snake, I told myself, he not only slithers off to the tropics with his beloved shrink, he <u>gets away with it</u>. He makes a success. Actually, in my parlance of that day, a fucking success. And there I was, in the murk of Cleveland winter slogging away on the deep interior of Edith Wharton and her friends. Days, weeks seemed to pass when I hardly saw anybody but Bart and the department types, they only in scholastic passing, as I martyred my way through freshman writing sections, then burrowed back to Cleveland Heights and up to my hide-out on the third floor. It was about this time when I realized Bart wasn't leaving lights on all over the house out of carelessness; he was crying out for some light, some semblance of life where he lived.*

*Yes, Sloan I was bad, and I don't have to tell you how thoroughly and utterly I wanted you to feel all of it, to feel as bad as I could possibly make you feel. Not proud of this at all, but of all the demons' gifts, their ability to open the doors to bottomless self-righteousness, self-pity, and vindictive rage is their greatest strength. I hope you haven't saved those letters, and if you have, I hope you will deep six them as a gesture of conciliation.*

*I was crazy, Sloan, mentally ill. In the same fifteen minutes I could want you dead, want you ruined, want you back. Like practically every other betrayed divorcee-in-the-making, money became the currency of my hurt. Even the incredible Vitak – I will tell you now, selected from the legions of predatory personal injury and divorce lawyers on the sole strength of Angie Mowra's telling me "he is without any conscience, totally ruthless" – even he had to admit to me that you would be hard to fault on financial grounds. From what he could tell, you seemed to have given up everything you owned and were sending me all the money you had. Tell me, if you feel you safely can, could this have been true? Was Naomi loaded? I know her husband was, but he can hardly have been in the mood to set you two up on the island, poor as I hear most Jamaicans are. By the way, did I tell you I met him – Nathan Weingart? He was at an opening at the Institute of Art. He seemed an absolute doll, courteous, soft, well spoken. Handsome guy from central casting. I wonder what's wrong with him.*

*Though none of my business. Back to good things coming together, which is nicer to talk about. H. tells me Doubleday wants to do a <u>This Island</u> book from your NPR pieces. Now that has to feel terrific. And guess what – a book by my hand is also in the works. U. of California press has made an offer to do my thesis. Wonder of wonders, and they don't even have a lot of suggestions for changes, except I have to do some excruciating reference checking. It's the kind of thing that I can imagine going poof and disappearing like a dream, except I have an actual contract in my file. A year from this very month if all goes well. I suppose lots of people will buy and read your book and you will be on talk shows. Only University libraries and eleven Edith Wharton scholars will buy mine, but, honestly, it still feels fantastic, as if my little boat has slipped into the same harbor where the genuine scholars and writers are moored. And as if I needed to say it again, God please commend Ted Krupansky's soul to the highest reaches of heaven for guiding me through my lonely toils and endorsing my thesis to UC Press when he has no special interest in Edith Wharton. Too many unfathomable mysteries.*

*Nice, very nice when you can feel things coming together. There's something uncanny about it, too, and the good things start to cluster so that you allow yourself to <u>expect</u> nice surprises and bright outcomes. Yes, this is me saying this. And while it is late, I have had very little to drink. The truth of the matter is that I never thought I could be in such a place. I think I am beginning to see that living well is less about doing things than it is about not having to do things. It's alignment, not construction. On my best days, and I have some, I can feel the walls coming down, walls I spent a lot of time and tense effort putting up. When I was working so hard to resent you, I think what I really resented was the walls, especially after you started your therapy/Naomi thing, because then it was getting clearer and clearer that you were figuring out the wall business, your own but also mine, and you were ready for them to come down. Because you got there first, either because you were lucky or braver than I was, I panicked. I thought you loved me and knew me well enough to expose me, and once I was exposed – out of the depths the shrieking demons arise – I would be seen for the worthless fake I felt I was. I remember once you were* *talking to me in the kitchen when Bart was maybe a ninth grader.  You were telling me that social boundaries didn't matter so much, that if you were honest and real you could cross them.  You were trying to say, I think, that you could break out, risk, sin, and live.  It was something I could actually feel in you, feel in the room as you were talking.  I remember the clammy scared feeling that you could leave me, at the same time fully aware that I was shrinking back from you, doing everything I could do to keep you distant.  Even as I was doing it, I _knew_ I was doing it, that I didn't want to stop, and then you said something about, I think, paradise, and that you felt you could actually get there.  I can remember shutting down, right on the spot.  You were talking about longing, and I had the distinct feeling that you were about to get somehow deeper and richer than I was, that you were going to be able to fly and that by doing that you would be proving that I couldn't.  If you follow that at all, you see how my mind worked.*

*But at a deeper, truer level, a level I couldn't begin to see then, an important and good thing was happening, a life saver.  You were, as I was starting to see and fear, getting ready to give up the indirection and negativity in our relationship, and that told me at a deep level that I was going to have to do that too.  But I wasn't ready.  I was afraid.  Even though I was feeling more and more wretched, more isolated from you and the boys and everybody else, more cocooned inside a self I didn't much like, I held fast to that status quo, because, as the cliché goes, it was the devil I knew.*

*I haven't told you, but it's really been getting better for a long time now.  It's been a thawing out, and all the crazy hatred was just a last ditch effort on the part of the demons to hold onto the old walled self.  I think I realized all that was over when H. came back from Jamaica full of all your news and his own wondrous tales of life at the Cliff Hangar.  I can't even begin to tell you the doubts and fears and misgivings I had about his going to you for the summer.  I suppose at the bottom of it was the dark dread that I would somehow lose him – as if I had him – forever, that he would in some vague, final way be you all over again.  But bless his heart, he sensed what I was afraid of and managed to let me know it was all right when he would call.*

*I must say he made a very attractive account of your set-up in Negril.  The photographs of your roost above the cliffs, all that water and sky look lush and* *gorgeous beyond my ability to take in. I will tell you again that my <u>objective</u> impressions of Naomi, which I must work hard to isolate from all other impressions, are very positive. She is almost too beautiful to look at, and I have to pass over the photographs in which she appears very quickly. H. is careful not to wound me, but he obviously finds Naomi true blue. He is very impressed with her Mission and was <u>mad</u> for the children, especially the littlest ones – yet another surprising and wonderful facet of H. Perhaps I should have suspected it. Or maybe it was something he was not about to disclose to me in my guise as jaded person about everything openly loving. At any rate, he is crazy about those Jamaican kids. Moreover, since you will no doubt be getting a proposal from brother Bart soon, I should warn you that H. has been telling B. about his fantastic adventures and that B. has to spend time in Negril working at the Mission. B. is drooling to do it, probably at this point more under the spell of the Cliff Hangar stories than the prospect of Mother Theresa-like good works at Naomi's Mission. At any rate, be warned. But before I leave the topic of H. and his tropical transformation, I want to share another touching thing. H.'s room, which is still not likely to be featured in <u>House Beautiful</u>, is now moderately presentable – <u>and</u> he has, to my knowledge, added his first carefully considered decorative touch. In noting this, I simply exclude out of hand the hastily taped up rock posters or near-pornographic cut-outs from <u>Rolling Stone</u>. H. has taken a photograph of himself and one of the Jamaican boys from the Mission – Eddie? Ernie? – to the developers and had it blown up to 18" X 24" and then had it framed. In the picture H., all bare and brown on top, is smiling dead into the camera with Eddie/Ernie riding piggy-back, clutching Henry's neck for dear life. Do you know the picture? I find I can't get enough of it. I keep creeping into his room at odd hours to look. It's one of those images that gives off more than what is pictured. I suppose it reveals H. as a lover of souls. H. as an evolved being, out in the world, connected. It stops my heart.*

*Now is this the longest letter you have ever received? I know my hate letters were substantial, but isn't this better? Don't worry, the end is in sight. I want you to know how much I have resisted this kind of thing. For the longest time I felt that if I reported any amusing or endearing development in life here, it would send out a huge message to you of Approval and Permission, which, in* my crazed smallness, was equivalent to losing everything forever. The thaw came with the realization that Approval and Permission are and never really were mine to give and that thinking they were was part of my scared-stiff, power orientation to life. What I have learned (at ridiculous length) is that getting over the Great Awfulness was not a gift or concession to you, it was the beginning of me. Maybe the realization started when it was so clear that in constricting myself, I was constricting Bart, making his world small and airless, too. And then it started to break over me like a tidal wave: this is what I have been doing for a long time. I did it to you, especially to you. I did it to H. I spread my own edgy, doubtful self around and made sure everybody knew it and nobody could forget it. And thank God that you helped me break that vessel, though I really did think I would die at the time. It was so strange and so wonderful the way it began to happen. There was a realization that even the seeming worst things – worries about $ and getting along, loneliness, what will I do on Saturday night – are also weirdly alive-making. Can you understand this, the feeling that you are on your own, no props, no easy assurances, not even the dull, heavy status of being a wife – and then discovering it's not a void, but a world, and it's full of life, and if you career around in it without defenses, let it wash over you, it's interesting, it's amusing, it's a mystery in the best sense, and (shudder, shudder, blush, blush), it's sometimes amazingly sexy.

Maybe that's old business to more evolved souls, but it is new and life-saving for me. And you know what else? The first person I wanted to tell when I started to feel the lift and the thaw was you. Of course I didn't do it. I wanted it to last for a while and be real. But this summer when I realized what was happening, I also realized I never felt more in love with you. Not needy love (you can relax, mop that brow), just the connected, close, solidarity kind, the kind that only wishes well. Once I was able to admit to that kind of feeling, other grateful realizations began shining through: that you never did anything to divide the boys' affections and loyalties. Both of them so consistently reported back – usually when I was in high-bitch mode – how unwaveringly warmly and respectfully you spoke of me that I used to scold them for it. And as Vitak, king of the pit bulls, pointed out, you have been preposterously generous with money. At the time I told myself you weren't generous, you were just too goo-goo eyed with your new love and too lazy to look after your self-interest. I think I am beginning to see exactly what you did and the spirit in which you did it. I am starting to see that there were trials for you, too, and I am sure trials for Naomi, trials you spared me. You also spared me any reports of what I know has been your great happiness with Naomi. If a little gingerly, H. has managed to let me know that she is a terrific person and that it is a joy for him to be in your company. He is especially admiring of Naomi's work at the Mission, her touch with the children and staff. Actually, I am putting it mildly. I'm not sure I don't detect the tiniest crush on her on H.'s part. Do you?

For a while it helped a lot that the idea of you in Jamaica was, despite all the catastrophic troubles on the surface, largely unreal. I needed that. But of course it is real, just real beyond my imagining. But now I am able to imagine, and your world is starting to seem not only real, but vivid. Those beautiful children at the Mission, purple bougainvillea cascading down the side of your house, the deck over the cliffs and the aquamarine. Henry has a photograph of a doctor bird that hovers over the outdoor shower on your deck. He told me, "Look at this amazing bird." I look, and it looks exactly like me.

I better close before this effusion of positivity gives out and I return to the slitty-eyed Jen of memory.

Just let it be said this night, now this morning, that I am happy and so hopeful and so fond of you. I think you gave me a gift --no, you didn't give it. The collapse of my anxious, mean-spirited safety was a gift.

I'm sending a whole batch of fixed-up notes and references to U. Cal. Press in the a.m. Say a prayer. The boys send love. H. makes a great sauce.

Jen

P.S. Bart has decided where he wants to go – Amherst.

# 20

## WISE/FOX

Sloan was aware that the rain had stopped for some time when he finished Jen's letter. He ordered a Red Stripe and read the letter again, very slowly. The sea beyond the beach was mottled blue, black, and lavender as bright sky emerged between tumbles of cloud. Sloan felt a swelling in his chest, a confusion of love and sadness and gratitude. For an instant he considered walking over to his office at *This Island* and writing Jen in response, an impulse followed immediately by a wave of doubt that he could find the words.

Down the beach front near the waterline the slender young woman, now covered modestly by an outsized white tee shirt, was smoothing out a blanket while the little girl pulled beach toys from a cloth bag. An invigorating gust swept under the awnings of the café, and the clearing sky blanched the length of the beach with white light. Fletcher had gone.

Walking back over the bridge to the roundabout, Sloan peered reflexively about for Buster's cab, and as his mind turned imprecisely on the vehicle, its exterior faded to the color of pale tomato soup, the familiar bumps and lurches, the smell within of sweat and garlic and motor oil, he had it: a *This Island* piece on Buster and his Russian Lada. Sloan felt the agreeable confluence of impressions. The crudely engineered, now decrepit but still haltingly operative vehicle represented something hopeless and majestic in the old Soviet system. He pictured the new Lada, gleaming in its fresh red paint, rolling off the assembly line. The plant workers, the foreman – he would be a Party member – might have noted its passing through their midst as work well done. They would imagine it carrying fares through the littered squares of Moscow or Leningrad, possibly Belgrade or Prague – certainly not Jamaica, not the roundabout in Negril. Or Buster. Sloan smiled. He would begin that evening after dinner. *Buster's Lada: Glasnost comes to Negril.*

Though the air was drier now and cooled by the rains, the sunlight overhead was a radiant force, and steam was rising from the damp macadam. Sloan scanned the line of public cabs idling at the cab stand and, not seeing Buster, decided to take a private cab, at least to the lighthouse, then walk the final mile or so in brilliant light high above the sea.

The electric blue private cab that swung around to Sloan's side was a new-looking British Ford. Leaning inside to talk to the driver, Sloan could feel a chilly hint of air-conditioning.

"It will cost 300 J to da light house," the driver said, "or ten American."

"300 J," Sloan agreed, and got in the car. *Ten American,* Sloan mused, for two or three miles up the West End Road. Cabs were cheaper in Manhattan.

"Where you live?" the driver asked.

"I live up by the cliffs, off Magic Caves Lane, but I'm getting out at the lighthouse."

"Da lighthouse is far from Magic Caves. What you gone do?"

I feel like walking a bit."

"Sa long walk, mon."

The cab moved past the Hi-lo, rickety shops and jerk chicken stands and was soon climbing a less settled stretch of narrow highway.

"Dat Magic Caves," the driver said, "Dat's where da German he was killed."

Sloan remembered. "That's right." The German, Krebbs, had rented the little brightly painted house a few hundred yards from

the turn off to Sloan's and Naomi's villa. Sloan had met Krebbs
a few times, invited him up for a drink shortly after he moved in.
He guessed Krebbs was in his early forties. His hair was oily and
mussed, and his stubble had not proceeded into a beard. Sloan
thought there was something evasive and wolfish about him, his
conversation agreeable but guarded. Krebbs told them he was a
dentist, but when Sloan said Negril badly needed dentists, Krebbs
face had clouded, and he said he would not practice again. He had
come to Jamaica to change his life. It's a good place to change your
life, Sloan had told him.

Sloan and Naomi did not see much of Krebbs after his visit to the
house. Among their friends who lived along the cliffs there was periodic speculation about the German's means of support. He hired a
gardener and a cook and then abruptly let them both go. He did not
seem to work. At night, he was known to frequent Club Compulsion, a
rooftop dance bar down near the roundabout, where he was reputed
to ask the locals about women for hire. Since Club Compulsion was
also known to be a hub of drug traffic, it was assumed that Krebbs
might be a dealer, or an addict.

Sloan had not thought about him much until, a few mornings
earlier, the lane down to West End Road was blocked by a cluster of
police cars and uniformed officers streaming in and out of Krebbs'
house. One of them recognized Sloan and told him that Krebbs
had been found early that morning outside his own gate hacked up
brutally with a machete. His hands and feet had been cut off, and
his severed scrotum was stuffed in his mouth.

"Das bad, dat kind of murder," the driver said suddenly, eager,
Sloan thought, to get some information from him. "I hear dat
German he got all cut up bad."

"Yes, I think he did."

"Dat feller he got no friends, I tell you. Dey cut you up like dat, is
not to steal your wallet or da TV. Dey kill you like dat when you been
bad, when dey is out to get you."

Sloan did not want to think about or talk about the German's murder. Like the driver, he had felt certain from the moment he heard the gruesome account that Krebbs had made some dark, unsavory trespass in the criminal realm. There were forces at work in Jamaica that he did not understand but which he respected.

The driver had raised his head and inclined an ear in the direction of the back seat. Sloan could see his raised eyebrows in the rear-view mirror and knew some kind of response from him was expected. To his relief, the sign for the lighthouse and then the lighthouse itself loomed up on the right. Sloan paid the fare and stepped out onto the deserted road.

"You be careful now, mon." The driver maneuvered the car around and sped back toward town. Little needles of radiance penetrated Sloan's brow and cheeks as he strode westward into the sun.

The road and surrounding scrub had a pleasing washed look, and he felt a lightening in his chest. Dark things. The driver had wanted to descend into dark things, to take Sloan with him into the bloody tangle.

The grade of the West End Road was steadily uphill, and soon Sloan was breathing deeply. There was a familiar, faintly pleasing ache in his calves and thighs, and he felt lubricated, loose in his joints, his sandals moist and pliant against the soles of his feet.

At the Magic Caves turnoff, the roadbed reverted to earth. Slender fingers of rainwater meandered down a network or ruts, and parakeets made a shrieking canopy of sound overhead. As Sloan passed Krebbs' gate, he heard the skittering feet and choked growls of the Rotweillers, now installed inside the fence by the shaken landlord. For a moment the slobbering complaints of the dogs and the image of the mutilated German lying at his gate seemed to Sloan continuous, related.

Sloan banished the thought. Pausing at the foot of his drive, his gaze came to rest on the carved wooden sign – WISE/FOX – and he remembered Jen's letter and that Naomi would be up in the house.

197

The kitchen, when Sloan entered it, seemed unusually full of life. He greeted Harriet, the stout and sturdy Jamaican woman Naomi had hired to cook and clean, Monday through Thursday. She was cutting limes at the sink, and Sloan noted with interest that she was wearing her shiny pink nurse's dress and cap. When, a week earlier, she had first appeared in the nursing outfit, Naomi had questioned her about it, wondering if, perhaps, Harriet had been a nurse. Harriet, Naomi told him, shyly disclosed that she was not a nurse, but her sister Edith was, and she had given her sister money to purchase the dress, cap, stockings, and shoes from the Hospital supply center. She confided that she had always wanted to hold a position requiring a uniform. When Naomi assured her *she* did not require a uniform, Harriet had looked hurt. "I believe a uniform is best," she told Naomi firmly.

Harriet's son Phillip, still in the starched white shirt and black shorts of his Ignatius Loyola School uniform, peered up over the floor of the parrot cage where he was, at his mother's bidding, attempting to pull out the retractable tray in order to clear the seed husks and droppings.

"You be careful wit dat," Harriet said to her son, "We don't need dat business on da flaw."

Booboo, the parrot, was perched on top of the refrigerator door, a bright crazed eye monitoring the movements of Phillip's delicate black hands.

Across the room sitting upright on the floor and silhouetted against the brilliantly illuminated glass doors to the deck was Roberta, almost two, who, since she was the youngest and smallest, Naomi sometimes took home from the Mission when there was a shortage of beds in the nursery. Sloan made noisy giant steps in Roberta's direction until he was standing over her. "*Ro-bert-a!*"

Roberta shouted with pleasure, and Sloan picked her up by the waist and held her high over his head. "Roberta's flying," he said. She met his eyes soulfully. Her immaculate little braids fell forward over her brow like antennae.

Sloan set Roberta down, glanced out over the empty deck and asked if Naomi was around.

"She taking her shower, outside," Harriet said.

Sloan closed the glass door behind him and stepped out onto the deck. Moving to the rail, he could see the sunlight making a rainbow in the mist of the spray from the dangling showerhead. There was a shower stall and bath upstairs in the house, but Naomi preferred the improvised outdoor shower, enclosed by a rough circle of mismatched boards, over which Sloan could see the glistening nape of Naomi's neck as she inclined forward to rinse her hair.

Sloan pulled two deck chairs away from the house and arranged them so that they were angled into the sun. As he stepped back inside to prepare rum and limes, Harriet was scolding Phillip for scattering Booboo's detritus onto the floor as he carried the tray to the trash bin.

"Now you clean dat right up. Da broom is in da closet under da stair."

Sloan was about to ask Harriet if she had any limes to spare when a shrill cry from Phillip electrified the air. He was back-pedaling clumsily from the open door of the utility closet, his eyes fixed on the floor. He shot an agitated glance toward Sloan and his mother and said, his voice wavering, "Sa forty *leggah.*"

Sloan moved to the open closet.

"It down deh, by da vacuum," Phillip said, then very solemnly: "Sa *red* forty leggah, dat can kill you."

"It's O.K., Phillip, we'll take care of mister red forty legger. I think you should go over by your mother for a minute." Behind him Sloan heard the squeaking and slapping of Roberta's hands and knees moving over the tile floor. "And do me a favor. Pick up Roberta, and take her over to your mother."

Surveying the shadowy closet, Sloan eyed the push broom on the back wall and gingerly lifted it from its hook. He was aware of his exposed feet as he scanned the dark closet floor. Forty-leggers. Sloan found that something about Jamaican life allowed him to suspend all concern about ambient terrors – deadly centipedes, sudden incursions of rats, the occasional snake in the cistern – until they were present.

Sloan tapped between the buckets and paint cans with the broom handle. As he levered the broom under the body of the vacuum cleaner and raised it off the floor, the forty legger, about the size of a bill fold and the color of an open wound, passed like a shadow over a paint can and disappeared down against the baseboard. Leaning forward into the closet but trying not to step inside, Sloan began prying the cans away from the wall with the broom handle. Then, like a sudden stripe, the centipede was moving up the wall. Startled, Sloan tried to spear it with the broom end, made only glancing contact, but managed to bat it back down onto the floor. Sloan watched it move to the corner, where it appeared to bunch itself into a mound. Taking some care to be accurate, he thrust the broom end into the corner. For a second Sloan thought he had missed, as the creature's legs and papery carcass appeared to be moving up the shaft of the broom toward him, but then he saw that he had skewered it, that the legs furiously opening and closing over the broom end were stationary. Streaky bits of the ruined centipede now stained the painted baseboard. Sloan made a sawing motion with the broom handle, and when he pulled it away, he saw that the forty legger had been severed in half. He watched, perspiring, as first one half and then the other grew still.

Phillip handed Roberta to his mother and stood over Sloan's shoulder as he brushed the remains of the centipede into the dust pan.

"He dead now?"

"He dead now."

Harriet said, "It's O.K. to put da bebby down on da flaw?"

"I think it's all right," Sloan said. "Trouble's over.

Sloan poured rum into two glasses of ice and, dropping a slice of Harriet's limes into each, carried the drinks out onto the deck. Naomi was reclining bare breasted on one of the deck chairs. A brightly patterned sarong was cinched loosely around her hips. Her wet hair was swept back from her face, and she was smiling, eyes closed, into the sun.

"You look like a happy cat," Sloan said.

"I am. Don't let Phillip come out, please. I'm not dressed."

Sloan knelt down next to Naomi and gently placed the cold glass on her belly.

"Oh!"

Sloan watched with a tenderness that weakened him as Naomi's lips drew back from her teeth. She did not open her eyes. As her fingers curled around the glass, Sloan brushed a light kiss across her belly. Naomi made her lovely hum.

Sloan rose to his feet and walked to the rail of the deck. The hardwood was brightly beaded with the afternoon rain. The decking, cornices, the sharply angled gables over the second floor windows combined to make him feel that he was standing at the prow of a ship, a substantial ship. Mellers, the sanitation engineer who designed and built the house, had been devastated when he was called back to England. The house somehow still held an air of great hope and release. It seemed to Sloan less to be settled onto the cliff rock than to be riding the grade up into the horizon, propelled from behind by the force of green inland heat.

The afternoon's storm front had now receded to the far horizon. The clouds were broken up and striated into what looked to Sloan like a mountain range giving rise to a still greater mountain range, its peaks outlined in metallic fire by the declining sun. Moving to Naomi, Sloan slipped out of his sandals and lay back on the adjacent chair. As he closed his eyes against the sun, there was an iridescent after-image of the cloud mountains, an impression of worlds beyond worlds.

Inside the house Roberta raised a cry of delight.

CPSIA information can be obtained
at www.ICGtesting.com
Printed in the USA
BVHW03s1418210618
519655BV00001B/9/P